CLUELESSLY UNSCRIPTED

A SHOWBIZ ROMANCE MYSTERY

PATRICIA PUENTES

To Xavi. You always get me

1

March 2023

There was **nothing Sol liked more** than a tight schedule with just the right amount of much-needed leisure time in it. And that Monday morning, the week ahead looked finally promising. She wasn't planning on writing anything else that day, having just addressed all the suggestions her editor made to her last Oscars reaction piece.

It had been a long busy weekend following Hollywood's glitziest movie celebration and writing about it. And even if, for the most part, she'd been working from her sofa, the whole affair had been exhausting.

At least this year she hadn't had to attend the actual ceremony. She hated red carpets and schmoozing in equal measure—and awards ceremonies were essentially *that* plus extremely uncomfortable attire and unbearable footwear.

Fortunately, awards season was finally over and Sol decided to celebrate by decompressing before the hecticness of the afternoon. She was already dreading the social media strategy meeting scheduled for 2 p.m., and she needed to start pitching stories that would answer such pressing queries as "Oscars 2024 Predictions: The TK Movies to Watch" and "The Best and Most Talked-About Movies of 2023 So Far," even if it was barely mid-March. Just thinking about it made her want to go back to bed; it had been a long night made even longer by the eight-hour time difference between London and Los Angeles.

After a light breakfast of yogurt, seasonal fruit, and her customary Mariage Frères French Breakfast tea with almond milk, she dressed in her most stylish athleisure wear and grabbed a big gray designer weekender bag. Nothing was ever too hip when she went to see Josie. And since spring wasn't making too much of an effort yet, Sol completed the ensemble with a quintessentially classic Burberry trench coat.

By the time she left her small terraced two-story cottage in the South Bank, it was mid-morning. She didn't normally have the luxury to escape to see Josie in the middle of the day, but she relished her walk through the quiet streets and across Waterloo Bridge, with its imposing views of the London Eye and the Houses of Parliament on one side, St. Paul's Cathedral and the City borough's skyscrapers on the other.

The short peregrination to Covent Garden from her house in Roupell Street was absolutely worthwhile. Before finding Josie, she had tried all the studios within a thirty-minute walk from her place. She had even braved the Tube and trekked to Islington to find a much-raved-about instructor dull and the session insufficiently arduous. Josie was the absolute best.

She'd found Josie's boutique Pilates studio, which catered mostly to a movie-and-TV-centric clientele, through a source. That piece of information had been by far the best part of a tedious interview with the semi-famous CEO of the dominant streaming service Supreme Video.

Josie's studio wasn't otherwise advertised and lacked any social media presence, so Sol was still thankful to the CEO even if she'd begrudged the many hours spent reading the manual they were promoting on the nature of the hyper-competitive business of streaming, and writing an article which she and her editor knew well wasn't exactly her best piece.

The man who'd been standing on a quiet corner of Roupell Street for the previous two hours was starting to resent some of his professional choices and lose feeling on his toes. Not even his usual perusal of real estate porn on the app Rightmove could appease him that chilly morning.

He had a new, slightly better-paying job and still absolutely zero chances of affording a one-bedroom flat in a neighborhood like that one, even if he'd never choose to live on that side of the river voluntarily. He was despairing at the pictures of a place where the micro kitchen hadn't been renovated since the nineties and the asking price was still of palatial proportions, when he saw the mark leaving her place at an unusual time. He made sure to remain invisible, put the phone away, and followed her.

She would typically be huddled up in her home office this time on a Monday morning, which was why he'd been caught by surprise. She was wearing leggings and an ultra-cropped oversized sweatshirt underneath a long honey-colored trench coat. She looked chic even if the ensemble was casual. But fashion appreciation thoughts aside, the outfit indicated that Sol was probably on her way to their main place of interest.

He trailed her from a safe distance for about twenty minutes as she walked briskly between the narrow streets and crossed the river.

The studio was on the second floor of a Georgian building on Henrietta Street. She got there with only five minutes to spare.

He followed Sol inside to see who else was there. Since he had been assigned to that particular job, he'd been in the habit of carrying a holdall that could also double as a commuter bag. Inside the bag were a pair of slim-fit, sweat-absorbing joggers and an equally fashion-specific and ridiculously pricey T-shirt. Something more ordinary would have cast suspicion in a place like that.

He barely had time to get his alter ego, Greg Knight, enrolled in the half-past-eleven Pilates mat group class, get changed, and try to get a spot preferably next to the mark. If only that would bring him closer to figuring out whether the journalist had been the one pulling off the theft.

2

Sol had always been curious to know** who had the luxury to attend the mid-morning classes at Josie's studio. As an entertainment journalist for a mid-level publication with a sort-of-regular nine-to-five-on-most-days job, she seldomly had the time or opportunity to catch one sweaty session in the middle of the workday. But the class that Monday morning appeared to be populated by the same mixture of middle-aged career women, stay-at-home moms, and active elders who also frequented the afternoon and evening classes Sol regularly favored.

She even recognized and promptly greeted two of the studio's assorted group of hardcore regulars: Philippa (or was it Phyllis?), the social media empress and person with the most flexibility Sol had ever met; and Agatha, the impossibly nice TV agent. Sol wondered once again how they both made it to pretty much every single class.

Only one person in the group of six students—Josie's classes were expensive and unfilled by design—gave the impression of being a bit out of place: the Tall Dark Stranger (TDS). Sol had him pegged as a banker or lawyer from the

City area of London with the sort of structured schedule that wouldn't allow for many daily indulgences. Yet there he was.

Sol had seen him for the first time a couple of weeks earlier during her regular reformer session at 5:30 p.m. on Wednesdays. It would have been impossible to miss him, not only because he was indeed tall, thoroughly bronzed, sharp-jawlined, and fetching in a nearly Mediterranean way she'd come to miss in London. He was the only other student with her taking the exclusive two-people class with Josie.

He'd tried chatting with her after the sweaty, grunt-inducing, fifty-five-minute class. Sol had smiled at him politely, agreed mildly to whatever banal observation he'd made, grabbed her stuff, and made a quick escape. She'd been a bit short on time to get home that evening. She still needed to have a quick shower, get changed, and make it to her 7:30 p.m. dinner reservation. Regardless of his good looks, she didn't have the inclination or time to grant attention to a man who undoubtedly wanted someone to patiently listen to him and marvel at his many talents and high-earning job.

And yet the TDS had decided to sit next to her in class that Monday morning too. He placed his thick Pilates mat close to hers and imposed himself on her yet *again*. There sure was something with young handsome men like himself believing any woman over forty must be happy to pay attention to whatever they had to say.

"Hello again," the TDS said.

She smiled demurely. In close range, she had to admit that he was objectively gorgeous, but there was something off-putting about the clean-shaven-ness and poshness of him.

"We were also in class together the other day, right?" the TDS said, taking Sol away from her contemplations.

She needed to remember to add lemons to her grocery list. If only Meyer lemons could be found anywhere in London. She sighed inwardly.

"The weather is looking much better today. Such a splendid March morning," he went on, and Sol considered pretending she hadn't heard him.

The irredeemably polite person in her simply half smiled. She really couldn't handle inconsequential conversation and hoped to be as unencouraging of further tedium as possible. Even after three years in London, she still hadn't comprehended or adopted the natives' ease for weather talk.

The mark smiled uncomfortably at him, and he felt embarrassed. A bit stupid too. Why couldn't he stop babbling in this particular gig? He was a professional. He *knew* he should be inconspicuous, watching without arousing suspicion, disappearing in the class's background.

He also knew that was literally impossible. He was good at blending in and becoming invisible, but he was a fish out of water in that particular fitness-for-the-middle-aged-and-somewhat-wealthy milieu.

He'd rather go for a run or join a crowded, Chaturanga Dandasana–filled yoga class than endure another Pilates session with its boring footwork, swan dives and mermaids, and painfully crushing hundreds and side-leg series. Yet here he was, about to suffer from a very sore arse and not making much progress in deciphering her. Sol was either a writer with a set routine and a very grown-up social life, or she was the best mark he'd ever met on the field at pretending they had nothing to hide.

She wasn't the only one to be observed that morning though. Philippa was also there. Some people at the agency referred to her as Trophy, yet he resented the nickname—even if Philippa's husband was one of the most prolific and successful producers in television. No one at the agency seemed to realize that Philippa had amassed her own money as a lifestyle influencer and entrepreneur. Maybe no one had bothered to look her up online.

He also had seen Agatha in attendance. The TV agent had had a semi-promising career a couple of decades before, but the size of her agency and the number of her clients dwindled by the day. You would never know judging by her lifestyle, though. He didn't think Agatha was all she let on at first sight. Yet he couldn't attribute that sensation to anything more than a mere gut feeling—and that alone didn't solve cases.

Josie, on the other hand, was *definitely* hiding something. That didn't mean he thought she was the swindler he was trying to catch, although like in Agatha's case he was basing that belief in mere speculation. Josie was probably in her sixties—even if she could pass as someone in her mid-to-late forties—and she taught most if not all of her classes personally (partially because some of her students had a cult-like adoration for her and preferred that she was present during all of the sessions). Yet she barely broke a sweat and seemed to have no problem keeping up with the demands of teaching several times a day.

What he *really* wanted to know wasn't if Sol, Philippa, or Agatha were involved with the case the agency was currently investigating, but how Josie managed to keep up with her own schedule.

3

There had been a glorious week in 2019 when Sol's two major preoccupations had been finding a new cleaning person who suited her arbitrary standards, after the retirement of her previous housekeeper, and succeeding in scheduling an elusive interview with the tremendously busy Zoe Saldaña.

For years, Sol had been the epitome of first-world problems: shopping for the right party gown for an awards ceremony, finding the appropriate way to phrase a question about a possible return to William Shakespeare adaptations while chatting with Kenneth Branagh, remembering never to ask Harrison Ford about Star Wars during an interview (but only pre–2015's *The Force Awakens*) and making sure to be invited to all advanced movie press screenings even if she wasn't planning on always attending.

Yet during the last three years, luck and meaningless problems had been more elusive. First, she'd realized she no longer loved—or even liked—the man she'd been married to. He'd actively contributed to that dislike. So she left him

and decided she needed to put the whole American conti-
nent and the Atlantic Ocean between the two of them.

There was also the matter that she'd been homesick for
Europe in a way that living in California could not appease.
So she moved to London in the run-up to a global pandemic
that made her realize she liked herself a lot but perhaps *not
that much*. She had moved to London after all, not to
Barcelona, and the number of people she knew in the
British capital was limited. But she couldn't find a way to
move back to her hometown and salvage her career as an
entertainment journo. London had been the compromise.

In the end, she'd managed a divorce, an international
move, career survival, and isolation. But now came this.

She was starting the day in the worst possible way:
opening her email and realizing there was no need to go
over the transcription of the interview she'd done with
Melanie Lynskey a couple of days before. Or to shoot a third
email to the Supreme Video publicist who'd been ignoring
her requests of access to press screeners of their latest YA
paranormal show.

Sol had been fired. *Again.*

It wasn't as if she hadn't seen the looming signs of layoffs
coming. This was her second time being "impacted" (the
euphemistic corporate lingo of media conglomerates) by
restructuring, re-strategizing, or simple bad luck. It stank
and it happened at the worst possible moment. She loved
her work and (most of) her colleagues. She had finally been
able to carve a position as a critic and to write (mostly)
about what she liked. And she was supposed to finally interview Emma Thompson the following week!

Now she wasn't. Her former micromanager and over-
editor-in-chief had made sure to send her one last and very
ironically thoughtful email assuring her she shouldn't worry

about Emma Thompson. They'd take care of the interview in-house. If she could only send them the contact information for the PR people who made it possible and remind him where and when it was supposed to happen...

"Al igual," she yelled at her computer's screen in her native Spanish—the language that came more naturally to her when she was in a mood. She had no intention of surrendering *any* of her contacts.

She was on the verge of being officially not okay. She was forty-two, almost forty-three really. Here came the world of freelancing, pitching to unknowns, and looking for work. *Again.*

There were not that many positions in her line of work, let alone ones that paid well and were meant for people with her experience. Plus, she'd seen colleagues laid off left and right for the previous months. And rumor had it that all those jobs would be taken by AI robots soon.

Her industry was imploding just when her father had finally stopped asking her to quit the masochistic path of entertainment journalism and join the family business. And now she'd proved that he was right all along. Here it was: the moment in which she'd have to dip into her squandered fund. *Again.*

...

That night, Sol was meeting Laia at 5:30 p.m. at the bar of their favorite Italian restaurant in Soho. They had bought tickets to see James McAvoy at the nearby Trafalgar Theatre weeks before, and Sol had decided to keep the date with her friend and tell her all about the layoff during dinner. It would help her unwind.

She'd been dealing with the fallout of her newly found

unemployment for most of the day. On top of being the most vexing of things, layoffs always implied a lot of tiresome paperwork.

The play Laia and Sol were seeing started at 7:30 sharp —as plays do, Sol had made sure to instill that idea into her friend's mind—and it was an eleven-minute walk from the restaurant to the theater, hence the unseasonably early dinner reservation for a couple of Barcelona natives.

It was 5:35 p.m. and Sol checked her messages and waited alone at the bar of Bocca di Lupo, a glass of chilled Sauvignon Blanc in hand. Laia hadn't notified her yet of a late arrival, but Sol had no intention of keeping McAvoy waiting.

She decided she'd start ordering food if her friend didn't get there in five minutes. She'd go as far as eating alone if necessary. Laia was notorious for her chronic tardiness. It was one of her only flaws. But Sol hoped there would be no need to dine by herself. She *really* needed to vent and pour her insecurities into her friend.

Having one of her best friends move to London at around the same time Sol had chosen the British city as a home destination was the best thing that had happened to her in the last decade. Plus, Laia had always been unabashedly reassured in herself and her friends. A bit of her friend's uncompromising certainty was what Sol needed most at the moment.

"No hi havia forma que acabéssim la peça d'avui," Laia told Sol when she finally rushed into the restaurant.

Being the newly minted correspondent in London for the biggest Catalan public TV channel came with strings attached, and Laia had been working until that very moment. She'd been delayed more than expected because she was shooting a feature on Catalan businesspeople working in the city.

Sol knew she had rushed there. Laia's hair was a bit disheveled. But she was still in full camera makeup and she only remembered to say hello and greet Sol with the customary two kisses on the cheeks after detailing the reason for her late arrival at 5:37.

Had they been in their hometown, Laia wouldn't have given such a reasonable explanation, Sol thought. It was a mere seven-minute delay! But they were in London now—and they had tickets to see McAvoy.

"Who's with the kid?" Sol asked Laia in Catalan as her friend sat on a stool next to her at the bar and checked the menu.

It wasn't lost on Sol that her own move from Los Angeles to London had been easy in comparison to her friend's. The Californian phase of Sol's life had run its course and nothing was binding her to a city she'd called home for more than a decade—other than a few friends she missed dearly. She'd grabbed her clothes, some of her books, and her vintage cerise-colored Le Creuset kettle, and left.

For Laia, things had been different. She'd been offered the kind of position she should have gotten years earlier— an opportunity hard to get in the small, nepotist-ridden, sexist market they both knew so well. Yet she was a single mom and moving to London from Barcelona meant being far from most of her friends and her family, who more often than not pitched in when someone had to stay with Laia's three-year-old if she was working.

"Paula is with the new nanny. Wish us luck," Laia said, making eye contact with one of the waiters and alerting them that they were ready to order.

The last few months had seen a coming and going of nannies, none resilient enough for the demands of the capricious but adorable Paula.

"We know what we want, right?" Laia asked Sol when the waiter approached. They'd been meeting regularly enough at the place. It was one of their newfound routines in the city and a habit that made them feel more at home.

"Absolutely yes. McAvoy is waiting! But I need to tell you something," Sol said.

They ordered first and then Sol detailed her news to Laia.

"How could this have happened to me *again*? When they offered me the job, they guaranteed me their finances were in order. At the end of last year, we were swimming in money apparently. Not that the editorial team saw any of it. And all of a sudden, poof!"

"Don't worry. You'll find something else," Laia said in her most reassuring tone.

"I wish I could be so certain. And I'm a bit terrified of the search, to be honest. Shouldn't things be easier by now? We're in our forties! We struggled through our twenties taking the most hideous jobs, and in our thirties things never completely got comfortable. You know how it is. I was at a point in my career where it looked like I was finally able to settle down and enjoy the journey. But no. Here I am, treading water again."

"We're constantly treading water, Sol," Laia told her in all seriousness. "With every new story, every deadline, and every fight with our editors. That's why we chose this job. It wouldn't be fun otherwise."

"Not sure I have the energy to keep having so much fun with this profession. Thinking about turning to a boring one."

"Are you sure about that?" Laia asked, and Sol couldn't help but smile. She knew her friend would lift the burden on her shoulders, if only a little.

4

Luke unpacked the fiber- and protein-filled granola bar, wondering what Sol and her friend would be savoring at that same exact moment. If he'd been the one dining there, he'd be devouring the bruschetta with sheep ricotta and the sea bream baked in salt. But the alternative wasn't that grim thanks to his foresight of always carrying provisions.

He'd started making his own snacks after two months at the agency. He'd realized that all the surveillance work he did meant eating on the go and not getting to sit in any of the swanky eateries that his marks invariably frequented. The agency would never reimburse him for it. The options were either homemade refreshments, fast food that would appall his former longtime yoga teacher, or starving.

Luke had landed the spot at Thompson & Thomson—one of London's biggest sleuthing agencies—after years of contracting work for some of the less renowned outlets. It didn't take long to realize T&T's bread and butter was the same mixture of divorce cases, child custody disputes, background checks, and work-harassment inquiries he'd been devoting his hours—basically his life—to for the last eight years as a contractor for smaller firms.

At T&T, there were still endless hours watching subjects from a distance, following them, attempting to take incriminatory pictures, and more often than not trying to rule them out as culprits.

He'd been assigned to this particular case feeling his luck was finally about to change. The dominant streaming service Meshflixx had hired T&T to look into the theft of one of their screenplays. The first episode in the second season of one of Meshflixx's hit TV shows had leaked online mere hours after one of the show's creators noticed a physical copy of the script missing. The last place the creator had been with that copy of the script was Josie's studio. Sol had been at the studio that evening.

But here he was, watching his mark sip white wine while he was freezing outside—the weather had turned vile that evening—and feeling very much like a perfect stalker.

He'd been watching Sol, along with some of her Pilates colleagues, for over two weeks and could not find a fault with the woman. She was a sharp dresser, always on time, and seemed equally devoted to her profession, fitness, and friends.

He had even caught her reading the intriguingly titled *Come as You Are* by Emily Nagoski Ph.D. and was now page-turning it himself when the job permitted it. The Kindle app on his phone tended to carry the latest best-selling crime book, but he found Nagoski's work enlightening.

He was starting to dread not having met Sol under different circumstances even if the sometimes uptight and somewhat bohemian-yet-posh journalist was nothing like his usual type. And, of course, he shouldn't omit the fact that she was possibly a thief.

"Dreading the gig already?" Divya's voice interrupted Luke's inner musings as his colleague approached from behind, ready to fill in for him on surveillance duty.

"Not dreading this one actually," Luke said, catching another glimpse of Sol talking with her friend.

"I see." Divya had a knowing smile on her face. "I personally also have no objection against following Sol around the city, especially when she's dressed in leggings and cropped tank tops."

"It's not that!" Somehow, he could feel his whole face turning red.

"Relax, mate. She's a good-looking person," Divya said.

"But it feels somewhat strange to think about, considering she doesn't know she's being watched. Doesn't it?"

"I keep telling you: Don't. Overthink. The. Job. Learn as much as you can. Don't spend everything you earn. We don't get paid that much, but still... save a little. Try to get as much access to the clients as possible. Make contacts. And one day..."

"Here's for that agency we'll hopefully open one day, yes," Luke said, toasting her with his half-eaten granola bar.

He'd met Divya when he'd started working at T&T two months before. They'd gotten on well from the start and somehow had already talked—half-joked, at least—about the agency they'd run together and how they'd do things so differently from their managers.

He left the stakeout, checking the window of Bocca di Lupo one last time and pulling up the collar of his tweed coat. Spring would still make herself scarce for a few weeks. He had over thirty years of experience with London weather and tried to always dress for it, but his hometown still managed to catch him ill-equipped sometimes.

5

Luke was at the agency's kitchenette making himself the strongest possible cup of tea. He kept his own JING Assam Breakfast bags in a locked drawer at his desk because the regular office-provided PG Tips wouldn't cut it. He took his brew without any milk or sugar and went as far as steeping his black tea for six minutes, not the customary five, for maximum strength and a hint of bitterness.

Luke carried his favorite *Talented Mr. Ripley* mug to the conference room. The debriefing meeting had just started when he got in. Divya's image was projected on the room's big screen. She was connecting from home after working until late the previous night while trailing Sol, codename the Stringer.

"They left the restaurant a bit after seven. The Stringer was pretty eager to get moving." Divya checked her notes. "The friend, on the other hand... Not sure how those two managed to become friendly with the Stringer being such a great believer in punctuality."

"They met at uni," Luke added, feeling like a nosy

voyeur once again. Had he been doing his job when he'd tried to find out as much as possible about the mark's background? Or had he been extra zealous?

He knew Sol was around forty and, according to her LinkedIn and more than a decade's worth of online clippings, she'd been working as a journalist for almost half her life. She had lived in Los Angeles for about ten years. Yet, with all his digging, he hadn't figured out what had made Sol leave that city and relocate to London. Not that he thought anyone needed a reason for that.

"The play was over a bit after ten and they left the theater with the bulk of the audience. They seemed pleased with what they saw, in case anyone wants to check McAvoy's play at the Trafalgar," Divya said when she clearly couldn't offer anything meaty on the subject. "I think they may have considered going for a drink in a nearby bar, but the friend checked her messages and decided against it. It must have been something important because, in a matter of seconds, the Stringer hailed a black cab, gave the friend a couple of air kisses, and sent her away. From my past surveillance, it normally takes these two a minimum of forty-five minutes to actually say goodbye."

Luke half smiled. He had witnessed the same.

"And would long goodbyes make the Stringer more likely to be our thief?" interjected Thompson. The agency's founding partner was wearing one of those bespoke three-piece suits that were expensive even to look at, and yet it did nothing for him. Luke hadn't been able to pinpoint what it was, but there was something inherently unkempt about his appearance, even fresh from a £200 wet shave and maintenance haircut.

"Er... no," admitted Divya. "In any case, the Stringer

grabbed another taxi and was home by half ten. What really puzzles me though is how she can afford to live there."

"She manages to make a decent living," Luke said. He'd also been surprised at Sol owning the two-bedroom, two-bathroom house. It had sold for almost £1.5 million at the beginning of 2020.

"As a journalist?" asked Divya, still obviously in disbelief.

Thompson chuckled.

There was nothing their fifty-something-year-old boss liked more than rejoicing in the many things others couldn't afford with their choice of profession and their family background, especially when he could easily afford it.

"She comes from money," added Luke, and Thompson stopped snickering.

There was nothing the co-founder of T&T liked *less* than the possibility of an improbable person having more money than he initially assumed.

"Explain," said Thompson curtly.

"Her family owns an import and distribution company. They focus on the US market and specialize in gourmet and traditional Spanish foods. Arbequina olive oil, Marcona almonds, and the like." Luke checked his notes, thankful for the research he'd put in.

"It's a lot of oil and nuts for a £1.5-million house, don't you think? And it's not like she works at the family's company," said Thompson. Luke was sure something about the idea of a Southern European journalist and uncoupled woman with independent wealth didn't sit well with the manager.

"I think she may be a trust-fund kid," admitted Luke. "But I can try to look into the specifics of how much her family's company is worth and dig a bit more into her economic situation."

"Do it. Was she a cash buyer who used all that family money, or does she owe a big mortgage? That would give her incentive. I like her for this."

Luke cringed at his boss's lack of investigative rigor. He *liked* her as the thief in their investigation.

"But let's not get ahead of ourselves," Thompson continued. "Who else may have the motive to steal?"

Luke grabbed the dossier of the case once again and tried to put names to all possibly involved in the disappearance of the leaked script besides Sol Novo. There was the wife of one of London's richest TV producers, Philippa Majors. There was Agatha Condon, the minor TV agent who'd seen better times in her career. Then Josie Ruiz, of course, the Pilates studio owner and the one who'd been teaching the night of the theft: Thursday, February 23. And there was Sara Daniels, one half of the duo of siblings and co-creators of the Meshflixx show *The Privateers.*

The period detective drama was co-run by Sara and her twin sister, Bryana Daniels. A copy of a script of the show with Sara's name watermarked on all pages was inside the creator's bag when she went to Josie's class the evening of the theft. Sara could no longer find it there when she left to go home. Her bag had been inside a locker the whole time. The contents of the script were published online a few hours later.

It had been a particularly full class suffering to Josie's whims at the studio that night. Among the other attendees was Martha Broch, a visual artist and title designer who'd recently won an Emmy for her work reminiscent of Saul Bass in a Christopher Nolan sci-fi miniseries. Mark Green had also been there. He was a veteran director with more than twenty hits under his belt, although none of them had been released during the last decade. And then there was Lashana Fletcher, a perfectly put-together PR consultant who was all straight white teeth and not a single wrinkle in her flawless skin or designer clothes.

All of them had close ties to London's film and TV industry, and all of them were regulars at Josie's small outfit for the fitness enthusiasts and worried-wells. Lashana was the newest addition and had only been to the studio on two previous occasions before the night of the theft. But she had remained a dedicated client since then.

Luke, Divya, and their T&T colleague Sanjay had followed them all intermittently to see if something in their behavior could link them to the theft. So far, no investigator had anything to report other than the marks' recurring sweaty visits to the Pilates studio and a taste for going out to lunch and dinner to some of London's most popular spots.

"The client wasn't happy with our first bill," said Thomson. T&T's other founding partner wore his customary no-efforts-given mix of baggy jeans and not-necessarily-clean hoodie. He tended to be in charge of delivering controversial decisions. "Too many hours billed. And I happen to think they're right. So we'll probably start eliminating surveillance in the next couple of days."

"Whom do we feel should still be on top of our list of suspects besides Sol?" countered P, adjusting his cufflinks. To distinguish between their bosses' too-similar last names, the junior partners openly referred to Thompson as *P* and Thomson, without the *p*, not so openly as *Sweatshirt* due to his apparel decisions.

"The has-been successful agent keeps fitting the profile," said Divya, and Luke was happy to see he wasn't the only one with the same feeling about Agatha. "She lives in a three-bedroom apartment in Notting Hill, she pays for Josie's ridiculously prohibitive monthly membership, she keeps a maid on staff part-time, and she's just back from a trip to St. Barts. Yet she barely seems to be at the agency or have any clients left…"

"Let's not forget Mark has a beef with Meshflixx," added Sanjay.

A few days prior, Sanjay had overheard a disgruntled phone call in which the filmmaker complained to his agent about his movies being available on the streaming service. Apparently, Mark wasn't getting much money off that, and he didn't like the format in which the films were made available on the service.

Thompson and Thomson agreed to keep intermittent surveillance on all subjects with the idea of dropping it on Martha (too successful in her career), Lashana (too well-connected in her profession to even contemplate such a self-sabotaging plot as theft), and Philippa (simply too rich due to her marital status) in the upcoming days if they kept looking uninvolved with the affair.

6

Sol flew economy plus instead of business because she hadn't been feeling completely like herself when she booked her plane ticket. She felt something similar to hesitation for spending her *other* money when at present she had no immediate prospects of earning any with her work.

She normally had no qualms about spending the sum that had been so generously given to her. It helped her maintain a more comfortable life than if she'd had to rely on her profession alone. She was grateful for it. She would perhaps have chosen a different career path—a more lucrative, safer, easier one—had it not been for the *other* money. Writing still felt like an occupation for the bourgeois.

But regardless of her relative wealth, which forced her to employ a finance guru and pay the government an indecent amount of taxes, she considered herself quite down to earth.

She led a simple life. She wasn't extravagant. She had only gotten used to a few minor luxuries really: air conditioning, radiant heating, a connected car, delivered groceries, and occasional visits to an excellent cosmetic dermatologist. Her biggest propensity toward splurging was a taste for four- and five-star hotels—and flying first class. Nothing major.

Her preference didn't come only from the extra comfort and room provided by the most expensive type of airfare, but because statistically there were fewer chances of encountering yelling children. And, most importantly, she wasn't at risk of having to interact with and fight for space against one of the many relentless man spreaders who abounded on planes.

But that was exactly the situation at her current economy plus seat. She had opted for that seat while booking her last-minute flight because the semblance of a belt-tightening gesture was needed after having lost her job —especially considering her financial illiteracy had prevented her from finding out how much money she still had in her fund. Plus, the flight was only two hours. Surely, she could endure economy plus during that time. Right?

Not really.

Not if she didn't find a way of isolating herself from a man spreader who wouldn't shut up about the rise of conscious Artificial Intelligence while being oblivious to the non-written rule of never crossing the invisible border that divides two seats occupied by strangers on a plane.

Sol retreated in her seat in the direction opposite to the man spreader, adjusted her KN95 face mask for the umpteenth time, and reapplied hand sanitizer. She grabbed her oversized handmade BIBA leather bag, took out her Bose noise-canceling headphones, and put them on. She retrieved Taylor Jenkins Reid's latest novel, which was also inside her excellently outfitted purse, and completely blocked her neighbor by strategically placing the book in front of her face.

They landed an hour later. The moment she saw the city's nocturnal coastline and the wheels contacted the runway, she felt better. It was almost absurd how, after so many years being a consummate expat, the moment things turned sideways she always felt the same urge to get on a plane headed for one particular destination. But she could finally breathe now. Everything would be okay.

She was home.

Things had started to look bad for Sol. Luke still wanted to believe the journalist had nothing—or at least not much—to do with the disappearance of the leaked script, but he was beginning to doubt his good sense. Especially when so many things pointed toward her.

First, there was a lavish lifestyle that would put her in need of cash unless they could confirm where her money was coming from or that she was indeed receiving funds from her family. Because Divya was right. No writer who wasn't more of a brand name could afford to live, dress, shop, and eat out the way Sol did.

And now, after a couple of hours of exhaustive online digging, he'd found ties to her and *Voyeur*, the same dubious internet outlet that first uploaded a series of badly taken photographs of Meshflixx's stolen script with Sara Daniels's name watermarked on it. The script had disappeared from the studio on a Thursday evening. *Voyeur* leaked its content the following morning.

It appeared that Sol had written several short articles for said outlet in the early 2000s. The collaboration had only lasted for a few months, according to the results yielded by a deep search of internet archival material. Sol Novo–bylined articles at *Voyeur* were no longer available with a simple

Google search, but the digital trace was there and it linked the Stringer with the leak.

"Found anything juicy?"

Luke jumped at P's approach. He hadn't known he was being watched.

"Not sure yet," Luke said, even if he was certain what he'd just unearthed wasn't just juicy but quite the bombshell. He also knew it was something he needed to tell P right away. It could be the kind of stunt he needed to keep the good graces of the partner. "I'm checking something on the Stringer's online CV."

In the process, he found mention of all sorts of random and minor jobs like Sol's tutoring job during her university years, but the CV contained no mention of her being a contributor at *Voyeur*.

When Luke shared his findings with P, his manager *liked* the Spaniard even more for the job and found the whole omission of *Voyeur* suspicious. Especially after he had spent half an hour playing with the company's drone and realized Sol's place on Roupell Street had solar panels recently installed and a parking space in the back garden where a brand-new Tesla Model Y currently resided.

Luke could understand that someone who had made a career in writing, like Sol had, would like to avoid including certain less reputable mediums like *Voyeur*, but he didn't try swaying Thompson or sharing those views with his manager. Luke couldn't afford to antagonize the friendlier of the partners at T&T.

It was no secret that Sweatshirt wasn't exactly a fan of Luke. He wasn't a fan of anyone, and Luke should have investigated more thoroughly before taking his job at the agency. He'd only discovered Thompson & Thomson's tendency of going through contractors and letting go of detectives *after* he joined the team.

But he couldn't afford to lose his job. Even if it had already been almost a year since things with his ex had fallen through, he was still penniless. After the separation, he'd had to look for a studio flat on his own and all his savings had gone to buying furnishings and covering an astronomic deposit. Plus, the salary at T&T was nowhere what he thought it would be and he had no savings to speak of regardless of Divya's insistence that he set aside a bit of money every month.

He didn't want to think about the possibility of losing his job and having to crash on his youngest sister's sofa or—even worse—being forced to return to his parents' place.

7

So far, she was having a glorious stay. She had landed late the previous night, grabbed a taxi, and immediately remembered the lack of politeness that so often characterized her fellow Spaniards. She must have been especially homesick because not only didn't she mind that her taxi driver wanted to take a longer route than necessary to her destination, she almost relished it.

She immediately felt the slower pace of the smaller, more laid-back Mediterranean city. Barcelona was still an international capital, but a place where one could stroll at a calmer pace on occasion.

She had woken up that morning, walked to the Oriol Balaguer bakery that had opened a few blocks from her place in the city, got a croissant, and was now devouring it while bathing in the morning sunshine that graced the rooftop terrace of her small but splendidly lit penthouse apartment.

She couldn't help but feel it was a different city from up there—a slower, more genuine one. You could spy on half your neighbors while they were watering the lemon or olive trees and tending to their urban gardens or simply hanging out the washing. The map of the city was laid at your finger-tips. She had views of the Tibidabo and Carmel hills and the Sagrada Família cathedral and never got tired of looking at them.

She had secured the two-bedroom, one-bathroom apartment a few years before, seduced by its location at the heart of Eixample and its views. She had made substantial renovations since she bought the place. There were one and a half bathrooms at present and only one decently sized bedroom. She had also opted for an open-concept kitchen that bled into the dining and living room areas and went against most Barcelona floorplan standards.

Several members of her money-savvy family had first questioned the renovations, approving of them only after they saw the final result, and informed her that the intelligent thing to do would be to sell the apartment for a profit and invest in something else, something bigger in a quieter neighborhood. She hadn't listened.

They also suggested she should rent the apartment while she was away, which was most of the year. But she hadn't listened to that either. She kept some of the books and clothes from her youth as well as some family heirlooms there and couldn't bear the idea of a perfect stranger going through her things, through a part of her life, without her even being aware of it. Plus, she liked the option of having the apartment ready when she felt like flying *home*.

She was nowhere close to solving her lack-of-a-paying-job issue but somehow feeling less stressed about it just because she was there. She'd always been unconventionally minded when it came to following her own path, but also about making and having money. While she took another sip of her tea, she looked at the space around her and felt something close to contentment. She only hoped she'd be able to keep both her place in Barcelona and her house in London considering her lack of money smarts and her professional odds.

"She's fled the country," announced Thompson, making his triumphal entry into the office that morning and holding his brand-new, big-by-any-standards premium phone.

"I'm sorry what?" replied Luke when he realized his boss wasn't making a random announcement but talking to him. Luke had spent the previous two hours trying to piece out who was still one of Agatha's clients. So far, he had two names and neither of them had worked consistently in the last few years.

"The Stringer is no longer in the UK," enunciated Thompson with the same pomp as before.

"Where is she? How did you find out?" Luke spoke with perhaps too much exhilaration. He hadn't gotten his second tea of the morning yet and was trying to compensate for his lack of wakefulness. He was also disappointed in himself. How could someone as generally inept as Thompson have found out that Sol had fled when Luke hadn't realized?

"She's in Barcelona. I follow her on Instagram." Thompson showed the picture of a street-floor tile, depicting four tablets with four circles inside them, on his phone.

Besides Sol's Instagram handle, the only other copy that accompanied the image was the word *Home*.

Luke was convinced that the senior detective was probably following the Stringer on social media from his own personal account, not even realizing she could notice she was being watched by investigators. But also, how hadn't

Luke thought about creating a fake account and keeping an eye on Sol that way too?

He was uncharacteristically unfocused when it came to the case at hand. Fortunately, Thompson was so high on his own discovery, he hadn't realized Luke should have been the one doing the social media monitoring.

Luke couldn't afford any other lapses of concentration if he wanted to keep his job. But even if he knew T&T was going to start downsizing the investigation soon in response to Meshflixx's request for a lower bill, he couldn't quite understand why the streaming giant had hired them in the first place. Why investigate the theft of a script that had already leaked online?

But not only did not Thompson offer any explanation for that, he also ambushed Luke with a most inconvenient request.

8

L uke frantically texted Divya before he needed to shut his phone down.

Luke Contadino: Had to leave in a rush. Will you keep an eye on Agatha?

Divya's reply was graciously fast. He loved that she was always on top of her game. Not that the same could be said about him lately.

Divya Bakshi: Already on it. Just dug some juicy info on her

Of course, she did. He was dreading not being there and not being able to assist her in any way.

Luke Contadino: What info?

Divya Bakshi: We can talk when you're back

Luke Contadino: Don't make me wait! This trip wasn't my idea

Divya Bakshi: You've got to admit our stringer is looking dodgy. She's got ties to Voyeur. She flees to BCN. She was sacked…

Luke Contadino: Journalists get sacked all the time

Divya Bakshi: …

Luke wouldn't wait for Divya's answer. He wanted to be able to wrap up that conversation without his fingers hurting from all the rapid typing.

"You really can't wait…" replied Divya when she finally picked up his call.

"What's the juicy info you got on Agatha?" he asked, trying to learn what Divya knew before he was forced to surrender his mobile phone. "You *know* I can't wait to talk about this until I return. I don't even know how long this will take. Packing was a nightmare."

"Sorry you had to get your luggage ready in a rush and are not sure if you're carrying enough socks or the right type of shirts," teased Divya. The thing was, she was right. Luke was conflicted about what was inside his suitcase. He was sure half of it would be either too warm or not warm enough.

"It's a serious issue!" he protested, hearing how ridiculous he sounded. But for some reason unbeknownst to him, he wanted to look good during his stay.

"Divya, what have you got on Agatha?"

"She was Sara and Bryana Daniels's first agent when they started."

"What?"

"They dumped her a couple of years ago when they got hired by Meshflixx to develop *The Privateers*. They're at one of the big talent agencies now and share an agent with guess who?"

"No idea," said Luke, taking mental notes of everything. He knew there had to be something about Agatha.

"Emmy-winner Martha Broch," Divya announced triumphantly.

"And this is important because..."

"No idea yet. But I'll keep digging. You know I don't believe in coincidences."

"Mate, I need to go," Luke said when a flight attendant's voice started asking passengers to put their mobile devices away.

"Not so fast! Why would our Stringer be sacked if she wasn't involved in leaking the script?"

"It's my understanding that job insecurity is a common occurrence in the profession," said Luke. He'd been told so by several friends of his oldest sister, Gaia, who'd all dabbled in the field and ended up deciding on greener and better-paying, albeit much less fun, pastures. Yet he seemed the only one at T&T to know what he thought was a truth universally acknowledged about journalists.

"And you have tried telling that to our bosses?"

"Several times," he admitted.

"Any luck?"

"Why do you think I'm sandwiched in a middle seat on my way to Barcelona right now?" Luke tried not to raise his voice. But that comment got him looks from the two women sitting on either side of him.

He really was trying to make himself as small as possible and not interfere in anyone's personal space. It was not an easy task for a six-foot person flying in the smallest kind of economy seat.

"Tell me, how is it that we were supposed to start cutting back on surveillance and they decided to send you to Barcelona?" Divya sounded a bit annoyed. But he would have happily exchanged his place with hers and stayed in London. He wasn't fond of flying—or any other aspects of traveling. But Thompson hadn't given him the option of saying no.

"Well, you know how things are at the agency..."

"Nothing ever makes any sense," said Divya, voicing Luke's exact thoughts. "How did you figure out Sol had been sacked?"

"I didn't. Thompson follows her on social media, and she's written about it on Twitter apparently."

"You weren't following her socials?" Divya's tone reminded Luke about his many failings.

He'd been supposed to take the lead in all the marks' online presences. He'd found Sol's landing page as an entertainment critic, as well as her LinkedIn profile, and he'd ascertained that she was in none of the most commonly used dating apps, yet he'd managed to forget all other social media.

"A flight attendant is giving me an evil look. Talk to you when I land. Keep me posted on Agatha. Cheers."

He hung up, put his mobile on airplane mode, and attempted to read without invading any armrests.

9

She was meeting **Miquel** to visit the World Press Photo yearly exhibition at the perpetually hip CCCB, but first they were catching up over a glass of wine at one of the terraces at plaça dels Àngels.

She had gotten there on time after zigzagging among the many skaters who flocked to that particular square in the Catalan city as a skateboarding destination.

She was anticipating the wait so she was comfortably seated, had already ordered a glass of Albariño, and was catching up on her reading of the fourth volume of *Heartstopper*—the creaks and smacks of the skates against the concrete a constant, if not quite melodious, background theme—when Miquel finally appeared.

"Benvinguda," he said when he finally got there, bending down to kiss her on the cheeks and flash one of his most alluring smiles.

"Fas tard," answered Sol. She had lifelong immunity to his many charms and hated the fact that he was always invariably late everywhere.

"London is not agreeing with you," he continued in

Catalan. "I'm only twenty minutes late and I texted you. Plus, you're the one who wanted to see me." He sat down next to her.

The smile hadn't abandoned his lips for a second. His hair was longer than the last time Sol had seen him, and even though she doubted he'd seen a hairdresser for months, his long, mussed locks worked for him in a way not many people could have pulled off. She'd always been jealous of his simple, undemanding beauty.

"I need one of your pep talks," Sol told him.

"What happened?" Real worry blemished his expression for an instant.

"Got laid off again," Sol said. "Been looking for a way to tell my parents. You wouldn't want to talk to my mom, right?" she half-joked.

"I mean, she adores me... and I'm sorry about the job. But why tell them anyway?"

"They'll want to know what I'm doing here."

"You work from home most of the time. You can work from your Barcelona home. Especially now that awards season is over. You've done it in the past."

"I guess. Wouldn't I be lying to them though?"

"Not if they don't ask you about it."

Sol remembered how his mind worked.

He continued, "Don't rush to tell them until you're ready."

Miquel hadn't imparted a proper inspirational speech yet, but Sol was already feeling better. Was it the sunshine? The wine? All the beautiful fashion-forward people walking by?

"What's so bad about being jobless this time? It's happened to you before and you've always managed to find something else. And it happens all the time in our line of work," said Miquel. He sipped his beer, and Sol remembered why she'd called him.

He never panicked and always downplayed things. Nothing rattled him, and she envied his sunny views on everything. It was almost as if he'd been untouched by life drama and midlife crisis, by age itself. And the thing was, he pretty much looked the same way he had twenty years before. He was the only friend Sol had her own age who could make her forget they now lived in the land of yearly mammograms, knee pain, back problems, kitchen repairs, endless bills, infinite laundry that needed folding, and all the other insufferable adulting stuff.

"What happens is that this time I'm older than the previous time, and our profession doesn't reward seniority," she said more for herself than for him. Saying it out loud helped Sol understand why the layoff had hit her so hard.

"I know you don't like me reminding you about it," Miquel said, "but you don't have to worry. You have more contacts now than you had last time precisely because you're older. So what if you have to freelance for a few months?"

"I hate freelancing!"

"We all do. The difference is, you don't really need to worry about the pay at the end of the month. Can you at least try enjoying your family money for the rest of us? You know I'd gladly be in your place." He flashed that smirk of his once again.

"Don't get used to this, but I think you may be right," said Sol, even if she knew Miquel was considerably magnifying whatever money he thought she had.

...

She had said goodbye to Miquel after a tedious forty-five minutes of him insisting on mansplaining the whole photographic exhibition. Sol was reminded of why her first marriage had imploded.

He was captivating and had a bright take on everything that mostly made life easy, and she'd been madly in love with him when they were younger. But he was better in small doses.

She needed to make sure to go to the museum another time during her Barcelona visit though. The exhibition appeared to be fascinating without the imposed audio guide.

That evening, she was meeting her friends Laura and Lali for drinks at a quaint gin cocktails bar in one of Eixample's quintessential corner buildings near her place. Her friends were already having basil-infused gin and tonics when she got there. She knew she should have opted for water—she always drank too much when she was home—yet she decided to join them.

They talked about relationships, gentrification, fast fashion, inflation, and shared custody as the ideal but flawed co-parenting formula after divorce for couples with children. They touched on work, but what really kept them engaged was a lively conversation about strength training, anti-inflammatory nourishment, and wood therapy. Lali swore by the wooden technique in her fight against cellulite, even if it was apparently painful, and Sol resolved to do her own online research.

Lali was sharing the name and contact info of her personal trainer in case Sol wanted some guided-workout suffering during her visit to Barcelona when the conversation took a turn Sol didn't see coming.

"Are you worried?" Lali asked her in Catalan.

"About my job? A little," Sol admitted. She'd briefed her friends on her newly attained unemployed status.

"I actually meant about the theft of *The Privateers* script," Lali explained. "Wasn't it stolen at the studio you go to all the time?"

"Yes, so?" Sol didn't understand what her friend was trying to tell her.

"Aren't you worried they're gonna think you had something to do with it?"

"With the theft? Why would anyone think such a preposterous thing!" Her friends could be so ridiculous sometimes. They didn't have the first idea about how things worked in the showbiz industry.

Sol was still musing about what little her hometown friends knew about certain aspects of her life when she saw someone who looked familiar sitting at the bar.

"Do we know him?" Sol asked Lali and Laura.

The friends didn't even pretend to conceal their curiosity, turning rapidly to look at the person Sol was referring to. His profile was visible from the table they occupied, and Sol hoped the bar was too busy for him to notice their scrutiny.

"I don't think so," said Laura.

Lali agreed and implied she wouldn't mind getting to know him.

"I didn't think we knew him," said Sol. He was too young to be one of their peers from school or college. "But he looks familiar."

She never forgot a face and hated it when she couldn't place someone.

They got a message from Lurdes—yes, Sol was aware of the remarkable affinity she felt for people whose names started with L—swearing she'd be there in the following ten minutes, right after dropping off her kid at her parents'.

"I'm gonna get us something to eat," said Sol, knowing they were going to be there for a while. She headed to order some food.

When she got to the bar, the guy who looked familiar saw her. He seemed surprised, but it looked like he recognized her right away.

"Ens coneixem, oi?" she asked him in Catalan, her go-to language in the city.

"I'm sorry, what?" he muttered in English. Sol placed his husky voice and Estuary English accent.

"Oh, we know each other from London. Now I remember!" she said. "You're the guy from my Pilates class, right?"

He looked different than she remembered though. Hotter.

"Yes," the TDS muttered.

10

What was Sol doing there? Luke had landed that afternoon, checked in at the hotel, went for a walk and got into the first bar he saw when he felt like having a pint only to realize he was in a fancy gin and tonic place where there were no beers to be had. And suddenly, there she was.

As a Londoner, he had the habit of thinking about other cities as small and even provincial, but could Barcelona really be this minuscule? This couldn't be sheer chance. He wasn't supposed to start looking for Sol until the following morning.

"I'm Sol," she said, and he was a bit perplexed. He knew who she was. "And I'm sorry because I don't remember your name," she added after an uncomfortable pause.

It dawned on Luke.

For her, he was just a random bloke from Pilates.

"I'm Luke," he said, and right away he realized he'd used his name instead of his alter ego's. Finding her there had totally caught him off guard. She didn't seem to realize he was called differently at Josie's though.

"What are you doing in Barcelona?" she asked.

She was by far the chattiest and nicest she'd ever been with him.

"Work stuff," he said, hoping she wouldn't go all journalist on him and ask a thousand follow-up questions about what exactly his work or the *stuff* was. "What are you doing here?"

"Oh, I don't need a reason. I'm from here," she said.

Was she giggling? No, he had to be imagining it.

"Hold on a second, I need to order some food and the bartender is finally paying attention," she said, then proceeded to talk to the only waiter behind the bar.

Luke tried following the rapid-fire conversation. He spoke Italian with his parents and sisters, so Catalan couldn't be that hard, right? It was. He did discern something about eating, perhaps? At least something sounded like *mangiare* and now a couple of women sitting at a nearby table were also participating in the frenzied conversation.

Perhaps he was wrong and his family wasn't as unbearably loud as he'd always thought. These people were vociferous.

"We're gonna have to go," Sol told him. "Apparently, they don't have food here. Not even some chips and olives." She rolled her eyes. "We still haven't had dinner. We're leaving in search of another place so we can eat and wait for our other friend to finally arrive. She's gonna be late. She always is."

Did Sol always talk this fast?

"If you're staying in the city for a few days, give me a call. I can show you around," she added.

Was Sol asking him out?

His impression of her during their brief interactions at Pilates had always made him believe that she barely tolerated him and found him annoying.

"I—I don't have your number," he muttered. "Should I DM you?"

He didn't want to seem too eager, and he really didn't understand what was going on. But if she was asking him out, he was game.

"Right," she said and left.

Luke didn't know how to play it cool with her. He had to have said something wrong. But what?

She was back almost immediately though, with her mobile phone in hand. She unlocked it and gave it to him. He looked at her.

"Your number," she said, as if what she'd just done was the most obvious thing.

And it probably was, but Luke's brain wasn't functioning in a particularly expedient way with Sol in front of him. She wore a black slip dress on top of a white T-shirt and classic Dr. Martens boots, and he had a soft spot for anything with a nineties flavor.

He made sure to type his first and last names the way he liked creating contacts in his own device, added his number, and gave her phone back. She called the number and his own mobile vibrated in his back pocket.

"Now you have my number too. Need to go now. Adeu!"

She left with her two friends, and Luke hoped they wouldn't have to walk much before they found a place to eat. They were obviously pissed.

He was about to grab his phone and message Divya about the whole encounter when he realized that not only had he given Sol his real name, but he'd also given her his personal phone number. And he'd done it with no qualms even if she fitted the profile of the thief he was trying to catch.

11

When Sol snoozed her cell phone alarm for the first time the following morning, her headache was difficult to ignore. By the time she'd snoozed it three times, she realized she was hungover. She hadn't even drunk that much the previous day! But she could no longer pretend she was still in her twenties.

The night had been fun though.

She'd had dinner with the girls and had promised Laura she'd join her that week for a Zumba class at her gym. Sol must have been euphorically tipsy to have agreed to *that*. Her lack of coordination had kept her away from Zumba, barre, and all sorts of other group classes where you needed to show some rhythm and the basic ability to follow dance choreography.

"Aargh!" she protested out loud, covering her face with one of the bed pillows when she realized there was no way out of joining the Zumba class without offending Laura.

She grabbed her buzzing phone to snooze her alarm again when she saw the text message.

> Luke Contadino: It was great running into
> you yesterday. Does your offer still stand?

"¿Qué oferta?" yelled Sol in Spanish. She sat up, remembering everything that happened the night before and realizing she had *indeed* been drunk.

Had she really not only flirted—a little—with the TDS but also given him her cell phone number and offered to show him around?

She didn't even like him!

Right?

However, on second thought, he looked different the previous night. He was sexy in a way she'd never come to appreciate in London. He no longer looked like a banker/lawyer/dude who was at the studio following his doctor's advice to start doing Pilates as a way of exercising in a low-impact way. He almost looked... *cool*.

He'd been wearing washed black slim jeans and a clingy, distressed and equally dark T-shirt. His short black curls weren't styled into a gelled, rigid do like in London but were loose. And did he have stubble? He would have had to for Sol to have given him her number. It was against her moral and taste standards to behave in any other way.

She replied right away.

> Sol Novo: Sure, I have a super-curated list
> of recommendations that I can send
> you now.

Her initial reaction was always to try and get out of whatever new or unusual situation her more motivated self had created. She copied and pasted her many-times-shared email of Barcelona musts, crossed her fingers that all of it would fit into a text message or two, and sent it Luke's way.

She also edited his contact info on her phone to make him more recognizable. There were way too many entries in her contacts for L names, and she needed clarity.

> Luke Contadino (a.k.a. TDS): Any chance that you'd accompany me to one of the many bodegas and bars on your list?

Sol started typing an answer, but Luke was quicker.

> Luke Contadino (a.k.a. TDS): We could also meet for an afternoon snack if you prefer.

Coming up with an excuse would have been easy, yet she surprised herself by accepting.

> Sol Novo: OK, let's meet this afternoon for berenar. Are you free at 17?

> Luke Contadino (a.k.a. TDS): Yes

> Sol Novo: Meet me at the corner of ronda Sant Antoni and carrer Tallers and we can have some ensaïmades at Forn Mistral.

> Luke Contadino (a.k.a. TDS): Sounds delicious even if I don't know how to pronounce it. Are Catalan classes included?

Sol couldn't avoid smiling. She was downright enjoying the text conversation even if a part of herself, who was now completely sober, wanted nothing to do with Luke.

After her second divorce and the events leading to it, she had implicitly sworn off romantic relationships and cultivated a greater social life instead.

Conflicted as she was, she had no clue how to respond to that text. And she was supposed to write for a living!

Sol Novo: Only if you prove worthy of them.

She couldn't believe she had sent that last text. She locked her phone, put it away, and hoped that a long shower, strong tea, and a dosage of naproxen would help with that headache of hers.

12

Luke was at the designated corner at 16:51. He triple-checked it was the right intersection. There were so many narrow streets in that part of the city, and he wanted to be sure.

He would never admit it to anyone, but even if what he'd managed to pack could be described as *meager*, he'd changed his clothes three times before leaving the hotel to head there that afternoon.

He'd only been somewhat satisfied with his sartorial selection after calling his youngest sister, Martina, with the excuse of how poorly he'd readied his luggage for his last-minute work trip. She was four years older than him and worked as a wardrobe coordinator in reality TV.

Martina had been initially suspicious but didn't press him much. It was true that he hadn't sought her advice on how to dress since he was at uni, but it was also true that he'd never been out of the country for business. So she seemed to deduce Luke wanted to look the best in the hip Mediterranean city.

Luke's sister had told him to keep it simple and he'd

listened. He was feeling confident in the same pair of dark jeans he'd worn the day before paired with an open black-and-white checked shirt over a gray T-shirt.

Then he saw Sol approaching and felt simultaneously hot and underdressed.

She had on a leather jacket over a flowy long black and blush-pink dress tightened at the waist. She walked the tiled street in her high-heeled espadrilles with the confidence of someone wearing the most comfortable sneakers. Barcelona clearly had a sunny dress code that no one had bothered sharing with Luke.

"Hola," she said.

Barcelona was doing something to him, and he almost replied *ciao* even though he never spoke Italian outside of his parents' place. He was a bit disappointed that she hadn't greeted him with her signature two kisses on the cheeks though.

She signaled the way they were going, and he followed.

"We're going to the sit-down location of this bakery," she said. "It isn't the most charming spot in the city, but the pastries are incredible and it's easy to find a table and have a calm conversation away from the hordes of tourists."

He nodded, trying to no avail to find something clever to say.

"Do you eat everything?" Sol asked him when they entered the bakery.

"Yes," Luke replied hesitantly, feeling there was probably only one right answer to that question.

"Do you eat pork?" she added curtly.

"Pork? Yes." He was a bit confused, but Sol didn't clarify.

She talked to the person behind the counter in her characteristic commanding-yet-polite Catalan flow.

"Do you want something to drink other than water? The

tea is mostly tepid, insipid water in this city," she said to him in English.

"No tea then, ta." That was the most decisive he'd been with her that afternoon, and he thought she smiled at his words.

He tried paying, but Sol didn't permit it. She played hostess to perfection, paid, grabbed a tray carrying two round pastries covered in powdered sugar and two bottles of water, and guided them to one of the upstairs tables away from the diverse crowd of families and tourists having an afternoon snack downstairs.

"This is an ensaïmada," she told him, pronouncing every syllable in the word while looking at him from across the table. Luke hadn't seen her hazel eyes from such a close distance before. They were warm in a way he wasn't quite prepared to take in. "It's made with saïm, which is basically pork lard, that's why I asked. Also, this is originally from Mallorca, so please don't do the whole 'I had this typical Barcelona pastry called ensaïmades' thing."

"I won't." He smiled and tried the pastry, convinced he was going to cover his clothes and face in powdered sugar. "This is so good!"

"Right?" she said, and he almost felt as if he'd passed a test. "Where did you eat?" she asked him between ensaï-mada bites.

"Lunch? Some place around the corner from the hot—"

"Some random place?!" Sol protested. There it was again —that elevated tone of voice that he was starting to take to, and which was much more common in her native Catalan and Spanish but could still emerge in English. "I sent you a detailed list with several restaurant recommendations this morning. There was a wide range of prices and types of food. I even added vegetarian, pescatarian, and gluten-free

options, and you go to a random place and have an unre-
markable meal?!"

"Sorry, I didn't know I should be—"

"Treating each opportunity to eat in this city as if it's a
religious event?" she finished.

"Yes..."

"Now you know." It sounded a bit like a warning. "Don't
waste any other meals in my city."

He nodded and looked at her intently. He got the
message. Also, those amber flecks in her brown eyes were
doing something to his core.

"Since we're on the subject of rituals. Where do I get a
proper English Breakfast tea in this city?" he asked,
genuinely curious.

"Nowhere. My place is probably the best option really,"
Sol said matter-of-factly.

"Can I come to your place for breakfast tomorrow then?"
He smoldered at her, his charming mode fully on.

"No, but I can recommend a couple of good enough
places. I'll text them to you later." For the first time that
afternoon, she wasn't making eye contact.

"Which one of your restaurant recommendations
should I put on top of my list? And is there any chance you'd
go there with me?" he asked. "You've seen that I need all the
guidance I can get."

"You're unrelenting." She smiled at him, cleaning some
powdered sugar from her cheek.

"You were the one asking me out yesterday!"

"As you probably noticed, I was drunk yesterday."

"Oh, I saw," he told her. "I knew there needed to be
something because you'd not give me the time of day in
London."

She started laughing in an infectious way that soon had Luke laughing with her.

"I'm sorry. I've been told I can be a bit snobbish and standoffish sometimes. It's just, I don't like small talk. I'm an introvert and it drains me to talk about insubstantial stuff with strangers."

He wondered how often she was so candid with someone she'd just met.

"I don't like small talk either," said Luke. When Sol looked at him with incredulous eyes, he felt obligated to elaborate. "I feel a bit out of place at Josie's. Everyone is so accomplished in their Pilates proficiency."

"The regulars take it very seriously."

"Are you one of the regulars?" he asked.

"I'm in my forties, which means I *have to* take all aspects of my health seriously. Josie helps me stay in good physical shape, so I treat my time there with respect," said Sol. She was a bit disarming in her security and commitment to fitness.

"I doubted joining Josie's place actually," said Luke. In a way, he felt that line of conversation wasn't a good idea, but he couldn't avoid going there. He was *supposed* to go there. "I read about *The Privateers* creator whose script was stolen there—"

"The one that leaked online, you mean?" said Sol. "Did you read the *Voyeur* article about the script being stolen at the studio? Everyone is pestering me about it. Even my friends yesterday wanted to know about my Pilates studio being the center of a Hollywood theft!"

"And what did you tell them?"

"That it's ridiculous. I'm sure it's just one of those rumors and *Voyeur* never bothered to confirm anything before publishing it. I don't think Sara or any of us could get robbed there. Plus, we all use lockers."

Luke had wanted to see Sol's reaction when he mentioned the theft. His inner lie detector believed her when she said the theft could not have happened at Josie's. Under normal circumstances, that would have been enough to convince him that she wasn't involved. But was he being his usual objective analyst with her?

"Sara?" asked Luke tentatively.

"Sara Daniels, one of the creators of *The Privateers*. She is a regular at Josie's. Haven't seen her since the script leaked."

"Do you know her?" He knew he could ask only so many questions without raising suspicion.

"I've seen her at the studio taking classes and I've bumped into her after class a couple of times. I already knew who she was before. I recognized her at the studio. I had interviewed her and her sister, Bryana, a couple of years ago when they were first promoting the show," she explained.

"So you're a journalist?" he asked, hoping it didn't show how much he already knew about Sol.

"Entertainment journalist, yes," she said, abrupt again.

"Don't worry, I'm not going to be one of those people and ask you who's the most famous person you've ever interviewed."

"Please don't," she replied, clearly relieved.

"I'm dying to know what Hollywood figure you've found most interesting in close conversation and whom you're still dying to talk to, but I'll wait until you feel like confiding that kind of information." He smiled. "In the meantime, do you have any other recommendations about your hometown you'd like to share with a very lost Londoner?"

"First time in Barcelona?" She looked like someone who wasn't in the habit of spelling anything out, not even facts about her own city.

"Afraid yes," he told her sheepishly.

"Don't tell me you went to Madrid years ago but never bothered coming here, and you like it there more than here..."

Luke had heard about the rivalry between the two cities but had never witnessed it firsthand. Judging by her tone, if he gave her a wrong answer, she'd probably let him go on the spot.

"Not that either," he said, the same abashed notes in his voice and manner.

He hadn't visited that many places and, even though he had never had a hard time admitting it, talking to a citizen of the world like Sol made his limited travel experience tougher to recognize.

"A bit of a reluctant traveler, are we?" Sol asked. He felt almost relieved because she didn't judge him and she seemed to get it.

"You could say that, I guess." He combed his wavy hair with his left hand. "It's just—I have a hard time leaving London."

"I see," she said, no sign of censure in her voice. "I guess my main advice is to walk a lot and everywhere. You'll get to know the city better that way. And look always not only in front of you but to both sides of the street."

"Are drivers so aggressive?"

"Yes, and there are also the tourists on scooters and the local bikers who don't care about traffic rules or pedestrians. But I didn't mean to be aware only when you're crossing a street. You don't know what art nouveau building or terrace in a hidden alley you may see if you pay attention to the small details. And they're often not only in front of you," she said.

"I'll keep my eyes open."

"Also, I don't care what travel guides may say, you *don't* walk La Rambla, and you sure don't stop there for a drink or a meal. You cross La Rambla on your way to somewhere else and, when you do, you try imagining how beautiful it was when Barcelonians could actually stroll there."

A family of five sat at the table closest to them, breaking their little bubble.

"Any chance I can impose on you a bit more and have you guide me in a walk through this neighborhood? I might get lost otherwise, and you can show me how to look properly."

"You're the worst, most tenacious flirt I've met!" Sol said. She stood and gestured for him to follow her. "But sure, I wouldn't want you to get lost."

He tried fooling himself into thinking he'd asked her for a guided tour in order to keep doing his job when in reality, not that deep down, he knew he simply wanted to continue spending time with her.

13

Sol got home with not much time to spare. They'd walked for hours. They started in Raval, strolling down carrer Montalegre, visiting the fifteenth-century chapel converted into a gallery on carrer Hospital, and meandering between the fruit and fish stalls at Mercat de la Boqueria. They then moved through many of the hidden spots of the Gothic quarter—the kiss mural by Joan Fontcuberta, the remains of a Roman temple on carrer Paradís, the steps at plaça del Rei—and finished by window shopping in Born.

They talked about themselves a bit—Luke had two older sisters, Sol was an only child—but it had been mostly about the city. Sol loved her peaceful strolls in the history-filled narrow streets of Barcelona, and Luke had behaved like the perfect companion, which is to say he'd listened but mostly he hadn't been intimidated by the long silences meant to let them enjoy their surroundings. It had almost surprised her how easy it had been to walk alongside him in perfect quietness. It had been comfortable in a way she rarely felt while meeting someone new.

He'd asked her—*pleaded* was probably a more fitting verb—to take him to dinner that night or he'd be forced to resort to eating in the first place he found again. She'd said no. She had plans that night. But she was smitten by him even if she had no intention of admitting it, and she'd agreed to think about having dinner with him the following day.

When Laia started video calling her, Sol checked the time and realized *she* was the late one for their date. They tried keeping their weekly meetings even when one of them was not in London.

"Fas tard. Què ha passat?" Laia inquired, surprised about Sol not being her usual extra punctual self.

"Nothing, I just got home. I took a long, beautiful stroll," Sol said.

"How's Barcelona?" Sol could hear the longing tone in her voice.

"Beautiful," Sol said.

"Do you realize this is the second time you've used that word in less than a minute? You're not the sentimental type who overuses adjectives."

"I guess the sun is proving me well."

"The sun? It's only March! You can't have sunstroke. What are you not telling me?" Laia asked.

"I doubt *that* has anything to do with me enjoying the beauty," said Sol, more for herself than for Laia.

"*What* do you doubt has anything to do with you becoming a peppy, tenderhearted person all of a sudden?"

Sol resented the implication of who she'd become because nothing could have sounded duller, but she told her friend about her day.

After Sol informed him that he should *not* have dinner before half past eight in the evening, preferably nine apparently, Luke headed to the hotel to kill some time and see if there was any work-pressing business.

He texted Divya first.

> Luke Contadino: How are things? Any new info on Agatha?

While he waited for his colleague's answer, Luke started a group message to his bosses. He needed to update them on his efforts to track Sol down and learn more about her involvement in the case. He phrased that last part as *an almost totally certain lack of involvement.*

Except he really wasn't that confident.

And if that lack of certainty about Sol's innocence wasn't bad enough, he doubted his approach with her would yield anything other than guilt. The encounter at the bar the previous day had been a welcome coincidence, and even though he'd managed to bring up the case with her, he felt bad about his deception.

He knew he should stop flirting. It was acceptable to make her acquaintance to gain information, but that should be all. And he was perfectly aware *that* wasn't all he was playing at with Sol.

> Divya Bakshi: Agatha has gone the stringer way.

> Luke Contadino: She is all chic and has a sexy accent?

> Divya Bakshi: Lol, no

> Divya Bakshi: She's left the country

Luke Contadino: ???

Divya Bakshi: I know. Sanjay was keeping an eye on her yesterday. She's in Tokyo

Luke Contadino: Is Sanjay there?

Divya Bakshi: In Tokyo? No! Too far and too expensive. Plus T&T keep convinced your stringer is the thief.

Luke Contadino: She's not

With that last message, he now found himself not being completely honest with his managers but also with Divya. He really didn't know if Sol was the thief or not, but he preferred his colleagues not to know.

Divya Bakshi: Did you find anything?

Luke Contadino: Not really. But I asked Sol and she seemed to genuinely think the theft didn't happen at Josie's.

Divya Bakshi: You asked her?

Luke Contadino: We had a sweet snack together

Divya Bakshi: Ring me

Luke did as he was told. He had two older sisters. He knew not to question or rebel against women's authority.

"What do you mean you've asked her and that you had a sweet snack together? You've talked to the Stringer about the theft?" Divya said as a greeting when she picked up his call. "You know we haven't been authorized to disclose our identity as investigators and interrogate any of the suspects, right?"

"I didn't disclose anything. I bumped into her yesterday by accident and we chatted."

"You bumped into her?"

"Yes, small city. Don't tell her I've said that though."

"Do I need to remind you this is *not* the place to meet people?"

"You don't," Luke said.

"Get it together, Luke. I'm not sure you getting closer to the Stringer is a good idea," Divya said.

"I was just trying to get some clarity." He knew his excuse sounded flimsy.

"Right. Did you get any?"

"No."

"If you're really so sure of her innocence, follow her around for one more day. Send a boring report to our managers and insist on coming back. There's work to do here," she ordered more than advised.

"You're right." Luke felt the vibration of his mobile as he received a text message. "Have to go now. Talk to you tomorrow. Cheers."

He read the message.

> Sol Novo: OK to dinner tomorrow. Meet me at La Panxa del Bisbe at 21 sharp. I'll take care of the reservation. Dress code: Effortlessly Hip

His response was instant.

Luke Contadino: Not sure I packed any appropriate clothes, tbh

Sol Novo: I'm sure you'll manage

14

Sol knew she should have taken the subway, but she didn't want to navigate stairs, crowds, and standing-room-only cars in her favorite pair of Vialis platform leather sandals. They added seven centimeters to her height and an extra dose of empowerment, but they couldn't be described as comfy—or balancing.

She took a taxi instead and hoped the traffic wouldn't make her late. She knew she should have left her place earlier, but she'd been ridiculously and uncharacteristically indecisive when selecting what to wear that evening. It wasn't a vanity issue as much as a confidence-building one.

Choosing the right clothes for an interview with a celebrity, a trip to the theater with friends, or an escape to a new city was her way of fitting in and feeling at ease. And right now, she wasn't confident about her rushed sartorial pick: a pair of ultra–high waisted flared jeans and a short-sleeved black jumper. It was too simple yet not effortless enough.

She checked the time, instructed the taxi driver to drop her off a couple of blocks from the restaurant, and made her way down the steeped carrer del Torrent de l'Olla with barely five minutes to spare. Even walking in heels on that particularly narrow and hilly sidewalk of Gràcia would be faster than stand-still traffic.

When she got to the restaurant, Luke was waiting for her on the street. She hated that she'd almost been late. For some reason—could be the stress-inducing traffic or her dissatisfaction with her ensemble for the evening—she was feeling a bit stirred.

Was it nervousness? Surely not.

She made a point of never getting nervous. If she hadn't felt any trepidation when she interviewed Jake Gyllenhaal or *Outlander* author Diana Gabaldon, she couldn't feel anxious at that moment. She was simply meeting an attractive man with whom she'd had a nice time the previous day. Those weren't grounds for nervousness.

"Ciao, come stai?" he asked with a smile. Sol tripped at the sound of his voice in Italian.

She almost fell, but she was able to recuperate a vertical and mostly dignified position before Luke reached out to help her. She dismissed his gesture and thanked the hours of Pilates that had ensured her some sort of balance.

"¡Malditas sandalias!" she muttered under her breath before finally addressing him with her best smile. She pretended nothing had happened. "Evening. I'm doing fine. I hope you love this place."

She made her way into the restaurant.

They were seated at a minuscule table and were given menus in Catalan. Luke could understand more in reading than he could just by listening to the language, but he'd decided to have whatever Sol chose.

She looked gorgeous and regal as always, even if he thought he had detected some tenseness on her part when they'd met on the street.

"The last time I was here, I ran into two different sets of friends. Well, some of them were just acquaintances..." Sol told him, her eyes focused on the menu.

"Don't take this the wrong way, but is the city that small?" he asked her with a daring smile.

Some humor was necessary at the moment.

"Of course not!" she protested, then realized he was teasing. "We're in Gràcia. The neighborhood was already hip when we didn't know what the concept meant. This is the kind of place where you'll find a good mixture of visitors and locals. So it's easy to run into people, I guess."

"You brought me to a popular place."

"I did. I had to *call* the restaurant to make the reservation," said Sol, finally looking at him. "And it's not like running into people doesn't happen in London. I swear I saw you one day at the corner around my place."

"And you didn't say anything?" he teased, trying to deflect from the fact that he was probably in surveillance mode when she saw him. "Where was it?"

"Waterloo," she said. Luke thought she was keeping it vague on purpose. She was probably still determining how much she could trust him and whether he was a nice bloke. It hadn't escaped him that they'd met in public places, and she'd always made her way there on her own.

"I like running by the river," he said to explain his presence in her London neighborhood. He didn't want to dwell too much on it. "I'm not paying much attention to the menu because I assume you'll decree the whole selection."

"You assume correctly," said Sol, smiling coyly. "And you still eat everything?"

"Yes," said Luke, trying to appear as assertive as possible.

"Red or white?"

"Red?"

"You sound unsure." Sol looked up from her menu, turning her eyes to him.

"I want to make sure I'm picking the right answer," he said with his best smile.

"We're talking about wine. All answers are right."

Sol ordered a couple of glasses of one of the Garnatxa options and a few items from the menu before asking him what had probably been on her mind the whole time. "So, you're Italian?"

"Why do you ask? It only took you weeks to appreciate it."

"I had you pegged as quintessentially Londoner," she said. "But I saw your last name on my cell phone, and I almost fell to my face on the street just now because you said hi in Italian."

"It happens." Except that had been the first time he'd used Italian as a wooing mechanism. "And I'm indeed quintessentially Londoner, but my parents are both from Southern Italy."

A waiter brought them wine and a few dishes. She explained what everything was with her usual competence, and Luke was happy with the switch of conversation. His identity as the son of immigrants wasn't something he wanted to elaborate on. But he liked her choice of words to describe him. He'd always felt that *Londoner* best described him.

"Do you watch *The Privateers*?" he said then, knowing he was threading a very thin line. "I overheard a conversation in the lift at my hotel and now I'm intrigued."

"Of course I watch," she said, splitting up the anchovies

and the croquettes between their two plates and grabbing a piece of pa amb tomàquet. "I'm an entertainment journalist and the show exploded. I *need* to watch it. Plus, I really liked it. Don't you watch it?"

"I don't," said Luke, and it was true. Since they'd started working on that case, he felt he should but hadn't found time for it. "Should I?"

"It depends on the kind of storytelling you gravitate to," she told him. "If you like period dramas, whodunnits, and shows featuring a couple of very sexy amateur detectives—and if you have a thing for the whole will-they-won't-they routine—then definitely yes."

"Will-they-won't-they routine?"

"Common TV trope, used often in mystery shows. You have a couple of investigators who tend to dislike each other but at the same time are attracted to one another, and the audience keeps wondering when or if they'll hook up. *The Privateers* did it with the two protagonists."

"Isn't it a show about eighteenth-century pirates?" asked Luke. He enjoyed how Sol explained things in an engaging way.

"It's set aboard a pirate ship, yes. The surgeon turns up dead when they're at sea. It looks like he got sick, but the captain, played by Murray Groff, doesn't buy it and starts sort of investigating. He suspects his new second in command, the quartermaster, did it. But the viewer knows the quartermaster didn't do it, plus the quartermaster is also suspicious of the circumstances surrounding the surgeon's death. In the end, the two of them investigate together, and you know the killer needs to be someone from the crew."

"Who plays the quartermaster?"

"Leonardo Pascual. He'd done a bunch of theater before this."

"And the will-they-won't-they is between the captain and his second in command?"

"Yes," said Sol.

"And do they?" asked Luke, trying on his best smoldering smile.

"I'm not going to spoil it for you."

"Please do. If you tell me they hook up, I'll probably watch. If not… the whole will-they-won't-they routine really frustrates me."

"It can get annoying when the writers stretch the whole thing for seasons on end. Blame it on *Moonlighting*. They made Cybill Shepherd's and Bruce Willis's characters hook up in season three, and the ratings plummeted after that. So now a lot of shows take their sweet time. It doesn't happen in *The Privateers* though." She was clearly enjoying the TV analysis. "At the end of the season, you know who the killer is *and* the two protagonists end up in bed."

"So, and tell me if I'm tiring you out with all these questions, why have I read something about the show being controversial?"

Luke lamented once again the specific circumstances surrounding his acquaintance with Sol. If things were different, he'd be asking about *Moonlighting*. He'd grown up on reruns of it and *Detective Montalbano* in Italian.

"That's because of the leaked screenplay. The one you *think* was stolen from our Pilates studio," Sol explained.

"I read about it being stolen, remember? The whole *Voyeur* article suggests the script disappeared from the studio during one of Josie's classes."

"And what, you think another class participant took it?" asked Sol.

Luke almost choked on the wine he was drinking. Was he telling her too much?

"Don't tell me you actually believed it?" she insisted.

"Why do you think it's so out of the question? What if one of the studio members who was in class that day stole it?"

"You're basing your whole theory on *one* article."

"Isn't *Voyeur* a credible source?"

"Not really," Sol said. "And I should know. I freelanced briefly for them back in the early 2000s."

With that admission, Luke saw a corroboration of his wanting to believe in Sol's lack of involvement.

"What about some kind of professional resentment? I think the TV agent who's always there used to represent the show's creators and doesn't anymore."

"You're taking the whole amateur sleuthing thing very seriously!" she said, smirking.

He felt a bit offended that she thought he was an amateur. And his discomfort increased at his lack of honesty with her when it came to his profession and interest in the case.

"People change representation all the time," Sol continued. "Especially when they get bigger opportunities. I mean, it's true that Agatha supported Sara and Bryana from the beginning and lost them as clients right when they started making more money. Agents usually get around a ten percent commission. But hers is a smaller agency, and the change made total sense for Sara and Bryana. And again, it happens *all the time* in the industry. Stop seeing weird things where there's nothing."

He registered everything Sol told him about the case, and even though he was very much enjoying the evening and the company, he also felt the need to confide in Divya soon. Money was a motive, and Agatha would have lost the potential to make lots of it when the Daniels sisters changed representation.

"I still don't think anything could have been taken from Josie's though," Sol insisted yet again. "She vets every single new member."

"Josie's is basically the perfect studio," he joked.

"Seriously, it is flawless. I can tell you nightmare stories about some of the Pilates places in London I've tried," Sol said vehemently, and Luke almost chuckled. The woman had a posh side he wasn't sure she was totally aware of.

"No nightmare stories, please. I promise never to leave Josie's," he said. "But tell me about the whole controversy with *The Privateers*. I can't decide whether to watch it or not until I know the whole story."

"And you are still okay with spoilers?" she asked, and he nodded. "I need to ask because complaints about spoilers make up about a third of the negative feedback I get from readers."

"Making a mental note to ask you about the other two-thirds in the future," he said, giving her the option to still talk about it if she wanted.

"*The Privateers* is a much more engaging subject, believe me. The whole controversy arose when people started reading the leaked screenplay. Everyone assumed the new season would have a new murder to investigate. More people can mysteriously die aboard a ship in the eighteenth century, no? But in the first episode of the second season, the quartermaster is the one killed off and the captain is presented with a new second in command, who happens to be a woman this time."

"So they killed Leonardo Pascual's character?" asked Luke.

"He's also a fan favorite, and they switched from a gay relationship to a more conventional one. Already in that first episode, there are signs pointing to a new will-they-won't-they dance between the captain and the new quartermaster."

"Now I don't know if I want to watch."

"Right? Production on the second season of *The Privateers* has been postponed after the whole leak, and there are rumors of rewrites," added Sol in a gossipy tone. "So you have time to decide."

He still had a thousand other questions for her that would help him with the case, but he was running out of a plausible pretext to keep asking her about that particular show. A waiter had just brought one last dish of rice and fish, and with it came the perfect excuse for a change of subject.

"I'm starting to understand why you got so upset with me yesterday when I told you about my sad lunch," he told her. "This is delicious."

"I'm glad you're enjoying the food." She smiled.

"Not just the food." He returned her smile with his best, most insolent one.

"Quit flirting or I'll ask you where you had lunch today. And you better not disappoint me." Her smile lit her whole face.

"Oh, I won't disappoint you this time. I went to one of the places you recommended on your list. It was good, but I'm not sure I chose wisely. I could have used your help..."

Luke knew he shouldn't be chatting her up so forwardly —not because he was worried she'd reject him, which she most certainly would, but because he was supposed to be working her in a different way. But he couldn't help himself.

Being far from home and from the office and his managers had almost made him forget everything that was at stake. He just knew he wanted to keep getting to know Sol.

15

Even if she was in her forties and twice divorced —or perhaps because of that —Sol was a bit unskilled and even mistrustful when it came to the whole dating scene. The mere idea of it both bored her and left her exhausted.

That could have been why the previous night she had accepted Luke's proposal to go for a walk after dinner. She'd shown him around the many charm-filled squares of the Gràcia neighborhood, but when he'd offered to walk her home, she excused herself. She'd hailed a taxi and made a rapid escape, even though a long, slow walk through the warm-lit streets of her hometown was exactly what she was longing for.

Thinking about it the following morning, Sol realized that the moment she said no to Luke's stroll proposal, he dropped the subject. He didn't try to persuade her with one of his charm-laden smiles. He waited with her on the street until he saw her inside a taxi and asked her to text him when she made it home safely.

She felt a bit weird about that. It was the kind of

thoughtful, caring thing she always asked friends to do when they were saying goodbye at night after catching a movie or going to dinner together.

She did text him with a simple *Home* when she got to her place, and then she put her cell phone away. She knew if he texted her, she'd respond. And she needed some distance. Too many things were happening at the same time.

Luke was the worst, most tenacious flirt she'd met in a long time. But she'd enjoyed his company during dinner. She knew it hadn't solely been because of the wine; she had been purposely pacing herself and didn't drink more than a glass. And the food was exquisite, but she'd been to that place several times and had never found herself madly enraptured with her companion before. It wasn't the ambience either. The lighting was soft and perfectly crafted to her liking, but that would have been the first time some warm illumination caused her to develop a crush on someone.

Could it be that she *liked* Luke? Surely not. And yet the main argument she could clearly see against him, other than the fact that she had just met him and didn't know much if anything about him, was that he was too young. And wasn't fancying a younger man a bit hypocritical of her, considering her not-so-recent-but-still-indelible latest relationship slip?

The harsh reality was that she didn't have the luxury to keep thinking about that hypocrisy. She still hadn't processed the whole being-out-of-job-*again* thing, and here came a gorgeous Londoner with Italian genes who was probably at least ten years younger than she was and the most attentive man she'd met. Perhaps ever.

The last thing she needed was a distraction from her

problem at hand. She had to focus on how to get her career back on track.

Plus, she hadn't allowed herself to brood too much over her latest divorce, and she wasn't even sure how she felt about it or if she was ready or willing to attempt a relation-ship ever again.

She felt flattered by Luke's attentions but she also couldn't quite believe them. There was something about him that didn't add up. It wasn't that she didn't think she was a catch—she *knew* she projected a sort of empowered Mediterranean image that was not *not* attractive. But she knew she wasn't his type either.

Luke was back at the hotel after an early morning run by the beach that had proved more distracting than he'd antici-pated. He was an exacting and disinclined traveler who was affectionately tormented by his family about his unwilling-ness to leave London. But why would he when his home-town could offer him pretty much everything he longed for?

Yet even Luke had to admit that Barcelona was living up to some of its hype. It had distinctive architecture, history-filled streets, beautiful people, and well, yes—the sea. He was starting to think he could easily get used to dinner dates with Sol and runs by the Mediterranean when he got a text message from Divya.

Divya Bakshi: This must be the most entangled lot we've ever investigated.

Divya Bakshi: Lashana Fletcher is Martha Broch's publicist. She only started representing her a month ago though.

Luke Contadino: Isn't that around the time Lashana joined Josie's?

Divya Bakshi: Yes. Maybe Martha was the one who recommended the Pilates studio or maybe it's another coincidence.

Luke Contadino: I thought you didn't believe in coincidences.

Divya Bakshi: And I still don't like it but I feel we have to hire an entertainment expert to consult.

Luke's heart leaped. He knew the perfect entertainment expert who had already helped him clarify a few things about the case.

16

Sol was sunbathing in the morning light while having breakfast on the terrace of her rooftop apartment. She was staying away from her phone on purpose and was contemplating the blue-skied view scattered with hills when she heard the tone of an incoming text. She couldn't avoid checking it out. So much for her screen-free breakfast.

> Luke Contadino (a.k.a. TDS): Ciao, can I call you? It's a work thing.

A work thing? She realized she didn't really know what he did for a living. Banking or corporate lawyering had only been her prejudiced assumptions when she first met him in London. But he gave a different vibe here somehow.

> Sol Novo: I'm free for the next ten minutes or so

She picked up the phone after a couple of rings.

"Hi," she said. "I'm intrigued."

"Hello. Sorry to bother you so early." He didn't sound

sorry, though. Sol wondered if he was as enthused to talk to her as she was to hear his voice. "Under normal circumstances, I would be texting you and letting you know how much of a good time I had yesterday."

"Okay," she managed to say.

What were the abnormal circumstances? Didn't he have a good time after all? And why did she even care if she'd already decided Luke Contadino wasn't a journey she was willing to pursue at this convoluted time in her life?

"And I did have a splendid time yesterday," he clarified.

Did he sound a bit flustered? Sol was determined to say the least until she started comprehending what was going on. After all, breakfast hadn't quite woken her up yet, and her mind could use a tad more lucidness.

"It's just that now I really could use your expertise," he continued.

"I can send you a dozen more restaurant, museum, and shop suggestions if you need them. No problem at all."

"Right, no. I meant your entertainment expertise," he said. He sounded serious. "What insight would you offer me if I told you the publicist from our Pilates place, Lashana, does PR for the title designer who also goes there, Martha?"

"Don't tell me you're doing it again!"

She loved mystery novels, but perhaps because she'd never been much of a true crime enthusiast she couldn't understand his whole fixation with the story about *The Privateers* script being stolen at Josie's.

"Doing what?" he asked.

"Trying to solve a mystery. It's no secret that Martha and Lashana work together. It was Martha who told Lashana about the studio and brought her one day to audit one of Josie's classes and see if she wanted to join."

"What about the fact that when Sara and Bryana left

Agatha, they went to work with the same talent agent who also represents Martha?"

"I'm thoroughly impressed by your level of insight," she told him. "There are only six or seven big talent agencies. In a way, it's just a probability thing. Plus, I think Sara and Martha were dating when Sara and Bryana got their big break, so it may have been Martha who introduced them to her agent."

"They were dating?" asked Luke.

"Uh-huh, it's all public info. Just search Martha Broch and Sara Daniels online, and you'll see a bunch of red carpet pictures of the two of them holding hands and looking adorable together."

"And they are no longer dating?"

Sol had to admit she had a soft spot for gossips.

"I don't think so, but they both are quite private and behind-the-camera people, so it's not like they're attending public functions and being photographed all the time or making statements about their relationship status."

"In any case, it's like this whole group is linked to each other," he said.

"Of course it is. You need to know someone to get in. Don't tell me Josie simply let you join without a recommendation?"

He couldn't have persuaded Josie just by leveraging his good looks, right?

Luke was once again carefully maneuvering a conversation that could compromise him.

"No, she didn't," he told Sol. Thompson had asked for a favor from a previous client with links to the movie and TV industry to get Luke's membership at Josie's.

"I thought so. Okay, if that's all, I should get going now," she said.

"Wait, one last thing, completely unrelated. Any chance you may want to see me today?"

A beat of silence had him holding his breath.

"I have a few things and a dinner with my parents that I cannot keep postponing," she said. He could almost hear her internally debating whether to say yes. "Maybe I could do one drink after dinner..."

"I'm probably flying back to London tomorrow morning, and I'd love to see you again before I leave your hometown."

He'd already contacted Thompson and Thomson about his intention to leave Barcelona. So far he'd found nothing substantial connecting Sol to the whole affair other than superficial appearances, and a part of him wanted to stop digging. He was waiting on his managers' approval but didn't anticipate much of a disagreement once they realized how much they were paying just for the hotel.

"I could meet any time after 9:30 if we do the same neighborhood where we met the first time," Sol said.

"The fancy gin and tonic place with no olives and no crisps?"

"Yes, in that neighborhood, but let's go to a different bar. I can text you a few options later."

"You choose, I'll be there. But wait, what time are you having dinner if you can meet me any time after half past nine?" he teased.

"What do you want me to say? My parents are old and like eating early. You should *not* follow their example."

And with that, Luke had another date with Sol.

What was the saying? When it rained it poured. It had started unequivocally pouring on Sol. She'd just had dinner with her parents and was saying her goodbyes when they decided to unleash some last-minute financial news on her.

"Sol, cariño," her dad started. "You don't need money, right?"

"Money?" she asked, confused. She'd just told him she'd lost her job.

"You have savings, right?" he continued.

"Of course."

"Good. Because with the news of your job, and while you find something else, you'll probably need that money," her mother joined in.

"I most certainly will," Sol said. They were acting strange.

Her mother took a deep breath. "Especially since your trust is not liquid at the moment."

"What do you mean it's not *liquid*?" Sol asked. Money

talk could be so confusing. Did she have a gaseous fund now or what?

"We've made some investments that haven't proved as quick and profitable as first expected, and part of the family money is entangled," Sol's dad explained. When she stared blankly at him, he continued, "The money in your trust was part of that investment, so your funds will be unavailable for some time."

"But fortunately you're a smart girl and have savings," Sol's mom said.

Sol decided not to disappoint them for a second time during the same day and tell them that her *savings* were actually the trust, and that she had counted on that money. She kissed them both goodnight and promised to call the following day.

There was nothing like being jobless and penniless at the same time. In a way, the news had almost been like being laid off all over again. The safety net she always thought would be there wasn't as immutable as she'd believed it to be.

She checked the time and decided to put the whole affair aside for at least half an hour. Once she got home, she'd have all the time to worry about being destitute.

...

Sol was trying to get there before Luke did. She wanted to partake in the whole early-is-on-time, on-time-is-late creed they seemed to share, but when she got to the terrace on carrer Parlament, he was already seated at one of the street tables.

"Hola," she said, bending down to kiss him on the

cheeks. He smelled musky, with notes of wood and lavender. "You found a table!"

"Ciao, bella," he replied, and Sol almost melted. "I came in early and grabbed a bite to eat here. I hope you approve."

"Absolutely." She sat down with wobbly legs.

She should have never kissed him. What exactly was she thinking? This wasn't a friend or family member, so there was no justifiable reason for such an intimate greeting. Plus, there was no way she could get that smell out of her mind. And he needed to stop with the Italian. Immediately. It was confusing her already incongruous thoughts.

"How was your dinner?" he asked, and Sol almost didn't hear him.

Did he look more tanned?

"Uneventful," she managed to say when she finally processed what he'd asked. And, of course, her answer wasn't even true.

"No remarkable food to ensure an appropriate out-of-body experience?" Sol recognized his playful tone.

"It's not that. The food was excellent. My parents wouldn't have it any other way," she said, smiling. "It's just... they are a lot."

She had left her parents' place feeling like they were too much. But the truth was, by the time she saw Luke there, she had pretty much forgotten all about dinner, her parents' unsettling money revelations, and their repeated pleas for her to move back to Barcelona for good.

They'd been intoning some variation of the same come-back-home theme for more than fifteen years, and Sol was running out of energy to deflect their attempts. It had been hard to come up with compelling reasons to say no when her whole argument for living abroad had always been her profession and, at present, she found herself without a job.

Should she reconsider and stay in Barcelona? It wasn't like she didn't love and miss her hometown, and her family and friends in the city.

A waiter came to take her order then. On her way there, Sol had resolved to stay for half an hour, stick to water, and leave early to mull over her newfound lack of money. Luke was a complication, and she couldn't deal with more drama at the moment.

But once she saw him, she forgot everything about her resolution. She ordered a glass of Mencía and reclined on her chair, making herself comfortable, relaxing perhaps for the first time that day.

They were seated on opposite sides of a small square table. Luke had both arms over it and was leaning forward, looking at her intently. She allowed herself to drink in his dark chestnut eyes. They were severely warm. And they didn't seem to want to move from her face.

Even though it was a chilly night and they were seated outside, she almost took her leather jacket off. Why was it so hot suddenly?

"I realized this morning I never asked you about your job," Sol finally said, averting her gaze after a few minutes of a too-intense stare play between the two of them.

"What about my job?" he asked.

"What is it exactly that you do?"

The waiter came at that instant with a glass of red wine for Sol and a bottle of beer for him, and Luke decided to tell her everything, even if it didn't look good for him and it could get him in trouble with his bosses. And probably with Sol too. Even if he couldn't be completely confident about her innocence. But it was about time he did it. The duplicity was killing him.

"Merda," she said suddenly, right when he was about to come clean. "Come closer!" She waved him toward her.

"I'm sorry, what?"

"Move your chair and come closer. I need to use you as a human wall," she explained. He did as he was told, moving his chair and seating himself mere inches from her. "There's someone I know and don't particularly like. I'm trying to hide."

"Let me know if this is too close," he said. She was literally making herself smaller behind him.

"This is why I hate hanging out in this neighborhood," she said in an almost whisper. "If it was during the day, I'd be wearing a pair of big sunglasses and it would be easier to go unnoticed."

"Any reason why you like going unnoticed?"

"I just hate small talk, remember? Especially with people I barely know and have never cared about."

"And this is better?" he asked, signaling her present situation.

"I know, I'm the worst... Okay, I think they went away." Her gaze was somewhere on the street corner, and her posture relaxed. "I'll admit, that wasn't my most empowered or social moment."

"I get it," he told her, and he sort of did. "My older sister has an aversion to certain acquaintances as well. Next time, do the opposite though."

"What do you mean?"

"Do the whole hide-in-plain-sight thing. It's easier to spot someone who is trying to conceal themself. And if they see you and recognize you, just pretend you have no clue who they are. That normally throws people off."

"Should I ask why you know so much about this?" She paused. "Oh, your sister probably told you all her secrets."

"You could say that. I'm very close to both my sisters."

"I gathered," she said with a smile.

"I feel like this keeps happening though." Luke realized he should probably move his chair back.

"What keeps happening? And where are you going?" Sol asked him when he started to shift his chair.

"You keep bumping into people," he told her, halfway to his previous position. "And I'm not going anywhere if you don't want me to, but I assumed you'd like to have your personal space back to yourself."

"I'm not going to argue with you about the size of my city *again*. This was just an unfortunate coincidence because I grew up in this neighborhood and know way too many people whose names I don't necessarily remember," she said adamantly. "And don't make assumptions about my personal space. I might still want to hide behind you, just to be extra prudent and avoid future unwanted encounters."

Luke moved back closer to Sol.

"Right. Sorry about that." He fixed his eyes on her again. "I really hope you don't do the whole hiding thing with me the next time we run into each other—here or in London."

He knew he should be going back to telling Sol what his profession was and why he was in the city, perhaps even trying to clarify some of the remaining questions he had about her. But this was much more fun.

"I promise I won't," she told him with a sly smile.

18

They stayed at the bar for a little longer, giving in to the urgency to keep staring at each other and sneaking in a few words about themselves—Luke had grown up in Islington and was paying an indecent amount to rent a cramped studio north of there, and Sol had grown up in Sant Antoni but she'd left Barcelona in her midtwenties.

It was her sixth night in the city and by then, Sol had lost count of how many times she'd felt perfectly content and at ease since landing in her hometown. And that was despite the fact that she was now not only unemployed but also cash-strapped. Barcelona soothed her soul in a way no other place could.

But even when the company, and the sights, couldn't get hotter, she couldn't keep warm as the night got chillier.

"Any chance you still feel like walking me home today?" she asked Luke, unsure what made her so bold.

She'd never been too much of an initiator. Both her ex-husbands were absolute opposites with not a single trait, thought, or opinion in common but would agree on that—and probably only on that.

She'd been younger when she'd met both of them. She was a different Sol now, a self-confident one. She also liked herself more than she'd ever done—and didn't care what others thought about her.

"I'm always up for a walk in the right company," Luke replied, and she could sense his charm being turned up.

"My place is very close, so it's going to be a short walk. But it has some killing views." For a moment, she didn't know whether they were still talking about strolling or if the conversation had moved to a more sex-adjacent level.

"Never been opposed to short walks with the promise of sightseeing," Luke said.

Definitely sex-adjacent.

"It's really just a few blocks down," Sol said as they strolled the tile-paved, pedestrianized street alongside the busy sidewalk terraces and the warmly lit interiors of bars and restaurants still in the middle of late dinner service.

Luke thought that, unlike two days before, she seemed to need to make conversation and fill the void instead of opting for a silent walk.

"No need for a long stroll, really," he said. Perhaps he also preferred to busy himself with words instead of opting for a quietness that felt loaded. "I went running this morning, and I've been walking around even more than in London. So I'm good for steps."

"It's good to get those in!" Sol sounded deceived at her own lack of imagination, not being able to come up with more inspired talking topics. "It's here," she finally said, sounding almost relieved, pointing to a glass and metal door. She started rummaging through a handbag that couldn't have room to carry more than a few credit cards and a phone and yet she seemed to have problems finding something inside it. "¿Dónde están las llaves?"

After a few more seconds of insistent searching, she unearthed an almost exaggerated set of keys. She chose one among them and unlocked the building's street door only to fumble with the set a second time, identify a new key, and open yet another door before they could make their way to a barren entrance hall and from there a narrow lift.

When the doors to the lift closed, they found themselves standing one in front of the other, not even ten centimeters between their bodies. From that distance, he could smell her—flowery but not overly sweet, woodsy but delicate at the same time, and intoxicating.

She was strikingly sexy even under the unforgiving fluorescent lights of the lift. Luke caught a glimpse of himself in the wall mirror of the elevator and thought he looked green-skinned, sweaty, and too eager to impress.

But Sol seemed to have composed herself and was back at her most regal state. She was no longer making small talk. She looked at him, straight in the eye, as if interrogating him. *Are we really doing this?* her gaze appeared to ask. *Are you as taken by me as I am by you?*

Luke's eyes simply told her: *More.*

19

After a short walk and the most sexually charged elevator ride ever, they were both standing on Sol's rooftop terrace surrounded by the flickering city lights.

"I feel I should offer you something to drink," she said, facing him. There were still only a few centimeters separating the two of them as their bodies didn't seem to want to get any farther after their confined trip inside the elevator. "But I only have water, unsweetened almond milk, and an opened bottle of white wine that's been sitting in my fridge like that for at least half a year."

"Saving it for a special occasion?" he teased.

"Haven't had many reasons for celebration lately."

How did Luke manage to loosen all her inhibitors? She couldn't refrain from revealing too much about herself.

"I presume you also have tea," he continued, his gaze fixed on her.

"Breakfast tea." With that admission, she lifted her fingers to his face, tracing the line of his unshaven jaw, the profile of his nose, his full lower lip. "Is this okay?" she asked, her heart pounding.

He nodded, smiling as her fingers descended. She took her time caressing his neck, the naked part of his collarbone. And even though his eyes were hungry, he seemed to understand that she needed to get acquainted with his body slowly.

As her hand lowered to his chest, over his T-shirt, she sensed his desire. She stepped on her tiptoes to approach his lips, urging his mouth to open to hers. He tasted like beer but also chocolate and something salty that made her smile. It was almost fitting that his flavor reminded her of the sea.

"May I?" His whisper sent a tickling sensation all over her body.

She acceded with an almost pleading stare and realized how much they'd said that night without actual words.

One of his hands was on the small of her back, almost burning to the touch even through the fabric of her black pencil midi dress. He pressed her against his body. His other hand had taken hold of her face, his thumb carefully caressing the sensitive area behind her earlobe.

They kissed under the Barcelona night sky. She reveled in the spontaneity of the moment. Her right hand made bold progress through Luke's anatomy when she felt something frantically vibrating in the back right pocket of his jeans.

"Your phone is..." she said, momentarily disentangling her mouth from his and about to succumb to the urge to bite his lower lip.

Yet she wasn't allowed to act on that yearning.

Even though Sol thought Luke was as much into kissing

her as she was into him, he detached himself when he grabbed his vibrating phone.

"Shit!" He sounded and looked frustrated. Or perhaps Sol was projecting her own thwarted sensations. "I need to go."

"I'm sorry?" She was convinced she had misheard that last bit. It happened sometimes—English as a third language and all that. Plus, Luke's London accent could be thick and she had always been better with a Californian drawl than any other English variant.

"My very annoying boss called, and he'll probably call me again in a minute," he said, not making eye contact and looking at his phone's screen. "I need to go deal with him and my trip tomorrow."

"Right, you're leaving tomorrow," she said, both processing the information and giving him an easy way out.

"I'm leaving tomorrow," he repeated absent-mindedly.

Sol walked him toward the entrance door to the apartment. She opened it with her best Californian fake smile.

"Is it alright if I text you?" he asked.

"Why shouldn't it be okay?" The smile was still plastered on her face. She pretended that a mere minute ago she hadn't been making out with the guest who was now about to leave.

"Will you answer?"

"Why shouldn't I?" she replied. The thing was though, it was getting late and her facial muscles were sore from all the faux grinning. She needed Luke to be *gone*, stat.

"Sorry I have to leave in a hurry," Luke started, and Sol really wasn't looking forward to whatever conversation he seemed to want all of a sudden.

"We all have things to attend to in the morning," she said. Her fake smile took on the cold-hearted glacial civility she knew she excelled at when needed. And the occasion screamed for Ice Queen Sol.

"Right, sorry to keep you waiting. Good night I guess, and thanks for showing me arou—"

"Good night!" Sol closed the door in his face.

What the hell had happened?

First, they were on top of one another. Was she so old, horny, and wrong in her reading of the situation? Because she thought they both wanted to have sex.

But then he had to leave in a hurry, only to decide right after that he wasn't actually so pressed for time and wanted to chat.

Perhaps she hadn't been thinking as sensibly as she normally would have done. But a lot had happened to cloud her judgment. First there had been a husband who had made her believe she wasn't enough. That was followed by the big fortieth anniversary and realizing society assumed her best days were behind her. Then she was laid off and there was *nothing* more grievous—and vexing—than having to answer the customary *What do you do?* after being fired. After that, her parents had told her they weren't as good at investing money as she always thought, and they'd somehow gambled with her security blanket. No wonder she'd been toying with the idea of shagging a perfect—if objectively gorgeous—stranger.

One thing was clear to Sol: Luke had never been interested in her in more than a friendship-light capacity. And that was precisely why she had a great number of friends and acquaintances whom she liked or in some cases tolerated, a diverse collection of sex toys, and no real desire to ever try combining the two of them again.

By the time Luke made his descent to the street, Thompson had called him a second time and given him the details of his flight for the following day.

He'd even dictated the six-digit confirmation code of the reservation, which forced Luke to stop and make a note on his phone and ask his manager to repeat everything twice.

After that, Thompson hung up. He wasn't interested in Luke sharing his findings about Sol. But he wanted him back in London the following day.

Why had Thompson decided to ring him when an email would have made the most sense? Especially considering Thompson hadn't even booked the flight. Luke knew Thompson's assistant would have done that, and he could have easily sent Luke all the details.

But precisely because a call in which you dictate a code was illogical, that's what Thompson did. By now, Luke knew T&T wasn't the well-run, slick detective agency it aspired to be.

It hadn't taken him that long to comprehend that the agency's founders and managers only made it in the business due to an equal-parts combination of luck and the right family connections.

But even if he was cross with his boss for the interruption, he was somewhat reluctantly pleased, even thankful, about it. Luke could have shut down his phone and ignored the call—but he didn't.

He liked Sol, more than he was ready to admit to himself. Lying to her about his profession and the reasons he was in Barcelona wasn't the best way of attempting to start something with her. In case she was interested at all, which—after that icy goodbye—he was seriously doubting. The woman could turn from Mediterranean warmth to glacial cordiality in a matter of seconds.

The best course of action was to return to London, hope for a fast wrap of the case of the stolen script that wouldn't get Sol implicated in any way, come clean with her, and keep his fingers crossed that she wouldn't be too cross with him about the whole duplicitous affair.

20

Luke had been standing on a quiet corner of Formosa Street for the previous two hours and was again mostly cold—even if perfectly dressed for the day's weather—and on a path of resentment against his professional choices.

He'd been on the seven in the morning flight from Barcelona to London that day and had barely had time to stretch his legs—he'd been relegated to a middle seat in a completely full flight again—when he got a call from his bosses. The executives at Meshflixx wanted the detectives to add a new possible culprit to their list of suspects: actor Leonardo Pascual. Luke was tasked with getting "anything compromising," Thompson's words, about *The Privateers* star.

Luke felt especially lousy as a result. He was just back from lying (or at least not telling the whole truth) to one person about why he happened to be in her hometown and now was supposed to trail another one, even if the evidence pointing to his involvement in the theft looked flimsier than in Sol's case.

Maybe Gaia was right after all, and Luke should have stuck to being a lawyer and given up the whole detecting vocation. It wasn't like it had taken him far. Had he read too many Agatha Christie novels at uni and was now paying for it?

It was never a good thing when he had doubts about his chosen profession. Fortunately, it didn't happen often, although it had become more common in those past months working at T&T. Even if, when he'd been offered the job, Luke felt like he was turning an important professional corner. But he now saw his position in a different light and, what was worse, he had the feeling he was trapped in that job. He couldn't afford to lose it.

Deciding to take a more optimistic approach and hoping there was still a way to salvage the Meshflixx case, he called Divya.

"I heard you were back," Divya said in greeting.

"You heard correctly."

"Were you feeling homesick?" she teased.

"Not really. They wanted me back here to start working on Leonardo Pascual."

"Oh yes. The new suspect," Divya said. "Apparently, Leonardo has been tweeting about the leaked screenplay and his utter dislike of it, and they aren't happy about it at Meshflixx."

"But how do they know he's involved with this? It's not like he was at the Pilates studio when the script disappeared, right?"

"Well, they want us to figure that out. But I overheard Thompson saying that Meshflixx could be trying to dupe us. He thinks the studio wants us to find some dirt on Leonardo, but instead of paying for a second investigation, they're keeping everything under one tab."

T&T had finally managed to get a client who could beat them at their own game.

"Should we try to talk to Agatha? She was the one with the most motive before Meshflixx started throwing new suspects at us," Luke said.

"She's still in Tokyo."

"What about Sara Daniels?"

"What about her?" Divya asked.

"Should we try talking to her? All the info we have on her comes from T&T's notes from their initial interview with her after taking the case. But you and me never heard directly from Sara about what went on that evening."

He'd seen firsthand how Thompson and Thomson dealt with clients, and he knew Divya had too. The founders were always invariably more preoccupied with keeping clients and their associates happy and unbothered than making any attempt at diligence. Luke was sure he and Divya could learn something from a chat with *The Privateers* creator.

"They won't be happy if we do it behind their backs," Divya said.

Divya's sleuthing interest was likely piqued by this case, and Luke knew she wanted to get to the truth of the matter just like he did. But she also wanted to keep her job.

"Let me talk to P," said Luke.

Thompson was universally acknowledged at the agency as the softer of the two name partners, even if Luke had started to suspect that malleability was only cosmetic.

"All right, but keep me out of the conversation unless he really sees no problem."

"Of course."

They hung up and he sent an email to Thompson, hoping his manager still hadn't figured out a couple of things when it came to operating his new mobile phone—work email being one of them.

And how could he have, considering that the previous night he'd called Luke and had dictated a six-digit confirmation code?

Hi P,
Making sure we're ready to have some new info on
the Meshflixx case by EOW. FYI, I need to talk to
Sara D ASAP to double-check something.
Luke

Nothing mystified Thompson more than acronyms. Half the time he couldn't decipher their meaning, yet he revered them. So even if he managed to read his email, the way Luke had written it should suffice to make his manager side with his need to talk to Sara.

With that out of the way, Luke sent the text message he'd been mentally writing and rewriting all day.

Luke Contadino: Sorry I had to leave
yesterday. Emergency at work.

Sol was having lunch at Bodega Sepúlveda, her favorite traditional Catalan cuisine spot in the city, with the company of a delightful Emily Henry rom-com. She knew that was probably going to be one of her last restaurant outings for a while, considering her new uncertain economic situation. But in the words of her favorite Laura Dern character, she wasn't ready to not *not* be rich and felt her lack of liquidity would materialize the moment she acknowledged it, so she was pretending nothing had happened for one or two more days of much needed self-care.

She received Luke's message then. She read it twice. Made sure she actually understood it correctly. Chuckled. Rolled her eyes. Smirked. Put the phone on the table, its screen facing down, and continued reading her book.

Ten minutes later, the device vibrated with the reception of a new message. Sol wanted to believe she was the kind of woman who'd ignore the smart device and simply continue savoring the baby squid croquettes and the sobrassada over pa amb tomàquet. And, had she the inkling that the message could be from anyone other than Luke, she'd probably disregard it. She had only eighty pages left in the too-engrossing book, after all, and was in the page-turning phase of her reading.

But she couldn't ignore her cell phone. And she felt a bit aggrieved about it. Disappointed in herself as well.

> Luke Contadino (a.k.a. TDS): I realize I never told you what I do for a living. It's a long conversation. Would love to tell you about it when you're back in London.

"Aargh!" She was starting to feel irritated. "¿Qué necesidad hay de hablar ahora de esto?" she muttered. She put the phone down again.

It was perfectly adequate for her to have lunch by herself. To talk to herself out loud while eating alone, perhaps not so much. Yet the phone beeped again, and she couldn't resist grabbing it.

Luke Contadino (a.k.a. TDS): I know I'm probably ruining a delicious lunch under the sun and by the sea. It's just that I'd love to see you again when you're back in my hometown.

Even if she couldn't ignore him, he didn't have to be aware of it. She just had to stay silent. But she couldn't resist the temptation to correct him.

Sol Novo: I'm indoors and like forty minutes away from La Barceloneta on foot. I guess by taxi I could be there in 15… But you're still ruining a delicious lunch.

Luke Contadino (a.k.a. TDS): Feel free to send me pictures.

Sol Novo: Pass. I'm too old to start documenting meals now.

Luke Contadino (a.k.a. TDS): You definitely aren't too old for me.

"¡Será possible el tío!" she said aloud. She couldn't believe his gall. She was done pretending she wasn't interested in that conversation and that she wasn't speaking to herself. Also, what exactly had happened the previous night to this seductive Luke?

Sol Novo: Cut the flattery or I'll ignore your messages. I have a selection of cheeses in front of me that require my full attention…

Luke Contadino (a.k.a. TDS): I'll let you eat peacefully but think about my request.

Sol Novo: What request?! I'm NOT taking a
picture of these cheeses and sending it
to you.

Luke Contadino (a.k.a. TDS): I see. Not into
food fetishes, eh?

Sol was genuinely confused now. Entertained and
giggling, but still confused. She really was too old for that
kind of digital flirting. Too hungry too.

Luke Contadino (a.k.a. TDS): I was talking
about my hope that you'll want to see me
when you're back in London.

Sol Novo: I'll think about it.

Luke Contadino (a.k.a. TDS): Remember
you promised me not to hide if we run into
each other.

Sol Novo: Promise still stands

Sol Novo: Need to go now!

She put the phone down, this time for good. She knew
he wouldn't be writing again for a bit after that last answer.

But even if she pretended as if the previous night had
never happened and he hadn't managed to wound her
battered pride and sense of seductiveness—and that was a
lot of pretending—Sol wasn't sure when or *if* she was getting
back to London, so there was no point in replying to his
question with something more concrete.

Her career was everything she was willing to invest time
in and to think about from then on. And she didn't know
where the next step in her professional life would take her.

21

"**A**ny luck getting ahold of Sara?" Thompson asked. Luke almost choked on the strongly brewed tea he was drinking, his third cup that wretched day.

It was safe to assume that at some point during the last two months, Thompson had learned how to read his work emails, even if he hadn't figured out how to send one. But Luke, with all his supposed investigating skills, hadn't caught on to that fact.

"Not really. I've tried calling her office at Meshflixx a couple of times, and she's never there."

Luke was in T&T's conference room with his two bosses, as well as Divya and Sanjay. The full team in charge of the Meshflixx case was holding their weekly debriefing meeting.

"She's very busy, isn't she?" Thompson said, a knowing tone in his voice. Was Luke being scolded? You could never tell with P. "What did you want to double-check with her?"

Divya sent Luke an inquisitive look from the other side of the big table around which the five of them were seated.

Luke needed to tread carefully. Her gaze told him to avoid involving her in whatever was going on.

"I just..." Luke started to look for something on the dossier of the Meshflixx case. "Here! I wanted to go over the timing for that afternoon. According to your notes from Sara's interview, she said Josie's class was running a bit long that evening, but Sara left the studio at half past six sharp nonetheless."

"Yes..." Thompson conceded.

"I wondered why she left early and also about the other attendees' schedules. Did someone else leave with her? I'm assuming someone, if not the majority of them, stayed at the studio for the whole class. They are quite a devoted group." He decided to be straightforward with his managers. "Also, could we perhaps interview the attendees we've been following? They could tell us about their movements for that night."

"Yes, yes, that's all very interesting, but we don't have the bandwidth to follow through," Thompson dismissed him. "Meshflixx wants us to check on Leonardo Pascual because of his behavior. We suspect they may be cross with him for reasons unrelated to this case, but they still want us to eliminate surveillance hours at the same time and spend the minimum on this affair. We'll have a report ready for them in the upcoming days or weeks."

"But we haven't made much progress in discovering who stole the script," Luke said.

"Haven't we? We were hoping you'd throw some light since you've been in Barcelona for several days and the bill for that is, as I'm sure you're aware, quite hefty," said Thomson. Sweatshirt tended to remain quiet until it was time to show teeth.

Luke couldn't quite believe his ears. The idea of

leaving London in pursuit of Sol hadn't been his but P's. The whole time he'd been there, Luke had been in constant communication with his managers to try to get back home—even if he'd been enjoying his stay and wished the visit had taken place under different circumstances.

He'd only been allowed to return because he was needed to follow a new person. But now he was supposed to have made some sort of miraculous break? Luke was reminded once again of his precarious situation at the agency. An image of his parents' crammed and musty spare room flashed in front of him, and he shook it off.

"The only light I can throw on this is that we should be looking into a different person. I managed to interview Sol," Luke continued, preferring to leave the details of his conversation with her as vague as possible. "And she had no idea about the script being stolen at the studio."

"You're aware that thieves know how to lie, right?" countered Thomson.

Luke's heart rate increased slightly. It was never a good thing when Sweatshirt not only joined but remained in a conversation.

"And she still finds herself inexplicably out of a job and linked to *Voyeur*," Thomson added.

None of his managers had been listening to him. But he still had to try.

"I broached the *Voyeur* subject with her," he said, hoping no one would ask about the particulars of his so-called interview with Sol. "She volunteered the information that she'd worked there. She doesn't publicly advertise it on her LinkedIn account because I gathered it's not something she feels especially proud of."

"You *gathered*." Sweatshirt could always find a way of

exasperating Luke. He knew he should have never used such an imprecise term.

"I *deducted* based on our conversation. Plus, her connection with *Voyeur* occurred two decades ago. For all we know, not a single person she used to work with is still there." A cold sweat gathered along Luke's chest and armpits, under the same clothes he'd worn on the plane that morning. He'd had no time to change.

"Is that all you have to report from your three days in a foreign country?" Thomson continued. He wasn't even looking at Luke, his stare buried in his mobile phone, his demeanor annoyed.

"Yes," Luke said. He chose to leave out the part where he still wasn't one hundred percent certain of Sol's total lack of involvement in the case.

"We shouldn't be surprised though, right?" Divya interjected, to Luke's relief.

"I'm not sure what exactly you're talking about, Divya. I *am* surprised," Thomson said, strengthening his reputation as a total tosser. He lifted his gaze from his device to look at Divya inquisitively.

"I was here the morning *Thompson* made the discovery of Sol's trip to Barcelona," Divya continued, making sure to clearly pronounce the *p* in the last name. "Luke and I thought that perhaps Sol's move demanded a reaction on our part."

Luke was about to protest. He'd never thought such a thing, and he didn't remember her doing it either. But Divya's look prevented him from contradicting her.

"Thompson proved to be more of an experienced investigator, of course," Divya said.

"Did he now?" Sweatshirt asked doubtfully, and both Divya and Luke knew she was playing a dangerous game. It was no secret that no one at the office, not even Sweatshirt, trusted P's good nose.

"He manifested his doubts about Sol's involvement but still thought it was an unusual move on her part. He deemed it worth making sure we could eliminate her as a suspect, which is what Luke just did," Divya said.

Luke looked at his colleague across the table, conveying a thank-you with his expression. She didn't have to get involved. In fact, the smartest thing to do would have been to stay away and let Luke get himself out of a situation that he'd never wanted to be involved in in the first place. And Divya always made the smartest move, yet she'd decided to go against her own personal policy and risk it for him this time.

What was worse, he wasn't even sure the ruse was going to work. P was absent-minded enough that he could forget something he'd said or done three days before. And he was self-absorbed and conceited enough to believe he was not only a good detective but also an excellent mentor figure to his employees, but would he really buy Divya's carefully crafted tale?

"Yes, yes. I'm glad to have guided that side of the investigation and, of course, I was correct, wasn't I?" said Thompson. The man's delusional grandiosity had no limits and, for once, Luke was grateful for it. "But let's not get ahead of ourselves in eliminating the Stringer or anyone else from the investigation. I'm sure we can include all the info we have in our final report."

The many junior detectives the agency employed were normally in charge of writing the first drafts of reports for clients. And they took turns doing it depending on the case. Divya was in charge of writing this time. After that, the founders at T&T would make their best embellishing efforts so it looked like their staff and themselves had worked non-stop.

But Luke wasn't sure what would go into the content of this particular report with what they had. It was going to be a thin piece of writing for sure.

"I know I keep bringing this up." Sanjay utilized the silence to finally speak. "But Mark keeps looking shady to me."

"What is it now?" asked an eternally annoyed Sweatshirt.

"I heard him on the phone *again.* He was disparaging Meshflixx and their lack of transparency toward creators," Sanjay explained. "I think he was talking to a journalist."

"Yes, yes. He likes blabbing around. Sadly, I don't think we have the time—or the inclination, really—to follow this up," Sweatshirt answered, once again checking his phone. "We need to wrap this thing up, remember?"

"Why does Meshflixx want to wrap up the investigation?" Luke asked.

It was probably the fact that he'd had to wake up excessively early to make his flight that day and he wasn't thinking straight. But even if asking that last question hadn't been the most self-preserving thing to do, Luke needed to understand the sudden rush behind Meshflixx's decision.

"Is money not a good enough reason for you, Luke?" asked Sweatshirt.

It almost sounded personal, as if Thomson *knew* Luke's family wasn't wealthy and that he'd always been—and still very much was—on a tight budget.

"Of course, but why now? I never understood why they hired us in the first place, to be honest. The script was stolen but had also leaked. The damage was already done when they came to us."

"Thompson and I think they wanted to appease their creators and prove to them that they cared deeply about the show." For once, Sweatshirt was being helpful.

"So they hired us, unaware of how long these types of investigations normally take, and now that they have reached a certain budgetary threshold, they realize they don't care about *The Privateers* that much?" Luke asked, genuinely trying to understand the logic behind their client's decision.

Thomson nodded. "Pretty much. But I don't think they stopped caring about *The Privateers*. They just weren't expecting things to take this long to get resolved and, in their defense, I wasn't expecting it either." His arsehole side was showing again. "When they first approached us, I thought we'd be dealing with a fairly easy case, with a limited number of suspects. I still don't understand what's taking so long."

The meeting was dismissed shortly after, once Thomson finished dispensing his trademark hostility.

Luke still had lots of questions about Meshflixx's decision. If only he could ring his own private entertainment consultant again and get her perspective on the case.

22

Sol still couldn't piece together the whole thing—or believe her good fortune. Was her fate reverting to luck once again?

She'd woken up that morning convinced that she was about to have one final, idle self-care day that would be pretty similar to the previous one: delicious, slow-paced breakfast on the terrace, walk around one of her favorite neighborhoods, unhurried exquisite lunch, late afternoon date with friends over berenar and light conversation, perhaps another walk after that, and some window shopping to ensure she was still on top of all the latest fashion trends... All that before she really started figuring out some sort of freelancing work.

But other than the relaxed breakfast, it looked like she might have to forget about pretty much everything else on her tight schedule for the day which—up until that moment—had the right amount of leisure time in it.

After a delectable croissant from L'Atelier and tea brewed to perfection, she had checked her email, hoping her finance guru would have good news for her and confirm that her being unemployed would mean lower taxes that year. Also that her parents had been grossly exaggerating and she wasn't technically *that* broke or anything.

She wasn't sure when she'd become such a clichéd midlife embodiment, but there was no point in denying that she was indeed preoccupied to an obsessive degree with income, career development, and the unavoidable but still somewhat delayable aging process.

But she'd found something else in her inbox, other than the lack of news from her money guru. Something unexpected.

Conceit Fair's executive film and TV editor Fionna Bennett had sent her an email commissioning Sol to do an interview for the magazine as a contributor.

The subject of the interview would be the longtime Hollywood producer and director Richard Fynn, who was promoting the long-awaited sequel to his 2010 science-fiction box office success, *Revengers Reunite.* Fionna explained that their longtime Los Angeles correspondent had fallen ill after a too-demanding awards season, and Sol came highly recommended by Miquel Oriol.

Sol called Miquel after replying to Fionna and accepting the assignment.

"Bon dia, guapa," he answered the phone.

He was one of the only people she knew, other than both her parents, who still invariably picked up the phone and preferred a conversation to any nonsensical and infinite amount of back-and-forth texting. And she appreciated it.

"Tell me how the executive film and TV editor at *Conceit Fair* has not only my email address, but she's also asked me to do a big interview for them even though we've never met?" she asked.

"Fionna contacted you?" Miquel sounded even cheerier than usual.

"Yes. She needs me to do a last-minute interview in Los Angeles in a couple of days. Apparently, their correspondent is sick and they've tried other regular contributors but no one is available. And then she remembered you'd told her about me. How do you know her?" Sol was happy that there was enough trust and friendship between herself and Miquel that he would never feel offended by her directness.

He was also a journalist, but he'd made a career in music criticism in Barcelona. Sol couldn't quite comprehend how he'd come to meet a showbiz editor from an American publication.

"I met her a few years ago. The newspaper I was working for at the time was short-staffed, and they sent me to this boring junket in Paris for some big-budget fantasy TV show or other... I don't remember the name. It's probably long canceled by now," Miquel explained. "Fionna was another one of the journalists there covering the event. We started talking, she was planning a visit to Barcelona, I recommended a bunch of stuff, some music venues and shoe shops, you know..."

He had a talent for reading people and was much more of a connoisseur in all things Barcelona than she was. For one thing, he still lived there.

Every time Sol came back to the city, she made sure to ask him various questions. What new restaurants had opened that she needed to check out? What old institutions were in vogue again? What was the latest not-to-be-missed exhibition? So Sol could believe he'd probably offered Fionna insight on the best-hidden spots of the city tailored to the editor's liking.

"When she finally visited, I met her and her family and

showed them around, and we've stayed in contact since," Miquel added.

"Meaning you always send her a prompt message for her birthday and during Christmas."

"I'm good at keeping in touch. You know that," Miquel said unpretentiously.

And he was. He was good at connecting with people in a casual way. But even if Sol knew the theory behind Miquel's modus operandi since he'd share it with her and anyone who'd listened many, many, *many* times, she could never emulate it. Networking didn't come organically to her, but it was second nature to him.

"So what, you sent her an email and told her your ex-wife was looking for a job?" asked Sol.

"I did contact her, and a few other editors I know, and sent them your contact info in case they needed an entertainment writer. I always referred to you as my longtime friend and fellow journalist. I assumed you'd prefer I leave the being married and divorced part out of it," Miquel said.

"You know I like keeping things strictly professional with editors."

She felt a bit guilty about her comment to Miquel, but she was grateful he still got her. She followed a keep-personal-details-to-the-bare-minimum-or-risk-being-seen-as-weak standard when it came to editors, and it had always worked for her in her career.

"But thank you. You're the best ex-husband and friend."

"Considering who your other ex-husband is, the bar was very low in terms of best for that one."

"I don't disagree," said Sol. "But still, thank you."

"Are you going to see him when you're in Los Angeles?" Miquel asked.

"Who?"

"Ex-husband number two: David Sparrow."

"Are you crazy! Why would I do that to myself?" Sol protested. She knew that made Miquel happy because even if they were no longer together and she'd married David after him, Sol only kept in touch with one of her former spouses.

They hung up after Sol promised Miquel she'd made sure to bring him his favorite organic dark-roasted coffee from Urth Caffé.

She had to hand it to him, *Conceit Fair* was the sort of big publication she'd been pursuing her whole career. They paid decently well. And she had gotten the assignment when she was least expecting it—and most needed a source of income.

But Miquel's words about meeting David in LA had sounded almost like a menacing possibility. Sol knew that in a city with a metropolitan area of over thirteen million inhabitants, the odds of running into someone unintentionally were zero to none. She just hoped probability would be on her side during her brief work assignment in her former place of residence.

The last thing she wanted was to accidentally see David.

23

She landed in London the following morning after one last afternoon date with her hometown the previous day where she'd gone to her three favorite bookstores—La Central del Raval, Finestres, FNAC—to browse for books and do some Catalan- and Spanish-written novel shopping. She was always reading and writing in English, and she'd long feared she'd lose her mother tongues.

Sol was meeting Fionna that afternoon in London, where the editor was based, and flying to Los Angeles the day after.

She could have met Fionna virtually and traveled from Barcelona, but there were more flight options to Los Angeles from London and—perhaps more importantly—the majority of her closet and work attire was also in the British city. And Sol wanted to carefully select whatever she'd wear for the interview to feel completely prepared and at ease.

She was on the Gatwick Express train heading to Victoria Station from the airport, and affecting all the cool composure of the seasoned solo traveler, when she got a text from Luke.

> Luke Contadino (a.k.a. TDS): Ciao bella. Thinking of you. London looks especially gray today.

Sol looked out the window on the train—recalling the girl out of her favorite Paula Hawkins novel—and felt an instant pang of homesickness. Her adoptive home city was looking gloomy indeed.

> Luke Contadino (a.k.a. TDS): I bet you're sunbathing on a street terrace and having an aperitiu with some interesting, sexy and remarkably dressed people.

That message grabbed her attention. How did he know about the habit of having a drink and some tapas before lunch called aperitiu? Also, what was it with Luke that Sol couldn't keep her distance even if all her common sense told her to keep her heart—and her mind—away from him?

She knew she should just ignore him and he'd take the hint. Yet, she didn't.

> Sol Novo: As exciting as all that sounds, sadly, no. There's not a trace of sun and everyone around me looks out of a Marks & Spencer catalog or is in strictly black punk attire.

> Luke Contadino (a.k.a. TDS): Are you back in London?

> Sol Novo: On my way there from Gatwick.

> Luke Contadino (a.k.a. TDS): What! Are you really back in London??

> Sol Novo: I had a last-minute freelance work assignment and here I am

> Luke Contadino (a.k.a. TDS): Do you want to meet?

Sol read the whole message exchange a couple of times without knowing what to reply to that last question. She didn't know what she wanted, really.

She was too old to deny to herself that she was somewhat charmed—*infatuated* was probably the most fitting word—with Luke. But she hadn't forgotten their latest in-person interaction, and she still believed that he wasn't interested in her in the same way she was interested in him. Even if he sometimes confused her, indicating the contrary.

She had stopped depriving herself of what she most craved a long time ago though, and she wasn't going to start doing it again now.

> Sol Novo: I'm going to LA for a couple of days. Let's meet when I'm back.

> Luke Contadino (a.k.a. TDS): Any chance of meeting before? There's something I need to explain.

Whenever Sol tried not to prevent herself from enjoying Luke's company but, at the same time, put some distance between the two of them to regain some sanity and have a clear mind, he'd managed to curtail that attempt.

But his logic was perfectly reasonable. What about meeting before she left? Plus, she was curious to learn whatever he needed to explain. Perhaps he wanted to talk about how he had fled her apartment in Barcelona.

> Sol Novo: Tomorrow it's impossible but I guess I could do tonight.

> Luke Contadino (a.k.a. TDS): Can't. I'm working tonight :(

Of course, he couldn't. What high-functioning grown-up with a satisfying career and an even more satisfying personal life could meet on such short notice? Certainly not Sol, if she had been thinking straight before typing.

She still needed to unpack and then repack for the new trip. She had to prepare for her interview with Fionna and then prepare for her actual interview with a director and producer whose filmography she had mostly not seen or mainly just forgotten or ignored—or all of it. Plus, since she was going to be in London, she had decided to attend a press screening that evening for a new action-adventure rom-com starring Emma Thompson that she had been anticipating for months.

And to think she had almost considered rushing everything and making time for a guy she barely knew. And on a day when she needed to run a thousand little errands before her flight. What had she been thinking? Who was this carefree, improvising Sol?

24

"Guess what I just found?" Divya asked Luke.

He had been following his latest mark from a distance for most of the afternoon in what had to be the most boring shopping excursion around Jermyn Street and St. James's Street. When he'd eagerly picked up Divya's call, he wasn't sure if he could endure a visit to yet another upscale boutique.

"No idea," he said, keeping an eye on Leonardo Pascual —code name the Irrefutably Sexy—from a distance. The *Privateers* star was browsing through a selection of top hats even though Luke was sure no one still wore them, and they didn't go with the actor's bohemian-chic style. Luke had liked the silk pajamas Leonardo had just gotten in one of the arcade's shops though. "Did you figure out why Meshflixx hired us?" Luke added.

"Even better. I've got a bit of romance gossip."

"About who?" He hoped he didn't sound too keen. Could Sol be dating someone even if he hadn't found anything about it and she hadn't mentioned it in Barcelona?

"Sara Daniels," said Divya. Luke realized his heart rate had spiked at the idea of Sol dating someone.

Can you please keep it together? he thought.

"You still there, mate?" Divya asked.

"Yes, sorry. I was trying to find a better location while keeping an eye on the mark." He was becoming a natural at deceiving women. "What's your bit of romance gossip about Sara Daniels?"

"I know what happened between her and Martha Broch," said Divya. "At least, according to a couple of articles I found online on some obscure websites. Behind-the-scenes people are not the object of the main gossip rags, eh?"

"So what happened?" asked Luke.

"They met on the set of the Danielses' first show. Martha was a title concept artist there. Don't ask me what that means because I really don't know."

"Something to do with the design of the title opening sequence?"

Divya scoffed. "Please don't let the time you spent *interviewing* the Stringer get to your head and think you now know what you're talking about. Anyway, it looks like Martha and Sara met then. The series was shot in Atlanta, but Martha was based here in London. She was in Atlanta briefly at some point during production, and I reckon that's when they started shagging. When production ended, I think they did the whole long-distance thing, but then Martha moved to the US and they both lived together in Los Angeles for a while."

"So what happened?"

"From what I gathered, Sara and Bryana got hired to do *The Privateers* but the show was happening in London even during writing and pre-production. Sara broke up with

Martha—the internet says she didn't want to do long distance again—and moved here. Martha stayed for a while in Los Angeles for work and ended up moving back here. She's actually from London, so..."

"It makes sense," said Luke, who didn't require any justification when it came to people moving back to London.

"You know what the cautionary tale is, right?"

"Never move for love?" Luke asked, starting to walk again as Leonardo stopped to grab a coffee. "Never leave London?"

"No, mate," said Divya. "Never mix trade and courtship. The Daniels sisters offered Martha the role of title designer in *The Privateers*, but she declined."

"It looks like things have worked out for Martha anyway." Luke was a bit wound up about Divya's comment. He knew it was her way of telling him, yet *again*, that the job wasn't the place to meet people and that he should stay as far away from Sol as possible.

"Tell yourself whatever version you want," said Divya. "But Martha has more motive than we may have anticipated."

"If she was angry because of the break, yes," said Luke. "But would she be so bitter and still go to the same Pilates studio as Sara? The first thing I did after my latest relationship floundered was change yoga studios. My ex still goes to the other one."

"I guess it only makes sense for them both to go to Josie's if they ended the relationship on good terms and are still friends. Or if Martha wanted to remain close to Sara for some reason."

"Like stealing a script from a show where she has no involvement," Luke continued.

"Aye. Should we add Martha to our private list of main

possible culprits then?" She and Luke had their own analysis of the case. "Even if Agatha is still at the top."

"Yes, let's keep Agatha at the top," said Luke. "And you know that if Sanjay was also on the call, he'd bring up Mark Green again."

"But Sanjay is not on the call." Divya had always believed Mark was innocent because she'd grown up with his movies and was a big fan of the director. "I can't wait for the day when we can make these sorts of decisions without fearing what the nitwits at the top will think about it. Looking forward to getting rid of P and Sweatshirt."

"Unfortunately, I need to let you go. The Irrefutably Sexy is headed for Piccadilly, and I want to make sure I don't lose him in the multitude."

"Right when I was going to ask you about that ex of yours who managed to keep custody of the yoga studio, you decide to hang up," said Divya.

Even if Sol had been on a semi-crowded flight that morning and she hated the hustle of getting to the airport, security lines, and airline passengers unnecessarily crowding the gates, the day had looked more promising after the flying portion was over.

She'd had a productive meeting with Fionna, who'd given her all the necessary details about the interview with Richard Fynn and the angle and questions they were going for. Sol was scheduled for a twenty-minute one-on-one interview with the filmmaker and couldn't see an issue covering what Fionna expected from her.

She was almost packed, her outfit for the interview was pressed and ready, and her interview prep was in good shape. She was planning on watching a couple of Fynn films during her long-haul flight to LA. The movies were already downloaded to her tablet.

To top all that off, she'd just attended a press screening of the most entertaining and engaging flick starring one of her favorite actresses. She was a bit disappointed that no one had thought of casting Emma Thompson as a rom-com action lead before. The woman was classically trained and could do pretty much anything.

That wasn't the only reason Sol wasn't completely pleased though. She had finally seen the movie she should have watched a few days before when she was supposed to have interviewed Thompson. It was one of those interviews she had been waiting for her whole career and that would have made her seventeen-year-old self so happy and proud. She'd interviewed dozens of celebrities over the years and she was seldomly star-struck, but the idea of meeting certain people, like Emma Thompson, still thrilled her.

But she had been fired before that could happen. And even though she was fully aware that she was catching a flight the following day to do a big Hollywood interview, it wouldn't be with Emma Thompson. She would have bought a brand-new outfit for that. And she'd still be very much unemployed once the interview with Richard Fynn was done, written, and submitted to her new editor.

She was debating whether to walk or take the Tube from the Picturehouse Central movie theater on Piccadilly Circus where she'd attended the press screening. But she decided to drop by Fortnum & Mason first and get something for her tea-loving friend, Lola, whom Sol was planning on seeing during her visit to Los Angeles.

Once at Fortnum's, she was piling on the Royal Blend loose-leaf tea for both her friend and herself—managing to put aside that perhaps that wasn't the best budgetary moment to impulse purchase multiple £16 caddies—when she saw someone familiar browsing the big displays of honey and marmalades.

He was tall and thoroughly bronzed, and Sol recognized him instantly this time. If only he hadn't returned to stiff business wear and gelled, slicked-back hair. *Is this supposed to be London Luke?* He'd looked different and much more casual in Barcelona. If this was Luke's everyday look, Sol wasn't sure she was actually into him.

It would have been easy for her to slip by unnoticed. She was always wearing one of her KN95 face masks when she was in crowded indoor public spaces. They protected her from unwanted viruses while also offering some kind of anonymity that the introvert in her not only liked but had learned to relish. But she had made a commitment not to hide if they ran into each other again, so she decided to do the out-of-character thing and go greet Luke.

"Hola," she said after crossing half the store to stand in front of him. "I would have said you were more of a Twinings person."

There was something in Luke's face that didn't necessarily scream *So glad to see you here*, and Sol didn't think it was because she could now vindicate her own hometown as a big city and prove it was equally easy to run into someone in London as it was in Barcelona.

"I"—his glazed eyes fixed on something behind Sol—"need to go."

"I'm sorry?" she almost yelled more than asked, although this time she'd perfectly heard him.

Was she having some sort of torturous and exceedingly unfunny déjà vu? What was it with him that he wanted to run away when he was in her presence?

"Let's talk tonight," he said as he made his escape toward Fortnum's exit.

It could have been so easy for Sol to pay for her goodies and leave without saying a word to him. In fact, it would have been consistent with who she was. Yet she had decided to be social, and for what exactly?

She felt like a foolish and disdained woman in the middle of Fortnum & Mason. Somehow, being surrounded by colorful tins and sweets wasn't exactly lifting her spirits at the moment.

Had she offended Luke with her tea comment? It hadn't been Sol's most inspired joke. The brand she'd said she associated with him was six or seven times cheaper than Fortnum's tea. But she had been a bit nervous and said whatever occurred to her, and she had always thought Twinings one of the most iconically British brands. It was also her mom's favorite, so it kind of held a special place in her heart, but she preferred not to read too much into that.

She was sure of one thing though: She and Luke were never going to talk again—and she was okay with it. She had been humiliated one too many times against her better judgment, and she was convinced that he would not call or message her—even if he'd tried making an excuse while leaving in a rush.

Whatever it was, she decided to brush off the whole Luke affair as a pointless and discarded, if rather sobering, experiment.

25

Sol was halfway through watching *The Revengers*, Richard Fynn's first foray into that franchise of corrupt half-droid, half-human cops that was released in 2008.

She was battling her impulse to fall asleep, and it didn't help her case of somnolence that she didn't care for all the fast-paced, CGI-heavy action sequences. Plus, the flick was almost two and a half hours long. When did Hollywood start ditching the whole superiority of ninety-minute movies with people just talking?

She was about to shut the television off, search for the rest of the plot of the movie on Wikipedia, and go to sleep when she heard the doorbell.

It was after ten and she wasn't expecting anyone. She was rarely up that late at night, usually tucked in bed with the company of a good book—a health-conscious custom she'd picked up during her California days.

She wasn't in the habit of opening her front door for no reason either, especially not that late. She checked the camera on her smart lock and saw Luke at her front door.

She rolled her eyes impatiently but went toward the door. What on earth could he want with her? He'd called her a couple of times that evening, but she'd hoped he'd taken the hint when she hadn't picked up the phone.

She was not interested.

She stopped herself halfway to the door. She didn't want to chat with him. It was late, she was tired, and she had a long flight the following evening. She could simply not answer the door, and that would be it. He buzzed again and a question popped into her mind: How did he know she lived there?

She'd never given him her London address. She panicked a bit. She lived alone, and he probably knew that since he also knew *where* she lived. She didn't know that much about him at all. Luke buzzed a third time, and she talked to him through the smart lock app on her phone.

"How do you know where I live?" she asked, a tone of alarm she hadn't intended to show in her voice.

"That's what I came here to explain. Also, to tell you about my line of work and why I was so hasty this afternoon when I saw you," he said through the smart lock.

"I wouldn't call it hasty, I'd call it rude," Sol said.

"Listen, I'll be at the pub around the corner for a while. I'm sure it's still full of people, in case you want to come and we can talk in a public setting where you feel safe." It was as if he read her mind.

"How do I know you won't be waiting for me on the street when I get out of the house?" Sol asked.

"Because you can check the camera on your doorbell, and you've been alone with me before. You know I'm a nice person. And it's not like I haven't tried calling before showing up unannounced. I'll be waiting at the pub."

26

Luke had been nursing a pint for at least twenty minutes at The Kings Arms and was worrying about the pub's closing time. He was starting to believe Sol would never show up when she finally arrived.

She wore a long, oversized hoodie and baggy sweatpants. Her chestnut hair was gathered in a low knot at the nape of her neck, and her normally fresh-faced and natural complexion looked stripped from any hint of even concealer. Luke wasn't sure if that was her home attire or if she'd decided to wear the roomiest clothes and most modest look possible, not wanting to call attention to the fact that she was an attractive woman. She was trying for the opposite of sexy even though he wasn't sure if she could pull that one off.

She grabbed the chair in front of Luke at the small round wooden table where he was seated. She moved the chair a bit farther away from the table—and from him—before sitting.

"Before you say anything," she started, her tone not only icy but slightly angered, "my friend Laia knows where I am right now. She lives close by and has been instructed to call the police if I don't text her in ten minutes."

"I'm sorry I frightened you. I just wanted to explain what's going on. I felt awful after this afternoon." For the first time, Luke fully grasped how much of a terrible idea that late-night visit had been. He should have approached her in a public space and in plain daylight since she wasn't picking up his calls.

"You showed up at my place at night. How do you know where I live?" she asked. His apology had done nothing to soften her tone. She was furious.

"Let me start at the beginning. My name is Luke Contadino, and I'm a private investigator." He paused, giving her the chance to ask questions or direct more verbal attacks his way.

"I'm gonna need more than that not to file a restraining order," she said.

Luke was about to tell Sol that the UK's criminal system only allowed for restraining orders to be issued in conjunction with a criminal proceeding but decided not to. Sol had lost all sympathy for him, and it wasn't the time or place to be a know-it-all.

"The agency where I work is investigating *The Privateers* stolen script case. Meshflixx hired us." Again, he paused, giving her a chance to say something. But she didn't. "Sara Daniels, the creator of the show, says the script was inside her bag and was stolen at Josie's studio during a class she took there on February 23. We've been surveilling everyone who was at the studio that night to see if they could be implicated."

"Was I at the studio that night?" Sol asked.

If someone asked Luke what he'd been doing on any

given day more than a couple of nights before, he would have also been unsure.

"You were," he told her.

She was still zealously gripping her mobile phone, but he thought she seemed a bit less tense and not thinking solely about how to press the panic-button function on it.

"You've said you've been surveilling everyone who was at the studio that night. What the hell does that mean?" she asked.

"I or one of my colleagues have followed you and other Josie regulars for a few hours here and there during the last couple of weeks or so," Luke said as matter-of-factly as possible.

"So you've been stalking us or spying on us or something?" Her fingers were once again positioned on the side and volume buttons of her iPhone, ready to sound the alarm.

"It's not that. We needed to make sure you weren't involved. We've basically followed you to restaurants or to class at Josie's. That's why I was also a student there for a while."

"A terrible student," Sol said. "You may not have realized, but your lack of dexterity to follow a basic side-leg routine slowed everyone down."

"I'm sorry about that," Luke said, trying not to sound too flippant. But the woman had gone from fearing for her life to complaining about him being a drag in a Pilates class.

"So you followed me to my house?" she asked, starting to understand.

"A couple of times, yes. I also followed you once or twice from your house. Surveillance is one of the aspects of my profession I dislike the most. But sometimes it's necessary."

"It wasn't in this case. I've done nothing," she said, her

eyes flashing. "I don't even believe the script was stolen at Josie's."

"I know that, but I didn't before we started checking into you." He tried sounding reasonable. "This afternoon, I was following someone else and they left the shop when you approached me. That's why I left in such a hurry. I was working until an hour ago. I came to your place as soon as I was done." He wanted her to know that he hadn't lied when he told her he couldn't meet that night because of work.

"How long were you going to keep this from me?" she asked. There was less anger in her tone, but the iciness was still intact.

"I know it's bad. I know how it looks. I tried telling you in Barcelona. The night we kissed, I was going to attempt again before leaving your apartment, but you basically threw me out."

"Don't blame this on me!"

"I'm not. I'm sorry," he said. "I asked you all sorts of things about the case, but you just assumed I was an amateur."

Sol said nothing. Her look was fixed somewhere between her phone and the wood patterns of the table. And Luke took the opportunity to be completely honest.

"The thing is, I was intrigued at first, by you. I didn't see it coming. And then I was terrified. I *am* terrified."

"Terrified about what?"

She was the one who'd been terrified by *him* that night, and he still regretted his misguided judgment. He'd been impatient to tell her what had happened, to finally come clean. But he should have thought about her perception first.

"Terrified about you finding out the truth and never wanting to have anything to do with me again," he admitted.

"Is it weird that I've been somewhat watching you for weeks?"

"Yes," she said, and Luke could see that she was still processing everything he'd told her and wondering about what hadn't been said. "A little bit. Some things make sense now though. There was no way someone like you would have been remotely interested in someone like me after a couple of Pilates classes and after bumping into them at a bar."

"Someone like you?" he asked, not understanding.

"A woman over forty," she said, looking him straight in the eyes for the first time and finally relaxing in her chair.

"You know your age actually turns me on, right?" he said with a smirk.

"Okay, don't do that," she told him.

"Don't do what?"

"Don't flirt with me," she said, her eyes still fixed on his. The iciness of her tone still not giving way.

"Too soon?" he asked, but she didn't answer.

He could see her thinking, and he thought he knew what she'd say next.

"I'm so fucking silly!" she said. "Barcelona... it was all a sham."

"It was by chance," he insisted. "The encounter at the bar was by chance. They... My managers sent me there when you left because they found it suspicious, even though I kept repeating there was nothing weird about it. The night I ran into you, I had just landed. It was as much of a surprise to find you there for me as it probably was for you, believe me."

"Was it really?" she asked. "You *knew* who I was. You knew I was in the city. I had no clue who you were. Not sure if I do now."

"Everything I've told you is true. My parents are Italian immigrants, I have two older sisters, I only speak Italian at home—and with you—and *The Hobbit* was my favorite book growing up. What I didn't tell you is that in my late secondary school years, I switched from fantasy to mystery and really got into Patricia Highsmith's novels."

"But you lied to me in Barcelona," she reasoned. "You lured me... You—you seduced me. For what exactly, I don't know. I didn't steal Sara's script. I didn't even know she was going to be in class that night or that she was carrying sensitive material in her purse. And I sure didn't leak it to *Voyeur*. I may be jobless and possibly broke, but I still have integrity. And mainly I just hate their guts. They treated me beastly when I freelanced there, and they're one of the main reasons why journalists have such a bad reputation."

"Nothing I did in Barcelona was to get you to trust in me and gain access to some secret information," he said. "I was genuinely... I *am* genuinely interested in you, attracted to you. I felt bad in Barcelona because I wanted to keep seeing you, but I needed to explain myself and I didn't know how."

"You should just have left me alone," she said, her eyes avoiding him again.

He was about to remind her that she technically asked him out first, but he decided not to. He wouldn't put it past her to try and kill him with one of those frozen stares. And she had all the reasons to be cross.

"Do you need to text your friend?" he asked her, delicately. He would prefer the night to not end with him at the local police station.

"Not sure what to tell her," Sol said. The iciness had given way to frustration.

"What about, 'Bloke's not a psycho. Just a private detective. He seems genuinely sorry. I think I should give him a second chance'?"

"I have to go." She stood up to leave.

"Can I text you?" he asked.

"I'll think about it," she said.

Luke was about to offer to walk her home, but Sol didn't give him the option. She nodded to the bartender and left the bar.

When she got home and locked her front door, Sol texted Laia.

Sol Novo: I'm home. All is good

Laia: Girl, what a scare!

Laia: Let me call you

Laia didn't give her the chance to send her a thank-you text and tell her good night, and even if Sol wasn't in the mood for a conversation, she saw her friend's call and instantly replied.

"It's late," Sol told Laia. She knew her friend tended to go to sleep invariably late, but she didn't like being the reason behind it.

"Not really," Laia said. "What happened?"

Sol had previously told Laia about her bumping into a Pilates colleague in Barcelona, how the two of them had sort of hit it off only for him to split at the most inexplicable time. So she only needed to catch her friend up on that afternoon's awkward encounter at Fortnum's and on Luke's confession after his surprise visit.

"I don't really know what to say," Laia told her after Sol had finished gathering her thoughts.

"I'm confused, angry, and disappointed. But I really don't know how I feel about the whole deception, to be honest," Sol admitted.

"I don't like that he lied to you. But he was working," Laia said. It was on-brand for one of her most career-oriented friends to see things from the perspective of someone else while they were doing their job. "And I don't think there was ill intent on his part. But he should have come clean before."

"I know," said Sol. "I guess, in his defense, he hinted at his real profession a couple of times. And I kept calling him an amateur sleuth and not getting it."

"Of course!" Laia protested. "How were you supposed to know? I wasn't even aware that his was a *real* profession and not a made-up-for-fiction one."

"I still feel a bit stupid about the whole thing though." Sol's naïveté was what had most annoyed her from the whole situation. How couldn't she have realized Luke's profession? She *should* have.

"Don't," said Laia firmly. "This is not on you. *He* is the one who lied and showed up at your place late at night."

"Okay." It was impossible not to listen to Laia when she was so unequivocal.

"Sol, I know you like him…"

"Oh, I don't," Sol said and, the moment she did, she realized she wasn't being honest.

"Good, because I don't like him," said Laia. Her friend probably hadn't bought Sol's lie about her not liking Luke, but Laia was going with it anyway because it suited her position.

"So I guess I shouldn't even consider giving him another

chance, right?" Sol managed to ask and immediately regretted it. She wasn't sure she wanted to show so much vulnerability right then, not even to one of her best friends. "Forget I said anything."

"Let's talk about this over dinner and wine and when we're both not about to fall asleep," Laia said.

"I told you it's late."

"It's not that. Paula just finally went to sleep twenty minutes ago, and I still need to go over tomorrow's script one last time."

"Thanks for listening," said Sol.

They said good night and hung up, and Sol was left with her own mixed feelings. From the moment she'd started spending time with Luke, she sensed there was something off about him, about his interest in her.

She had decided to ignore that intuition. Only the undeniable fact that she was facing a looming midlife crisis could explain that carelessness and disregard for her own instincts.

Why can't an inordinately attractive and interesting man like Luke be into me? she'd thought and let herself go with the flow. But the reality was that she was a spoiled and possibly ruined trust-fund baby with meager work prospects and a sagging face that was showing her age even if she deluded herself into believing in another—more intriguing and glamorous—version of herself.

Sol reproached herself a little bit. Her rational, conservative self had been warning her from the very beginning, while her unconcerned, hedonistic self—the one she didn't know she so strongly possessed—took over.

Never again. She was going to forget that whole affair. Tomorrow would be another day, and she'd never been one to brood.

27

Ever since her second-to-last work layoff, Sol feared opening her email in the morning. Call it professional PTSD. So she'd started doing it *only* after breakfast. If the electronic mail carried bad news, let them not ruin the sweetest meal of the day.

She was glad she had followed that arrangement that morning because her breakfast would have been utterly sullied otherwise. When she finally opened her email—and after she sifted through an inbox filled with PR pitches bearing titles as catchy as "Michelle Yeoh gains over 450,000 Instagram followers after winning Best Actress Oscar," "Camila Morrone is the most influential cast member of Daisy Jones & The Six, new study shows," and "SEX EXPERTS REVEAL: The PERFECT Toy To Match Your Zodiac Sign"—she found a message from Fionna. Sol's interview with Richard Fynn was postponed.

Fionna told Sol not to worry about anything, which of course caused the journalist to panic. Fionna explained in her email that the studio distributing the movie Fynn was promoting would update them soon about the new date of the interview once everything was newly scheduled. But Sol would not be flying to Los Angeles that evening as initially planned.

She almost saw the whole postponement as a sign that the interview would never happen. Or it would happen, but it would not be her conducting it as one of *Conceit Fair*'s many regular contributors could become available then.

She also knew that sometimes in Hollywood's fast-paced, cut-throat environment when things started being a hindrance, they were simply scrapped. If the interview wasn't scheduled soon, they risked missing the magazine's tight publication deadline. Fionna believed that all would be set in a couple of days, but Sol knew that estimation was terribly imprecise.

If the interview didn't happen in the end, she would not be paid for it.

Her finance guru had still not gotten back to her since her parents had informed her about their new economic reality. The accountant was on a cruise in Antarctica, her out-of-office email said—and Sol was worried about money.

But the worst part was that there had been no need for her to fly to London. She could be trying to figure out her life—and career—from sunny and cheaper-than-London Barcelona instead of looking at the gray skies through the window in her home office.

She was still musing about the uncertainty she faced once again, upset because she didn't know *when* or *if* she was supposed to fly halfway around the planet, when her cell phone buzzed with an incoming call from Luke. She picked up, almost managing to forget everything that had happened the previous night between the two of them, along with her decision to move on from him and basically delete him from her mind.

"Hello?" she answered.

"Ciao." He sounded hesitant and apologetic. "I know I should be letting you decide whether you ever want me back in your life or not..."

"Uh-huh," Sol agreed. The *And yet...* was implied in her condescending tone.

"But my bosses really want the Meshflixx case finished, and I could use your expertise *again*."

"Is that what you've been doing with all these questions about *The Privateers*? Covertly prying insider information from me?" She suddenly realized the depth of his deception. "I thought you were just a regular person debating whether to watch a popular show."

"And I am *also that*, but I'm a junior detective with two incompetent managers who want to wrap up a case that's nowhere close to done." Sol felt he was sharing too much information with her this time. But she sort of liked this new, more transparent version of him.

"So you still don't know who stole the script?"

"No idea. And I'm afraid if we don't find something soon, you'll become suspect number one again," he said bluntly.

"What do you mean?!" she asked. "When have I ever been the main suspect?"

"When you found yourself out of a job and decided to leave the country."

"I'm a journalist. Being laid off is a common professional hazard," she said. "And I like going back home from time to time. Where's the crime?"

"I know. But try explaining that to two middle-aged, upper-middle-class arseholes with a not-so-moderate case of prejudice against immigrants and the will to overcharge Meshflixx while doing the least amount of work possible." Luke sounded frustrated.

"What sort of place do you work for?" Sol asked, alarmed.

"Not the one I thought it was when I took the job."

"Luke, this could end my career," she said. "If Meshflixx thinks I stole the script of one of their TV shows and then leaked it online, my days as an entertainment journalist are done. This time for good."

"I know," he said. "That's why I'm calling you. I need to get to the bottom of this. I know you're flying today, but—"

"I'm no longer flying today actually," she said.

"Could I ask you for an odd favor then?"

28

"Remind me again why I'm driving you to Hertfordshire?" Sol asked.

"I need your help getting introduced to Agatha," Luke said.

"She knows you from the Pilates studio." Sol's eyes were fixed on the motorway. "She remembers everyone who pops in even for just one class."

"She knows my surveillance persona: Greg Knight, banking lawyer and well-being enthusiast," Luke explained. He thought he saw Sol grinning. "But I need her to meet private investigator Luke Contadino and to ask her a few questions. *You* need that as well if you want to be cleared from this whole Meshflixx fiasco."

When Luke called Sol that morning, he'd hoped her flight would be scheduled in the evening and that she'd be ready to forgive him—or at least to put her disappointment in him temporarily aside.

He'd also asked her to accompany him to Harpenden since Agatha was finally back in the country. She'd gone directly to her vacation home in the quaint Hertfordshire small town.

Instead of wanting to take the train there though, Sol had offered to drive. Luke couldn't understand who would prefer to drive anywhere when there were public transportation options available, but he'd readily accepted. He didn't feel in a position to contradict Sol much.

Convincing Sol to come with him hadn't required much persuasion on his part, especially since it seemed that Sol's plans for the day had changed. He had the feeling she welcomed the distraction. If you could call that bizarre situation a distraction.

Luke was supposed to be at the office that morning. But he'd called P faking a terrible flu-like illness, and the germophobe in his manager had pleaded with Luke to stay home. Only Divya knew where he really was, and she'd helped him prepare for his chat with the elusive TV agent.

But before getting to Agatha's vacation home in Harpenden, Sol and Luke still had more than a half-hour drive, and he thought he could try and clarify a few more specifics about the stringer's story.

"Please don't take this the wrong way, but why are you no longer working at the same publication you used to a few days ago?" he asked, trying to tie up all the loose ends pointing to her.

"Why did I get fired, you mean?"

"Yes."

"For a moment there, you sounded more West Coast American than British in your indirect way of formulating that question." She smirked, and he couldn't help but feel he should have confessed his real profession to her earlier. She seemed to be taking it well enough. "I was laid off with another ten percent of the staff at my previous company. They got rid of senior-level writers and editors based in the US and the UK. We were making more money than junior peers or people based in other, cheaper countries. If you've been reading the news, it's been no picnic for journalists these last few months, not that it ever was."

"Don't get me wrong," he proceeded cautiously. But dreading the idea of being called an American for a second time, no matter from what coast, he opted for directness instead. "But how can you afford the car?"

"This car?" she asked. It was a dual-motor long-range electric vehicle with a driver assistance system that she wasn't currently using.

Luke knew the vehicle cost well above what he earned in a whole year.

"It was a gift from my parents," Sol said, as if she were talking about a bouquet of flowers or a toaster. "My dad thought that, after so many years driving in LA, I would miss having a car. He didn't consider that I may have a hard time adapting, with you folks driving on the wrong side of the road and all... But it's become convenient every time I need to escape central London. *If* I remember to take round-abouts counterclockwise."

"Clockwise, you mean," Luke corrected her.

"Whatever, opposite of how it should be," she said, eyes still on the road.

"Do you realize that money makes you look suspicious?" He ignored her remark about his home country driving on the left-hand side.

"What money?" she asked. She sounded almost clueless.

"All of it," he said. "You lead a somewhat posh lifestyle."

"Posh?! Everyone at Josie's is well-off!" It was as if the mere idea of being associated with poshness offended her.

"Have you seen what she charges for a semi-private Pilates class? Why is my money more questionable?"

"Because of your profession and because you're single, I guess." He hoped she wouldn't take that as his opinion. He was trying to put himself in his managers' minds, and that never led anywhere progressive.

"Twice divorced," Sol said, and Luke was surprised. He hadn't found a trace of one ex-husband, let alone two, when researching her. "My money came from my family business though."

"The Spanish products export company?"

"I guess I have no secrets." She sighed. "My parents sold part of it years ago before they retired and gave me an amount so I could live comfortably and still do what I like. They manage most of the money for me because they're supposed to be better at it."

"Sorry about the indiscretion," he said.

"No problem. It's not like you haven't been secretly following me for weeks."

"And for your information, you still do have secrets," he said. "I had no idea about the two ex-husbands."

"Let's keep it that way then." A trace of a grin spread on her face as she remained focused on her driving.

...

When they arrived at Agatha's place in Harpenden, they were faced with a handsomely proportioned Victorian home and an equally spacious garden surrounding it. A couple of big vans were parked up front. Sol parked on the street and they both headed toward the house.

Luke knocked on the front door since there was no doorbell. The door was ajar, and they could hear loud voices and a lot of noise coming from inside.

"She must have started with the renovation," offered Sol. "Agatha talked about swiping this place off the market a few months ago in class, but she mentioned it was a total teardown."

Luke knocked again and peeked inside the house when no one answered. He didn't think it would have been possible to hear the knocks with all the racket.

"Hello?" he said, not quite loud enough. He'd grown up surrounded by a family of yellers and had always been too subtle to imitate them.

"Hi! Agatha!" Fortunately, Sol didn't seem to share his qualms.

"Uh, hellooo!" they heard someone calling from the upstairs floor. "I'll be there in a second!"

Sol and Luke waited outside. They hadn't been officially invited indoors and their visit wasn't exactly social.

"Darling, you came!" Agatha received them with a smile when she made her way downstairs and saw Sol at the door. "And you brought even more people from class," she added, referring to Luke. If Agatha felt curious at the sight of the two of them together, she said nothing about it.

"I did," Sol said hesitantly. Luke realized Agatha had probably invited Sol over earlier, and—judging by Sol's people-avoidance tendencies and dislike of small talk—she'd managed to evade the awkward visit until that moment.

"The place is a mess," said Agatha, frowning. The TV agent wore dusty denim dungarees and was wiping her hands with a wet towel. "Carpets everywhere, including in one of the upstairs bathrooms—and the stairs, of course! A washing machine in the family room! Stucco on the sitting room ceiling! The house is from the 1870s, yet you'd say the previous owners wanted to cover or remove each one of its historical elements."

Most of Josie's students tended to be oblivious to how they sounded. Luke didn't think Agatha had considered that the previous owners might not have had the funds for an extensive overhaul like she obviously did.

"You should have seen my London place when I got it," Sol said. "The renovation was a nightmare. The American in me wanted to tear all the walls down, and the architect I worked with kept telling me it wasn't possible. I had purchased a grade-II-listed historical building and there were regulations! I hated her the whole time, but in the end, she did a great job."

"I wonder if it's the same excruciatingly obstinate architect I'm dealing with here," said Agatha with an eye roll. "But I'm such a bad host. Do you want some tea?"

Both Luke and Sol politely declined.

"Thank heavens," Agatha said. "The kitchen is in full disarray. It looked straight out of the seventies, but not in a good way. It *had* to go."

"Listen, Agatha," Sol finally said. "Unfortunately, this isn't a social visit."

Agatha's shoulders seemed to relax. "Darling, I feel a bit relieved. I thought you wanted to see the house, and right now it would be too much of a hazard. And I don't want the contractors even *more* distracted. But I can show you the garden and you can tell me all about this non-social surprise visit of yours."

"I guess I should start by telling you that Greg is *not* whom we were led to believe," said Sol as Agatha guided them around the house and toward a well-kept herb garden.

If the indoors were in the process of being rebuilt, the

outdoors looked immaculate, at least to Luke's untrained urban eye.

Once Luke's true identity and profession were disclosed, and after a few vehement exclamations from Agatha, Sol and Luke managed to tell the fascinated TV agent what Luke's purpose had been at Josie's and that *The Privateers* leaked script had been stolen at the Pilates studio.

"So the *Voyeur* article wasn't all smoke and overinflated gossip? I missed even more than I thought I had that day!" Agatha said.

"What do you mean?" asked Luke. That group never managed to stop surprising him. They never reacted the way he'd expected.

"The evening of February 23, of course. It was one of Josie's most inspirational Pilates mat group classes, the first and most challenging session to date in her ongoing program to have everyone in perfect beach-body condition by May. *And* there was a theft at the studio!" Her eyes sparkled. "Now I feel even more upset about losing out on the whole thing."

"I don't understand," said Luke. "What exactly did you lose out on?"

"Well, the whole thing, darling! I'm a regular at Josie's every Thursday at half past five in the afternoon, but that day I had a meeting with a former client. He wanted to see if I'd take him again," she said, implying that nothing was further from her desires. "He kept insisting and wouldn't let me leave! We were at the Rotunda Bar of the Four Seasons for what was supposed to be a cup of tea and a finger sandwich. But he wouldn't let me go for two hours and a half! I couldn't make it to Josie's that day. After that, everyone kept talking about how life-changing the session had been—for weeks! I was so upset."

"Of course you were!" Sol's Mediterranean warmth had taken hold of her while she held her hands to her face in dismay. Luke almost rolled his eyes; she could be so dramatic sometimes. "It was Josie's best, most challenging class to date. And you know that's a tall order. I absolutely loved it!"

"So you weren't at the studio the night of the theft?" asked Luke.

"I wasn't," said Agatha. "But Josie felt so bad for me and since I had actually enrolled and I'm there always, she had a recording of the class and sent it to me. So I was able to take the class after. It's not the same as doing it with her in the room."

"No, it's not," agreed Sol. Either the Spaniard was truly affected by Agatha missing *one* class at Josie's, or she was a genius at pretending she knew how to emote. "She always makes sure we hold the right position the whole time. And she *knows* if you are giving it your all."

"She does! Isn't she marvelous?" asked Agatha.

"Josie sent you a recording of the class?" Luke tried to get the interview back on track. For a city as stereotypically exercise-shy and non-fitness-prone as London, Josie sure had found some zealous acolytes there.

"Yes, isn't she a darling?" Agatha replied.

"Could you send me the recording?" requested Luke.

"Oh, I would if I could. You should better ask Josie, I'm afraid. She sent me a link with the recording. I did the class religiously, and now the link has disappeared in the immensity of my inbox with so many other things..."

"I see." Luke tried not to sound too disappointed. "There's one last thing I'd like to ask you, and I hope you don't take this the wrong way."

"Oh, she won't," Sol said. Luke frowned and narrowed

his eyes at her. Didn't they agree he'd be the one talking once Agatha knew who he was? But if Sol understood his gesture, she ignored it. "Agatha has very thick skin," she added.

"That I do," said Agatha. "Too many years in show-business."

"I see. I wanted to ask you about Sara Daniels."

"Oh, she's an excellent Pilates practitioner, but I haven't seen her at the studio since this whole unfortunate event took place and the script was leaked," said Agatha. "I hope she doesn't neglect her training for too long."

"I'm sure it's just temporary," Sol joined in *again*. "She's always been one of our best pupils, and she always can tell her right from her left, which is something I can't say I do. It's a plus in any group class."

"Right," said Luke, unsure how the subject had veered so far from his original question about Sara. "I meant that you were Sara's agent."

"Hers and her sister Bryana's, yes. I signed them when they first moved to Hollywood. I worked in Los Angeles for most of my career," Agatha explained.

Luke nodded. "But then they got hired by Meshflixx and changed representation. That couldn't have made you happy."

"On the contrary! I was so pleased." Agatha's words were gentle and overly cheerful, which Luke could only assume was the result of her exposure to too many friendly Californians when she worked abroad.

"You were pleased?" Luke asked doubtfully. "Wouldn't you have preferred to keep them as clients when they finally got hired by a big streaming service and were about to earn a lot of money?"

"Little secret, darling," said Agatha, leaning in. "Some of

the streaming services are famously stingy. I'm sure Sara and Bryana got a decent offer, but nothing like if they'd been hired to develop a show fifteen years ago by an American network TV channel, with the prospects of then selling the show internationally and getting syndication residuals on top of that."

"Was that why you didn't want them as clients anymore? Because they weren't going to be earning that much money?"

"No, darling. Who needs more money?" Luke felt he could give her a few names. His would certainly be at the top of the list. "For the past decade, I've been trying *not* to work that much. Some of my longtime clients are set on keeping me semi-busy, but I mostly managed to keep them at bay when I moved back to London from Los Angeles. All I really want to do is travel, finish this house, and keep being a regular at Josie's."

Luke found himself speechless for a minute. Of all the scenarios he'd contemplated regarding Agatha's possible involvement in the Meshflixx case, not having the least interest in making more money hadn't been one of them.

"So Luke, darling, not much of a Pilates person are we, after all?" Agatha asked. "That's such a pity. You were showing such promise by the end."

"No he wasn't," Sol said dryly.

"No he wasn't." Agatha chuckled. "But I'm always looking forward to new additions to our small group of fitness disciples."

...

Sol insisted on driving back to town after their talk to Agatha. And Luke was ecstatic to return to the London motherboard swiftly. He'd never gotten the allure of the countryside.

They didn't talk much on their way back. Luke was musing over the chat with the television agent, and he had the feeling Sol had her own things to muse about. There seemed to be a sort of unspoken understanding between the two of them to put everything else aside and work together to clear Sol's name. Or at least, that was how Luke saw Sol's lack of resentment at his deception.

She left him a five-minute walk away from his place on Seven Sisters Road by Finsbury Park. He called Divya when he got out of Sol's car.

"Tell me the TV agent did it!" Divya answered.

"I'm afraid it looks like she didn't," Luke told her. "She says she wasn't even there the day of the theft. Remember how I always thought there was something almost dodgy about her?"

"Yes," said Divya.

"Well, she was decidedly hiding something: that she wants to retire but doesn't want to admit it even to herself. Or to her remaining clients."

Divya made a thoughtful noise. "Retirement is tough, mate."

As soon as Sol dropped Luke off, she found herself thinking about him and her feelings about his lie. And she was reminded of how her brain worked sometimes.

She'd always been able to do her most unrestrained reflecting while walking or driving. Something about the need to reach a destination while being alert to the rules of the road, incoming traffic, and pedestrians kept a portion of her mind occupied but freed another one to bring her unconscious worries to the surface.

And even though the night before she had gone to bed set on forgetting Luke, she hadn't been able to keep her resolution for even a day. She'd answered his plea for help the moment he'd called her.

She could delude herself into believing she'd done it solely for selfish reasons—she'd be the case's main suspect unless they could prove otherwise. She could also pretend she'd said yes because she had nothing better to do that day after her trip's postponement. Both things were true, but they didn't show the whole picture.

That candid chat with herself behind the wheel made her realize that things were a bit more complicated. She seemed to still *like* Luke.

She was very aware of the fact that he'd lied to her, and that alone should be grounds for absolute extraction of his presence from her mind.

And yet.

She hadn't cared about his profession at all in Barcelona. She'd been more interested in how hot he was. She'd been awfully frustrated when he'd left her apartment after they kissed but, in perspective, it had been the right thing for him to do since she didn't know who he was. He'd tried talking to her after that kiss, but she'd basically thrown him out. *I realize I never told you what I do for a living. It's a long conversation. Would love to tell you about it when you're back in London,* he'd texted her the following day, and she'd been annoyed by that too.

He had still lied to her, and she was allowed to keep him in purgatory for as long as she deemed suitable, of course. But she could also dabble with the idea of forgiving him someday. She permitted herself to like Luke—but as a friend and only that.

She'd been so happy for the last few months after putting together all the broken pieces in her heart and her mind. There was no one worth risking being hurt again. Plus, she had far more pressing business: finding a new job and making sure her name was nowhere near the whole *Privateers* mess.

The chat with herself had tired Sol. Fortunately, she'd just arrived home.

She enjoyed the last hour of the warm-ish afternoon by having an Ippodo Ummon matcha tea in her small back garden and reading a Scotland-set Alyssa Cole novel she'd just started. She was sure she'd feel better after.

She would start the active job search process after that, even if she wasn't really looking forward to it. She thought of her conversation with Laia the day she was fired. She'd told her friend she didn't know if she had the energy to keep having fun as a journalist. Would it be such a terrible idea if she found a different profession to have fun with?

29

Luke and Divya had decided the night before to go straight to Meshflixx and talk to Sara themselves. Now that they knew Agatha was no longer an option as a thief—they had checked with the Four Seasons and at least three staff members remembered the agent staying there until late on the afternoon of the theft. She was a memorable tipper, apparently—they needed to know what happened on February 23. What *actually* happened.

Next on their to-do list was to get a link, copy, or whatever available medium of the recording from the class that night. Sol had promised Luke to ask the Pilates instructor for it herself and brief Josie on what was going on.

Luke had said yes to Sol's proposal because he suspected Josie would react better to Sol's request than his. Josie had known Sol for much longer than him, and Sol had never lied to Josie about her identity.

Plus, and Luke would not know how to express this in so many words, he'd liked Josie in his venture as Greg Knight. He'd admired her and didn't want to tell her that he'd lied to her. He'd already done that twice in the previous days—first to Sol, then Agatha—and it had been draining and exhausting even if Agatha had seemed not to care.

But coming clean had been brutal when it came to Sol. Their relationship had changed since that conversation, since his confession to her. He suspected she still tolerated him only because she needed him. She needed to be close to him to keep an eye on the investigation.

They had somehow moved from potential lovers with lots of chemistry to simple acquaintances who had a common goal and where one of them had betrayed the other. Perhaps if Luke managed to salvage Sol's reputation and keep her name out of the case, once it was finally wrapped, she would give him another chance as a potential love interest. He'd like that.

Divya broke him out of his reverie that Monday morning by handing him a to-go cup of tea as they met at the entrance of the Meshflixx building.

"I know you don't like just any kind of tea," she said. Luke rarely had tea on the go; it was never the right brand or strength, and he hated paper cups. "But I *know* you need another cuppa. You've been distracted. I need you sharp. Know what I mean?"

Luke could have objected. He and Divya had the kind of relationship where they were straightforward with one another but also joked constantly. But she was right about him being distracted. So he grabbed the cup and accepted her method of trying to get him awake and alert. "Ta."

Once they got inside Meshflixx's ultra-modern, ultra-minimalist building, the receptionist wanted to know if they had an appointment with Sara Daniels.

"We don't," said Divya. "We are from Thompson &

Thomson, the agency investigating the theft of *The Privateers* script."

"I see." The receptionist seemed to understand. "Let me get her people."

After fifteen minutes of idly standing in the Meshflixx lobby—there were no chairs or even stools in the whole reception area as the interior designers had taken the minimalist concept to an uncomfortable extreme—a petite person with turquoise hair and dressed in an immaculate lemon-colored two-piece suit and sneakers came looking for Luke and Divya.

"You are the detectives?" the person asked, and Divya and Luke nodded. "I'm Moon Scott, Sara and Bryana's creative liaison. My pronouns are they, she."

"I'm Divya Bakshi, junior investigator at Thompson & Thomson, and my pronouns are she, her." Divya smiled, and Luke recognized that smile as the one reserved for purveyors of good food, and beautiful people.

"And I'm Divya's colleague, Luke Contadino. He, him," he added.

"Follow me," Moon commanded, taking them through what looked like a maze of lifts, halls, and stairs. For such a recent construction as Luke knew the Meshflixx building to be—there was no way of overstating his real estate obsession—the place had been designed with the worst interior design choices of the seventies when it came to its floorplan.

"Please sit down," Moon told them when they got inside a cube-like room where all the walls were glass. A round plexiglass table sat in its middle, four equally transparent chairs around it. "The agency didn't tell us you'd be coming today," said Moon.

Luke decided to let Divya do the talking. She was better than he was at charming their way into getting something.

"They didn't?" she asked so convincingly that even Luke believed it. "I'm afraid our manager has been a bit preoccupied lately. New love interest troubles."

Luke didn't appreciate that Divya was using his own romantically caused distractions as a plausible excuse.

"I see," said Moon. "We've all been there."

"Yes, we've all been there." Divya smiled again, and Luke rolled his eyes a bit. She'd scolded him not a week before because the job wasn't the place to *meet people*, yet there she was in full meeting-people mode while performing her responsibilities as a detective.

"Unfortunately, Sara isn't at the office," said Moon. "She's been working from home."

"Would it be possible to get her address and talk to her at home?" asked Divya.

"That won't be possible." Moon returned Divya's smile, and Luke was thoroughly entertained. On the surface, Moon and Divya were having a cordial chat, but beneath all the professionalism were sparks between the two of them, even if they were on opposite sides. "But I can pass her any message you folks may have for her."

"We'd like to have her version of the facts one more time," explained Divya. "She mentioned leaving the Pilates class early that day, and we were wondering if she'd been the only one to do it. Also, was there any other thing out of the norm that day?"

"Other than her script being stolen, you mean?" asked Moon, not a single trace of sarcasm in her tone.

"Other than that," conceded Divya.

"The whole thing is so odd," said Moon. "Sara didn't normally go to Pilates on Thursday nights. Evenings tend to be very involved in terms of breaking and pitching new storylines. But that day we finished early, and she decided to go. She needed to finish some revisions of the script at night. She normally does that on her tablet or laptop, but the wi-fi was down that afternoon. That's actually why we finished early."

"The wi-fi was down?" repeated Luke. "Where? Here? Isn't that odd?" And extremely inconvenient for a tech company.

"Very odd!" replied Moon. "So Sara grabbed a copy of the script and left to go to Pilates. If only the wi-fi had worked, but she didn't want to risk getting home that night and not being able to access the latest version of the script on the cloud because of the wi-fi kerfuffle."

"Was it the whole building? The wi-fi not working, I mean," asked Luke.

"Not sure, but several people on our floor told me they also had problems."

Luke was about to ask Moon how unusual it was for the building to be without internet when they heard a knock on the glass door of the fishbowl-like meeting room.

Sara Daniels was the one knocking. It appeared she wasn't working from home after all.

"Oh, Bryana is here," said Moon.

Luke shook his head. Why had he assumed the woman at the door was Sara? He knew she had an identical twin, and he'd been told Sara wasn't there. But his detective's nose tended to veer toward not believing everything he was told. He must have assumed the creative liaison hadn't told them the truth.

"These are the detectives in charge of investigating the *theft*," said Moon, uttering that last word almost in a whisper.

Bryana introduced herself. Name, last name, job title, and pronouns. The detectives did the same.

"We'd love to talk to your sister," said Luke.

"She's been focused on writing," Bryana said. "As I'm sure you'll understand, the leak was a bit upsetting and she feels responsible, even if we've all assured her that it wasn't her fault. We're quite busy with *The Privateers*. But Moon and I will be happy to send her any request for information."

"Please, tell her we'd like to chat with her. It wouldn't be more than ten minutes, and a phone call would suffice." Luke gave Bryana and Moon cards with his phone number.

The cards read *Luke Contadino (he/him), Investigator* and included his phone number and email account. He'd had them printed when he was working as a contractor at another agency, and he was still using them since T&T had never bothered outfitting him with new cards.

"So you're busy writing the second season then?" he asked Bryana.

"Incredibly busy," she said, without offering any specifics.

"Any chance the quartermaster doesn't get killed in the end?" Luke still hadn't watched *The Privateers* but had decided to use all the information Sol had given him.

"A fan, are we?" asked Bryana, not giving anything away.

"You caught me," lied Luke. "I loved that you didn't prolong the whole will-they-won't-they routine too much, and that the quartermaster and captain finished the first season as a couple."

Divya shot him a look from across the round table. *Have you decided to start watching* The Privateers *without telling me?* her eyes asked.

"I wanted them to solve another crime together this season," added Luke, feigning the shyness of an overzealous fan. "I'm very much into whodunits with lots of romance."

He almost blushed. Those were the truest words to come out of his mouth that morning, which made him wonder why he hadn't started watching this show yet.

"That's what the fans keep telling us. That they want more of Leonardo Pascual and Murray Groff together doing their sleuthing bit," Bryana said. She was less guarded than before. She'd warmed up to Luke's demonstration of appreciation for her and her sister's work. "I won't spoil anything..."

"Please don't," fake-pleaded Luke.

"But don't worry too much," Bryana said.

Luke was about to express his fake relief when Divya thankfully intervened. He'd never been a good actor and wasn't sure he'd be able to pull off the authenticity of a comforted fan.

"Does that mean the leak made you change the script?" asked Divya. Nothing escaped her deducting skills.

"Oh no, no!" replied Bryana, back to her professional reserve. "But the version of the script that was stolen wasn't by any means a finished one, and there are many ways of keeping a character."

Before either Luke or Divya could add anything else, Bryana checked her smartwatch, stood up from the chair she'd taken, looked intently at Moon, uttered an apologetic goodbye to the detectives, and left.

"I'm afraid we have no more time," Moon told them. "We're meeting with Meshflixx execs in five minutes."

"Everyone looks so busy," said Divya with one of her sweetest, most adorable smiles, her amber eyes looking perfectly innocent.

Luke loved working with her because they could easily communicate. They always coincided with their reads of the interviewees, and they could take turns leading the questioning depending on who the person they were approaching responded to.

"We're a bit swamped," Moon said in their musical Southern US accent. "Lots of rewrites." She grabbed her mobile phone and stood to guide them to the exit.

"Are rewrites usual at this point in production or is it because of the leak?" asked Luke, afraid his eagerness may spook Moon. Divya sent him a killing stare that could only be read as *Back off!*

"I don't know about other TV productions," said Moon. "But rewrites have always been the normal way in *The Privateers* writers' room before and after the leak. And we don't start shooting for another few weeks, so there's still plenty of time. Sara and Bryana are the kinds of showrunners who may rewrite a scene during production just because they saw how an actor reacted to the material." Luke couldn't tell if she was being completely honest. Was the creative liaison tired of being swamped, perhaps?

On their way to the lift, they crossed a hall where movie and TV posters from some of Meshflixx's most popular productions hung from both walls.

"Is this a Martha Broch design?" Divya suddenly asked Moon. One of the posters did resemble Martha's work, even if it was for the first season of *The Privateers*.

"It's not," said Moon.

"It looks exactly like her work," said Divya.

"Unfortunately, Martha wasn't able to join our team the first season, and she didn't design the poster and title credits sequence of the show. She was working on that other show with Nolan, who was making his TV debut. He *really* took a lot of Martha's time," explained Moon.

"So Sara and Martha are still on good terms even though

they broke up and everything?" asked Luke. Divya shot him another irate look.

"Of course! The breakup was mutual," said Moon. "They are best friends. Martha organized Bryana and Sara's latest birthday party."

"Sometimes it's better to be friends than lovers, I guess," said Divya, and Luke almost rolled his eyes.

Moon saw Luke and Divya to the lift and badged them straight to the bare lobby with a warm smile. The moment the lift's doors closed and the detectives were alone, Divya said, "I was taking care of the interview with Moon!"

"I know. I should have let you deal with them, but I wasn't sure you'd ask about the rewrites."

"I wasn't going to because I knew they wouldn't answer," said Divya. "But I was going to ask them for their phone number, and you made the whole thing very awkward!"

"And here I thought the job wasn't the place to *meet people…*"

"Oh, shut up!" she grumbled. But even if Divya sounded annoyed, she'd forgive him soon enough.

30

Since Sol was still very much jobless and her job search hadn't borne any promising results, she decided to catch one of the mid-morning classes at Josie's. Sol had never been an early riser capable of being fully awake—let alone moving—before eight in the morning *and* a slow breakfast ritual. Pilates classes at 11:30 seemed to be designed for people like her.

She was a bit jittery and needed the pleasant endorphin release that came with strength training. Plus, if she was going to be flying to Los Angeles soon, and that was still up in the air, she wanted to feel well-exercised and properly stretched before the long flight.

Of course, there were other reasons to head to Josie's that morning. Sol had promised Luke she'd talk to the Pilates instructor and explain what was going on, asking her for that recording of the February 23 class. That would hopefully help her get closer to clearing her name from the Meshflixx investigation.

Mid-morning classes tended to be less crowded, which gave her a better chance to talk to Josie alone. That wasn't always possible during the more popular afternoon sessions because the most impassioned members at the studio tended to want Josie's attention by the class's end. They were a bit like groupies, hounding Josie for her longtime early morning meditation technique or the recipe for her latest antioxidant-packed green juice.

When Sol got to the group Pilates mat class, only Mark was there. He was an incredibly affable person with a long career in Hollywood, and Sol liked chatting with him.

"I'm glad to catch you here," she told him, placing her mat close enough to have a conversation with but prioritizing the most optimized view of where Josie would be. First things first. "I'm supposed to interview your old pal Richard Fynn in Los Angeles."

Richard and Mark had worked together in a series of immensely watchable, if not creatively compelling, action movies in the late 1980s with Mark as the director and Richard producing. That had been before Richard made his directorial debut.

"Oh gods! Why would you subject yourself to such a thing?" Mark asked, half genuinely concerned, half joking. Sol remembered reading something about their parting as working partners not being necessarily amicable.

"He's promoting this upcoming release," she said. "*Revengers Reunite Redo* or something like that." She couldn't remember the title of the movie because it had sounded too silly to be true the first time she'd read it.

"Did he finally manage to produce a sequel to that bloody bore *Revengers Reunite*?" Mark seemed a bit more interested now. "I quit reading the trades ages ago, so I know nothing about what gets produced these days until it shows up at my local movie theater or on my streaming device."

Mark had mentioned before that he no longer bothered

reading all the showbiz news. But he still loved gossiping about anything and everything industry related.

"He did. He also directed it—and wrote the script," Sol explained.

"Oh gods! He *wrote* it!" Mark chuckled. "Don't tell me you'll have to watch it."

"Fortunately not," Sol said, amused. "They'll play a trailer and the first twenty minutes of the movie for me before the interview. But that's it."

"Those are twenty minutes of your life you'll never get back," Mark warned her.

"I know. Well, that's if the interview ends up happening." Under normal circumstances she wouldn't share that many details, but she knew Mark was discreet. And it was always therapeutic to talk to someone who understood her struggles. "The interview has already been postponed once, and you know that sometimes when they start moving things around on the calendar, they end up never happening…"

"Yes," Mark admitted. "But don't be too concerned. If there's anything Richard loves, it's the limelight and feeling important. Nothing gives that illusion more than talking to a journalist."

"I see." Sol felt relieved after Mark's words. "Thanks again for the Hollywood perspective."

"*Old* Hollywood perspective, but anytime," he said with a smile. Mark seemed happier—and much healthier—since his retirement a decade earlier after a cardiac event, but Sol knew he still missed certain aspects of the industry. "One last thing about Richard. He can be a total tosser with pretty much anyone, so…"

"Papa, please don't tell me you're pestering your Pilates colleagues again with old stories. Nobody cares!" Oliver, Mark's son, interrupted.

If Mark was one of the most agreeable, nice, and even modern-thinking people—especially for a sixty-something cisgender, heterosexual, white man—Sol didn't quite comprehend how he could have produced a little rich brat of a son like Oliver. Fortunately, the thirty-something-year-old who claimed to be a documentarian but whose filmography was nonexistent only joined his dad at Josie's sporadically.

"Mark wasn't pestering me at all!" Sol said.

But she didn't have time to add anything else. Josie entered the practice room then and the unspoken rule at the studio was to shut up and stop what you were doing when she did so. The following fifty-five minutes would be focused exclusively on Josie's teachings, breathing and adapting to the increasing difficulty of the exercises. And Sol, evidently, did that.

She would talk to Josie and tell her about what she'd privately been alluding to as the TDS Mess after class.

...

"Do you have a minute?" Sol asked Josie at the end of class.

"Sure, but I really don't recall where I got this," Josie said, referring to the breezy V-neck tunic-like dress she wore over black leggings and a sports bra. She was used to Sol harassing her about her clothing.

"That's a pity," Sol said, and she really thought so. It reminded her of something she'd seen on the streets of Mallorca the previous summer that she hadn't been able to track down. "But that's not what I needed to tell you."

"Do you mind talking while I occupy myself with my middle-of-the-day strengthening routine?" Josie said as she unrolled her extra thick Manduka mat. She contorted her slender body in a stretching position Sol would never dream of achieving.

"Should I also have a middle-of-the-day strengthening routine, you think?" Sol asked, forgetting her initial intention for talking to the Pilates instructor.

"You just took a strength training class, Sol," said Josie, opening one eye to look at Sol while she did leg raises over a one-legged plank.

"I know, but I was wondering."

"Was that what you needed to talk to me about? I can draft something for you, if you need," said Josie with the extremely patient tone she used with all her pupils.

"No, but yes. Thank you," said Sol. "What I meant to talk to you about was Greg." She was glad she could easily recall Luke's fake name.

"Greg?" Josie was perched in a side plank, one leg and one arm in the air. "Brand-new divorcé with a less-than-healthy lean-body-mass percentage and the worst case of midlife crisis we've seen at the studio in a while? And we see *lots* of those."

Sol wondered where exactly in the mild-to-severe scale Josie would classify Sol's own midlife crisis, but she decided not to ask. *Sometimes it's better to live in ignorance,* she thought.

"No, that was *Craig*," corrected Sol. "I meant Greg. Tall, sun-kissed, and very sexy guy answering to the classical canon of male beauty but who looked like a posh, out-of-his-element lawyer or banker."

Josie, going through the flow of her routine, paying attention to her breathing with her eyes closed, opened one of her eyelids again to direct an interrogating stare at Sol.

"I don't recollect," she said.

"Doesn't matter because, the thing is, he's actually not called Greg and he isn't a lawyer or banker either."

"Oh, you mean the Italian model look-alike who is extremely clumsy and can't move through a sequence even if he tries," said Josie. She had finally remembered Luke. "I knew there was something shady about him."

"So he didn't fool you?"

"Sol, at my age and with everything I've seen and lived, *nobody* can deceive me anymore." Josie had been holding a forearm plank for a good two minutes and was still talking —and breathing—easily.

Before telling the Pilates instructor the whole TDS Mess, Sol wondered, once again, about Josie's age. And whether she herself had any chance of becoming such an unafraid and poised woman.

31

"Josie is extremely disappointed in you," Sol told Luke when he picked up the phone. "But she's open to letting you stay at the studio as a member under your true identity, *if* and only if you take a few private lessons with her to work on basic exercises and routines. You need to up your Pilates game."

These people seriously need to get their priorities in order, thought Luke. The more assiduous members at the studio were all suspects in a highly publicized theft—Sol's name at the very top of that list—and all everyone seemed to care about was that he took his Pilates practice seriously.

"Sol, thanks for that, but I'm not sure I'm Pilates material."

Ever since his confession to her, he'd been all soft around Sol and tried not to disappoint her even more. He was acutely aware that his admission had poured buckets of iced water into his and Sol's previously heated connection.

"I see," said Sol.

Luke's attempt at smoothness had been in vain, so he'd forgo the extreme diplomacy strategy altogether.

It wasn't as if the relationship was in such bad shape, after all. There was some bantering left between the two of them. And even if he *knew* he'd like to more than bicker with Sol, he could be content with that friendly quarreling while they worked at solving the case.

She added, "Pilates is too boring, right? What's your thing then? Workout wise, I mean."

"Uh, not much..." He didn't want to get into specifics about his muscle-toning workouts, frequent runs, and de-stressing and back-healing yoga classes. He'd be at risk of being perceived as vain.

"Please! At least have the courtesy to tell me you think Pilates is not enough for you, and tell me what it is that you do. I'm used to the whole workout-for-old-ladies rhetoric, which is absolutely wrong. But I *know* you do something. I've seen you in a tight-fitting T-shirt!"

Luke was about to protest at her use of qualifiers for Pilates, something he'd never thought, but decided to go in a different direction. He needed to know what Josie had said about the recording, but there was plenty of time to ask Sol about that. He wanted to enjoy the current conversation and its intriguing subject. Especially since Sol didn't sound mad at him at all. Perhaps things between them weren't as glacial as he thought and were veering in the direction of moderately warm.

"So, you've thoroughly checked me out," he said slyly.

"Mare meva! ¿Cómo se puede ser tan creído?" she yelled at his vanity, and he couldn't avoid a smile.

"Sol, as much as I'd like to, I can only understand half of what you say when you speak Catalan or Spanish. My Italian only helps to a point. You were saying I'm gorgeous..."

"I said not such a thing," she protested, her tone furious but sexy. "And you *know* it."

"I do," he admitted.

"I may have been thinking it," she added playfully, and he almost choked on the fresh cup of tea he'd just brewed at the office kitchenette. "But now is not the time to talk about that."

"It's not?" She'd just upgraded their whole relationship from lukewarm to scorching hot, but she didn't feel like talking about it?

"Aren't you at the office?" she asked him.

"I am," he admitted reluctantly.

"Not the time, or the place," she concluded.

He had escaped to the office's empty kitchenette away from anyone's earshot but was very much aware of his whispering on the phone.

"Do let me know when it's the time and place to talk about it," he said huskily.

"About what? Your gorgeousness?"

"And I guess we could also tackle yours…"

"Okay, enough, Luca," Sol said. It was the first time she'd used his name in Italian. He'd insisted his family should never use it when he was a kid, asking them to only use the English version of his name to better fit in British society. But suddenly, he realized he liked *Luca*. A lot. "Let's talk business," she added.

"Let's," he said, even if he didn't want to.

"Josie is going to try to get the recording for you," Sol told him in all seriousness. "It's going to be hard because apparently the classes only get recorded as part of the studio's security system. She never uses the recordings, and those get stored on the cloud and deleted automatically. She did use the recording for the class of February 23 because

Agatha would have died otherwise, and the system has proven useful in such occasions."

"You mean useful when an overenthusiastic member misses one class, not in case of possible theft, right?"

"Yes, the first one," Sol clarified. "Josie shares my opinion about the script *not* being stolen at the studio, by the way."

"Not sure if this is an opinion issue, but I hear you," said Luke.

"She's uneasy at the idea of a member stealing something from another member."

"It could also have been her," Luke said.

"What do you mean?" Sol asked. Luke thought she was being purposefully dense.

"Josie could have been the one doing the stealing," he told her.

"No! She could never. Why would she do such a thing? It could ruin her business. She's one of the best Pilates instructors I've ever worked with—"

"Big sample?" he interrupted, genuinely curious. Once again, his desire to know Sol better was interfering with his work.

"I mean, I wouldn't call myself an expert... but I've worked with some of the best ones in LA. And you know how fitness-conscious Californians are."

"Not really," Luke said. He realized the decade Sol had been living there was what gave her Spanish-infused accent a somewhat Californian musicality. But it also gave her many traits of character he was now starting to distinguish.

"And you really don't care," said Sol. "Bottom line, Josie is the best, and please rule her out as a suspect. It just doesn't make sense."

"Right. Let's say I listen to you and come to realize you're correct," Luke said, even if he hadn't been completely persuaded by Sol's arguments regarding Josie's innocence.

"I tend to be," she said. Luke suddenly understood it was Sol's security in herself that had attracted him in the first place.

"I'm sure you are." He was loving the non-stop banter between the two of them. At times it was flirtatious, at times quasi-professional. It was a lot of fun on every single occasion. "But tell me, who looks like a thief then? I mean, from the other possible suspects?"

"I don't know! I'm not even sure who the other suspects are," Sol said.

"You were there that day. Is there any chance you remember who else was there and what happened? It would actually help me." He should have asked her that before, but he'd been too busy trying to seduce her.

"What day was it again?" asked Sol. Luke could almost hear her thinking, trying to evoke the moment. "It was a Thursday class, right? I'm always there on Thursdays."

"We've been told the class ran long," Luke told her, hoping that information would trigger her memory.

"Oh, that day, right! No wonder Agatha was upset because she missed it. I was sore for a week!"

"That sounds weirdly sexy," he said, not able to shut up.

"Stop with the flirting, Luca." He really did love when she used that name. "We've got work to do."

"Sorry," he said. "I couldn't stop myself."

"Should I continue telling you what I remember?"

"Please do," Luke said. "Do you remember who else was there?"

"The usuals, I guess. Philippa for sure. She asked everyone if she could post a picture of the class to her Instagram." Luke made a note to look for that post. "Mark was also there. He's our only guy, so he's easy to remember."

"I feel left behind," Luke complained.

"Please," Sol dismissed him. "Martha was also there. I remember chatting with her after class about how strenuous the whole thing had been. And Lashana must have also been there because they're friends and work together... Yes, now I remember talking with her days after. She told me she had also been sore for days due to that class. And that's it, I guess."

"And you, Sara, and Josie were also there," Luke helped.

"Yeah."

"What time was it when Josie finished?"

"Not sure. 6:40ish? Not later than that because I normally meet my friend Laia on Thursdays for dinner at 7:30, and I still needed to go home to shower and get changed and all that. I remember thinking, 'If Josie is not done by 6:40, I'll have to make an apology and leave.' I hate being late. But, in the end, I didn't have to leave before the class ended."

"Would that have been an issue? Leaving early?" he asked. "We were told Sara left at half past six."

"If a member needs to leave before the class's end, they tend to ask permission out of respect for Josie. And she may advise them to do some stretching at home or whatever else she had prepared for the remainder of the session. But she's normally extra punctual and respectful of our time. She knows some members are extremely busy. Sara is one of them. I think I do recall Sara leaving early but, to be honest, by then my butt was probably on fire and I was just following the routine through the discomfort. Trying to endure the whole thing."

"Again, sexy," he said, his voice low.

"Okay, since we seem to be done with the professional portion of this chat, I feel I can ask you this now." She paused dramatically. "What are you wearing?"

This time Luke did choke on his tea.

"What?!" he asked.

"What are you wearing? Is it a pair of beige dress trousers with an ill-fitting shirt?" She sounded utterly disappointed, describing what he wore when embodying Greg Knight.

"Right now, I'm wearing a tea-stained striped gray T-shirt. Thanks to you, I've spilled my cup of tea all over myself."

"And?"

"And washed black jeans that my sister Martina insisted I should get from All Saints." He didn't add that he'd always resented Martina for insisting he buy such a pricey garment.

"I see," she said. He couldn't decipher whether she sounded relieved or still disappointed. "No slicked-back hair?"

He combed his tousled waves with his left hand. "No."

"So the way I've seen you all around London was a fluke? Your style is like the Luke I met in Barcelona? A bit grungy and distressed, indie rock with a vintage-inspired sensibility?"

"I wouldn't put it in those terms mostly because I can't. You *are* the writer," he said, amused by her description. Flattered too. "But I only wear *certain* clothes when I'm working and trying to blend in."

"Very ugly undercover attire?"

"I guess you could say that, yes." He laughed. "If you're not asking me anything else, could I—very much against my best instincts—ask you something strictly professional?"

"Sure," she said. Had he detected a hint of disappointment on her part for his unfortunate topic shift?

"Can you help me understand why Meshflixx has spent money on this case?"

"Why did they hire you, you mean?"

"Yes, especially when the script had already leaked online. According to my boss, they wanted to show the creators that they cared about the show, but I think there's something else. And you could give me a new perspective on the whole thing." He trusted Sol even if he still hadn't found definitive proof of her innocence in the affair. The only certain thing he knew was that he fancied her.

"Do you realize anything I know is public information? Whatever has been reported on this, right? I don't have a source at Meshflixx who's given me a scoop or anything of the kind. And I am *not* an investigative reporter. I write hot takes, reviews, and the occasional interview with a celebrity."

"I'm aware. You still have two decades in that industry and are able to see things in a different light than I do," he told her.

"Okay. But I have to agree with your boss here." Luke groaned in discontent. He hated when someone he liked agreed with Sweatshirt. "The first season of *The Privateers* broke several records in terms of audience for Meshflixx, and the show became their most-watched TV property in the US and the UK but also several other coveted international markets. The streamer is prioritizing international growth, so I can see how they'd like to make Sara and Bryana happy by showing them they care about the show."

"I see." He tried not to sound too disappointed.

Sol was searching online on her laptop while talking to Luke on the phone. She thought she remembered something else about *The Privateers* being on the news for reasons other than the usual casting announcements, trailer launches, and season renewals. She wasn't sure if the information would be relevant to Luke or the case but decided to offer it anyway.

"Here it is!" she said when she finally found an online article about what she was only vaguely recalling. "Not sure if this is anything, but when the show premiered last year, their Twitter account got hacked."

"Whose Twitter account? Meshflixx's?" Luke asked her, sounding engaged once again.

"No, no. The show's own account. The streamer's audience development team creates individual accounts for their prominent shows as a way of reaching more people. They can post a new trailer, release behind-the-scenes photos of the cast, choose GIF-able little clips from the show..."

"What did the hacker do?"

"Nothing major really. It could have been bad like posting insensitive or offensive things," Sol said. "In this case, they just put out one poll regarding the quartermaster, with a picture of Leonardo Pascual, the actor who ended up playing that character. He'd been rumored as a possible contender for the part for a few weeks but hadn't been officially contracted yet, even if there was a lot of online chatter about him. The post from the hacker was simple: Should this very beautiful man play one of the two leads in the upcoming *The Privateers*? *Yes* won by a big margin. Meshflixx was able to recuperate the account after that. They maintained that Leonardo had been hired before the results of the poll and that the hacker's action didn't sway them in any way."

"First a hack and now this," Luke said.

"Yes. Seeing how odd things keep happening, it makes sense that Meshflixx decided to have this latest event investigated. I guess they want to ensure that everything runs smoothly going forward," said Sol.

"But they may be halting the investigation soon."

"In this industry, it's all a matter of perception and image more than anything else. They don't necessarily need to do everything they can to clear the case of the theft. It only needs to look like it."

"Right," said Luke. He was probably determining how absurd the whole showbusiness industry could get.

"How much is your agency charging Meshflixx?" Sol asked.

"To be honest, I don't know," admitted Luke. "I'm nowhere near that kind of information. I can only assume as much as they can. That's why my managers shipped me to Barcelona and like surveillance work so much. It's easy to inflate an invoice that way."

"That may not agree with Meshflixx right now," said Sol. "They just reported their financial results for the first quarter of the year, and things don't look as comfortable as before. There's pressure to bring costs down."

"Thanks for all the insider analysis," Luke said. "We can go back to flirting now if you want."

"As much as I'd love that," said Sol, and she truly would, "I need to sort out this trip to LA."

"Is it happening soon?"

"It looks like tomorrow morning."

"Will you let me know?" Luke asked. "I don't want my managers losing their minds again because you're leaving the country, but it will hopefully look less nefarious if I tell them I already knew about it."

"Okay." For a moment, Sol had misinterpreted his wishes to keep him updated regarding her trip.

"Also, let me know when you're back. I'd love to see you."

Perhaps she hadn't misinterpreted anything in the end.

"I will. Need to go now. Adeu, Luca. Talk to you soon."

Ever since Luke had made his whole confession—and scared the hell out of her by showing up unannounced at her door—she no longer felt like there was something he wasn't telling her. And she liked that.

She still wasn't sure what to think about him, other than that she evidently had a soft spot for him. She hadn't verbally teased someone so hard since—never really. In fact, she couldn't remember being so openly flirty with anyone before. It had to be just some flirtation between two early-stage friends, but nothing else. There was no way she would have been so obvious with someone she really fancied. Right?

All that would have to be a thought for another day though because at that moment, she needed to focus on her upcoming trip to LA. The sun and waves called to her.

32

Clearing customs and immigration at LAX airport had been a breeze. After ten years living in California—and after her marriage to a US citizen—Sol was the proud possessor of a blue passport that made things easier when visiting her former home country.

Once out of LAX, the city Sol had called home for a decade greeted her in the most LA-idiosyncratic way possible: with gridlocked traffic. There was nothing like a seven-lane-per-direction highway completely full of cars to welcome you to Los Angeles.

Fortunately, she'd decided not to drive herself during that visit and was aboard a ridesharing vehicle that she'd hailed on Uber. She managed to soak in the sunny views of the 405 freeway, which had never been much to contemplate because it ran four miles west of the ocean. Sol must have missed Los Angeles more than she'd realized if she was really that taken by the freeway landscape.

She would have preferred to stay in Venice Beach or Santa Monica and be able to walk to the Pacific during her visit, but the magazine had booked her at the London Hotel.

The coincidence of the name wasn't lost on her; she couldn't escape the British city even in the West. The hip hotel was on the Sunset Strip in West Hollywood, and she would be walking distance from the indie bookstore Book Soup and a shortish hike away from the Chateau Marmont, in case she felt like celebrity watching. Yet, it contravened her longtime rule of never staying east of the 405.

Her interview with Richard Fynn would take place the following day, so Sol had time to sleep the jet lag off for a couple of hours but also enjoy the city and fall in love with it all over again.

She had brunch at AOC in West Hollywood with her friend Lola, who was a television screenwriter. They talked about a looming Writers Guild strike and the superiority of California hass avocados. Sol went to a referral-only Pilates class at the most sought-after and exclusive LA studio, which had opened *after* she left the city. She recognized at least a couple of minor celebrities sharing in the suffering of the class with her. From there, Sol headed to Venice for a stroll on the beach.

On her way from one place to another, she gazed at the many billboards on Sunset, Wilshire, Venice, and Lincoln Boulevards advertising an array of TV shows and films for the industry-insider Angelenos.

There would be no time to visit The Broad, the LACMA, or the Academy Museum. And she'd also have to leave her shopping at the Century City mall and on Melrose Avenue for a future occasion.

The one thing she hadn't done and still intended not to do under any circumstance was to meet her second ex-husband. The one who, on paper, had looked perfect but wasn't. The one who had deceived her.

During the last few months of their relationship, Sol had

been convinced that David was having an affair with a much younger woman, only to learn he'd concocted the whole thing to make her jealous and reboot their marriage, which had run its course. She *had* gotten jealous and extremely self-conscious. She'd still divorced him.

Avoiding David was the only way Sol was able to rekindle her fondness for Los Angeles.

She was a bit nostalgic at the thought of her daily morning walks on the beach when she'd lived there. She'd jump out of bed, throw on a pair of wide-legged sweatpants and an oversized faux-fur jacket that she would never dare to wear in London or Barcelona, and leave the house like that. Back then, that had made her feel like an Angelena while walking among the throngs of skaters, runners, yoga-on-the-beach practitioners, dog walkers, and tourists.

But that had been another life. It felt like it all happened to a different person—and it had. The Sol who had lived there wasn't the same as the Sol who was now visiting.

All the remembrance made Sol tired. She was ready to catch the sunset at the beach, head back to her hotel, order room service for dinner, and go to sleep early when she got Luke's text.

Luke (Sexy PI): How is Los Angeles treating you? Please don't tell me you prefer it to London.

She rolled her eyes and decided to reply right away. Being in LA had made Sol realize that her ex-husband's strategy—pretending to be involved with someone more than a decade younger than him and Sol—had been what caused her hesitancy when faced with her and Luke's own age difference. Her latest relationship's lack of success was also why she'd been so delusionally intent on keeping Luke in some sort of nonsensical friend zone.

She was ready to consider putting all that aside now.

Sol Novo: Don't get jealous. You're too attached to your hometown.

Luke (Sexy PI): Look who's talking

Sol Novo: Why are you still awake? Isn't it like past three at night there?

Luke (Sexy PI): We have a new case on top of the Meshflixx case and surveillance is getting out of hand.

Sol wanted to talk to Luke in person for this conversation, but texting would have to do for now.

Sol Novo: Don't want to offer my unrequested opinion but…

Luke (Sexy PI): Please do

Sol Novo: Have you thought about working for a different agency?

Luke (Sexy PI): Constantly

Sol Novo: I see. Are the options so limited?

Luke (Sexy PI): Practically nonexistent

Perhaps, even if their two lines of work were completely different, Luke's and her chosen professions had more things in common than she'd realized. They both did what they liked, even if that meant less stability, certain social stigmas, an unclear path for career growth, and financial uncertainty.

> Luke (Sexy PI): Need to let you go, sadly.
> The mark is on the move again!

> Sol Novo: Have fun!

She could practically hear Luke groaning all the way from England. She knew he probably wasn't enjoying his current assignment, so she decided to have fun for him and savor the salmon-colored skies during magic hour.

33

The following day, a car picked her up at her hotel and started down San Vicente Boulevard en route to Sol's destination. The car had stopped at a traffic light on Santa Monica Boulevard when Sol saw the almost all-glass building that doubled as the headquarters of Supreme Video in West Hollywood. It was an imposing building, and Sol was admiring its architecture when she caught a glimpse of a man who appeared to be in his sixties leaving a black electric SUV and entering the place. He looked like Mark Green.

Sol got only a brief view of him since her car started driving again, but she was almost sure she'd recognized her Pilates colleague. It looked like the retired director was having a meeting at the main office of one of the big streaming services. Mark hadn't mentioned he'd also be traveling to Los Angeles when Sol told him she was due for a work trip to the Californian city. Her colleague must have wanted the meeting to remain under the radar.

She was still intrigued about the whole thing when her

car left her at the main entrance of the Four Seasons hotel on the palm tree–lined Doheny Drive.

It was almost a full hour before the scheduled starting time for her interview, and she knew there would be a lot of time devoted to waiting. It was always like that with these kinds of celebrity interviews. Journalists were ushered early to the hotel where the event was hosted with the promise of food and gossip—either from colleague journalists or publicists. The PR people running the set of promotional interviews made sure there was always someone available and on hand to throw into an interview room.

Big promotional junkets entailed that talent—actors, producers, directors—were enclosed in lofty suites where a non-stop parade of journalists would interview them either in grouped interviews or more exclusive one-on-one settings like what Sol was scheduled for.

By the end of a press day, the talent would had been asked the same reshuffled questions dozens of times. What made a star, and a long-lasting career in Hollywood, wasn't only a compelling performance on the screen or directing a hit movie, but the ability to reply to those dozens of identical questions differently and graciously. Every. Single. Time.

Sol got to the hospitality room that the studio of *Revengers Reunite Redo* had booked for the press day and was immediately reminded of the somewhat social nature of these occasions.

She saw an old acquaintance seated at one of the tables and went to say hi. They talked about the dismal health of the journalistic profession, the prohibitive nature of Californian real estate, and how bad most of the movies they'd seen that year were. It was an unspoken rule among the members of the celebrity-interviewer circuit to never admit to liking anything—other than in front of eager publicists.

The journalist acquaintance told Sol about all the celebrities he'd interviewed in the previous few weeks. Sol had long observed that being so close to power and fame—even if journalists were still outsiders in that glitzy Hollywood milieu—caused her peers to sometimes enmesh themselves in that world and measure their success by the celebrity status of the people they got to talk to.

"You're here to interview only Richard, right?" he asked Sol. He'd been there since early morning talking to the full cast of the flick, and he had also spoken to the writer/director/producer. "He's been awful. That's why they're running so late."

"Oh no!" Sol muttered. She checked the time on her phone. It was almost an hour after her slotted interview time. But she had no occasion for follow-up questions with her colleague because a publicist came asking for Sol then, ready to finally take her to interview the filmmaker.

It had been a while since Sol had performed an interview of that kind. So many things had been happening over video conference, and Sol had missed the excitement and pomp of an event where you couldn't wear flip-flops, leggings, and a fancy, camera-friendly top. One-on-one, you pretty much put all your stock in your ability to connect with the interviewee and direct questions their way in a limited period of time.

She was confident in her interview prep and her power look, consisting of loose and perfectly straightened locks, a two-piece plaid suit paired with a T-shirt, and Munich platform sneakers.

When Sol got inside the suite where the interview would take place, there were already half a dozen other people there between the studio's publicists and Richard's team. Sol introduced herself and smiled at everyone, acknowledging them. She always did. You never knew who all these people could be or become. Plus, it was the polite thing to do. No need to snub anyone, especially not an intern.

She'd witnessed her fair share of celebrity surrealism during the years: a since-then-canceled two-time Oscar winner summoning his assistant so that she'd close the blinds in the room because he couldn't be bothered to stand up and do it himself; a young, up-and-coming *enfant terrible* vexing even the most seasoned Hollywood reporters with his bratty behavior; several established A-listers managing to answer all questions in the most boring and bland way possible, no matter what you asked them; and a midcareer TV actor who had decided a roundtable interview was the right venue to hit on Sol.

But she wasn't quite prepared for the sight of Richard Fynn seated on the long tuft-cushioned sofa at the center of that Four Seasons suite.

He was eating lunch—what looked like a quinoa salad on kale topped with fried chicken—and the lunch wasn't only in his bowl but also half in his mouth and on his clothes.

"I'm eating!" he declared when he saw Sol, after one of the many publicists in the room tried telling him Sol's name and her outlet before rushing off.

Sol wasn't sure if Richard meant he wouldn't stop his food intake during the interview or he was inviting her to leave while he finished.

She tried making eye contact with one of the many publicists standing in the background, but if they'd heard Richard, they pretended they hadn't. They were all absorbed by the luminous screens of their mobile devices.

Sol decided to go ahead because time was ticking. She sat on the Eames chair that decorated the room next to the sofa where Richard sat. The room had a California Modern vibe disturbed only by the director's rumpled bright green hoodie and neon yellow boardshorts. She placed her digital recorder and her cell phone, which was also recording, on her lap and started her interview the same way she'd done it so many times.

"Thanks for taking the time and talking to me," she said, a smile plastered on her face. She took notes of everything she observed while still keeping eye contact with the interviewee. It wasn't an easy task, but one she'd mastered after years of making the Hollywood rounds.

"It's not like I had too much of an option," the director grunted more than said, his mouth full of quinoa.

Sol giggled timidly, sure he was being funny. Another look at the publicists gave her nothing; they were even more enthralled by whatever was on their phones. For all Sol knew, they were messaging one another and commenting on her bad interview start.

"Do you like the promotional portion of making a movie?" Sol asked, trying to ask the director something mildly original that could still fit what *Conceit Fair* was going for.

"It's the numb, soulless act of trying to charm the likes of you," he said. Sol couldn't help but feel a bit slighted by the comment.

One last try to be nice.

"I understand we can be a bit repetitive sometimes in our formulation of questions, but I tend to ask what readers tell me they want to know," she said, only slightly defensive. "And in this case, they want to know what made you return to such an iconic franchise."

She'd managed to say *iconic* without laughing out loud and maintained her smile while waiting for Richard's answer.

"Why?" Richard muttered, attacking a fried chicken thigh.

"I'm sorry?" Sol was starting to sweat nervously. There would likely be no way of reconducting the interview. How much time had already gone?

"*Why* do the fans care about my return?"

"Perhaps you could answer that for me." She was *really* trying. These things were only this difficult if you had to find a way of asking a celebrity one last question about their parenting style or dating advice but never this early on and if no probing questions had yet been asked. There had been zero possibility that she'd offended him already. "Why do you think the *Revengers* franchise has been so popular over the years?"

"Fuck if I know!" Richard said. "Aren't you supposed to be the entertainment writer? You people are the ones who over-analyze every single frame of my oeuvre, not me!"

"Let's talk about your oeuvre then," said Sol, pronouncing the word the French way instead of the American way that Richard had used (and she'd always disliked). If he wanted to be difficult, she could be a total snob. "You first started in this industry as a producer working alongside director Mark Green. How did his directorial style inform yours?"

"It didn't," Richard replied curtly. Sol knew she shouldn't have gone there, considering how they hadn't parted on good terms. But she couldn't avoid it. Richard was being such a pain. "I stopped working with him ages ago."

"Why? You made several very successful films—"

Richard didn't let Sol finish her sentence, and for once

she didn't have to fight an answer out of him. "We were in different stages of life. Mark had gotten married and had a child, and families are such a drag!" Sol remembered that Richard had been married and divorced five times himself, but her own two ended marriages didn't permit her to judge him even if she was feeling inclined to. "All families are a nuisance, but Mark's especially."

"You definitely made a name for yourself with the first *Revengers*," Sol said, changing subjects and hoping her fakeness wouldn't show too much. She couldn't believe she'd found the energy to say another good thing about a director whose filmography she didn't care about and who was behaving like a total cretin. "How has the franchise defined you?"

"It hasn't," he said. Sol should have asked something different, but at least Richard kept talking. "*I* was the one who defined the careers of the cast. They were unknowns, but I saw their potential."

She should have taken the bait and gone with that and kept asking about the *Revengers*' original cast. Even if not a single one had returned to the franchise, regardless of the promise in its title. They had all moved on from action and sci-fi, devoting themselves to serious historical dramas since then. They now amassed eight Oscars, thirteen Emmys, and even a couple of Tonys between the four of them.

But Sol's editor wanted the piece to center around its tech aspects. Fionna had also mentioned they would prefer not to mention the original cast if possible. Apparently, at least two of the actors had slighted the magazine recently, declining to talk to their journalists. So Sol tried broaching the tech subject now that Richard seemed to have warmed up a bit.

"It's been thirteen years since *Revengers Reunite*. The fans and the critics had safely assumed the franchise was done. But you've just gone back to it. Did VFX technology pave the way this time?"

"No," he replied.

"Care to elaborate?"

"Not really."

"Okay. What you would like me to ask you about the movie?" She tried to sound conciliatory. And that was her last resort question. "What do you want to say about *Revengers Reunite Redo*?"

"I've been babbling about the damn movie all morning already!"

Sol tried not to look too directly at him as he disgustingly ingested another chicken thigh. His second or third during their chat.

"You haven't been babbling about it to me," she said, attempting to smile but not managing it.

"What do I care!" He stood up. "Ask one of the others for a recording of their interview. I'm sure you'll all write the same crap!"

And with that, he exited the room. A piece of fried chicken was still in his hand, and half a dozen publicists were still very much buried in their mobile devices.

Sol was deciding which one of the deeply engaged-with-their-smartphones publicists to approach when a new PR professional, whom she recognized from past press events and who exuded bossiness, entered the room. Her eyes were also fixed on her own oversized phone while she wrote what could only be an urgent email or other. The publicist approached Sol, still clutching her device, but stopped giving it her whole attention momentarily.

"Richard has been a bit grumpy today," she whispered.

"Grumpy?" Sol asked in disbelief.

"It's his blood sugar," the publicist continued in her secretive tone as if she was making Sol privy to some sort of valuable and exclusive information. "He participated in an online global press conference this morning, and we'll make sure to get you those answers. He was very cooperative then."

"What do you mean by an online global press conference?" asked Sol. It had just dawned on her that the piece *Conceit Fair* had commissioned would be pretty much impossible to write with the material she had.

"He answered questions from journalists all over the world via a chat platform," the publicist explained.

"Meaning there's no video of him replying to those questions." Sol shook her head. "How do I know he typed the answers and not one of the people on your team?"

"Sol, we would never." The publicist sounded almost offended.

"Yes, I know. I'm sorry." Sol really wasn't sorry. She had to ask because it was the kind of question her editor would ask her. "But he was being completely obtuse with me."

"The team told me," the publicist said, acknowledging the half a dozen people behind her. None of them lifted their eyes from their screens.

"I can't believe I'm saying this, but would it be possible to talk to him again?" Sol asked. "After he does a quick media training crash course reminder..."

The publicist laughed, but Sol wasn't joking.

"We can try, but he's said he's done for the day. There were ten other journalists waiting to interview him today and it doesn't look like it's gonna happen."

"Does he realize that, now that the movie is done, he needs to sell it?" Sol asked frustratedly.

"Part of the problem is that the movie is technically not

done," the publicist said. It had to have been a very bad press day when a publicist was being so candid to a member of the press. "They're still working on the effects, and Richard is nervous."

"I don't want to be difficult. You know me, I'm the opposite of difficult," Sol told the publicist. "But I don't know what we'll be able to publish with this!"

"I know, I promise to get you that online press conference." She exited the room with the gang of phone typers in tow, leaving Sol inside the now empty suite.

She gathered her stuff. The only thing left for her to do was to also leave. Not even getting into the same elevator as Sam Worthington or George Lucas, or running into Helena Bonham Carter or Christian Bale at the valet parking—all things that had happened to Sol at some point in her career in that one particular hotel—would make up for the horrible day and worst interview she'd ever had.

She decided not to dwell too much on the improbability of something nice happening that day, or she'd interpret it as a metaphor for the somber prospects of her career.

34

A couple of hours after what had objectively been the worst, most vexing interview of her whole career, Sol was in another car en route to the airport. She kept replaying the interview in her mind, each one of Richard's rude answers and her responses to them.

Sol was angry. She should have reacted differently. She had two decades of experience doing that kind of work, yet she felt like a total novice. An amateur would have probably handled the whole situation better—or left the room in tears. But perhaps if she hadn't tried being so accommodating and polite and she'd told Richard what she *really* thought about his *oeuvre* and his attitude, he'd have stayed for the whole interview and would have engaged with her. But it was too late now.

If only Mark had been able to finish voicing whatever advice he intended to give her about his former working partner, but that irritating son of his had interrupted him! But again, it was too late to start with the what-if route. What she *knew* was that she wouldn't be able to write much with what she had.

After a few minutes of nervous thinking, she managed to calm down a bit. She would explain to Fionna what had happened. There was still a way of writing something about Fynn and his unwillingness to promote a sequel that hadn't happened for thirteen years. There was a story there, even if it wasn't what *Conceit Fair* had initially commissioned from her.

She checked the time on her smart tracker. It was much later than she'd anticipated, and she was nowhere close to the airport. Traffic was bad, reminding Sol of one reason why she'd left the city.

She was beginning to fear she'd be late for her flight back to London when she received a message from someone she'd managed to mostly keep off her mind. And she was forced to recall the *main* reason why she'd left Los Angeles.

> The Boring One: I had to find out through social media that you're in LA. You could at least have texted. Your crap is still all over the place.

Sol frowned. The last thing she needed was having to deal with David, ex-husband number two and the number one person who made her lose her not-really-that-plentiful-to-begin-with patience. She was about to text him *again* that he could get rid of anything she may have left there and send her the bill for the expense—or better yet, finally ship her *her* remaining stuff—when she got another message.

> The Boring One: I'm sure you had the courtesy of speaking to ex-husband Number One when you were in Spain a few days ago

Not only was David the most exasperating person Sol

knew—he had an unparalleled way of irritating her—but it also looked like he'd been following her movements on social media.

When her phone buzzed again, she was ready to roll down the window and throw it out of the car. But the new message wasn't from the most annoying person she'd known. It managed to make her forget about Richard Fynn, David, and even the possibility of not catching the plane.

> Luke (Sexy PI): Still enjoying sunny Los Angeles?

A lot had changed in Sol's mood and feelings toward the Californian city since they last texted.

> Luke (Sexy PI): The weather in London is a balmy 13C right now and it should only be rainy for half of the week

> Luke (Sexy PI): But please don't hold that against us

Sol couldn't help but smile at Luke's messages. London's weather sounded terrible, especially if she compared it to the glorious Angeleno day. Yet she wanted to catch that wretched flight back now even more than before. It almost surprised her: she was actually longing for the British city and the home she'd made for herself there.

Being back in Los Angeles—the city she'd called home for so many years—had reminded her that she was no longer the person who left Barcelona in her twenties and LA in her late thirties. She was no longer simply Barcelonian or Angelena. Fitting in *anywhere* would be difficult because of that. But it was the path she'd chosen for herself.

Sol Novo: I won't :)

Sol Novo: Even if what you've described
doesn't sound too enticing.

Luke (Sexy PI): Did I mention I'm also here?

She laughed earnestly—her first authentic, not-at-all-fake laugh of the day—and was relieved when the driver pulled up at LAX. It looked like she'd be back in London soon after all.

...

She was at the gate waiting for her London Heathrow evening flight to start boarding when she got Luke's call. She promptly answered it.

"Ciao, bella," he told her in a way that made her smile. "Sorry to bother you during your Angeleno stay."

"I'm actually at the airport. No bother at all, but they may call my boarding group soon."

"I'll go straight to the point then. Especially since it seems you won't be abandoning us for California after all."

She couldn't help but laugh. "I most certainly won't."

"Happy to hear it. Feel free to criticize Los Angeles and compare it to London and its superiority any time." She rolled her eyes at his London pride and love even if more often than not it reminded her of her feelings toward her own hometown.

"Luke," she said, still laughing. "Group One just started boarding. Sadly, I'm not there but I'm in Group Three. You needed something...?"

"Josie sent me a recording of the February 23 class," he told her. "Thanks again for asking her."

"No problem," Sol said. The conversation could have been much more fun if she didn't have to board a plane momentarily and rush him. Then again, that plane would take her much closer to him.

"Let me know if you want me to send you the link so you can retake the class. I know you enjoyed the bum-on-fire routine." Amusement filled his voice.

Sol assumed he had called her to figure out something about the case, maybe ask her something else about *The Privateers*. Yet he was unabashedly talking about her ass.

"Luca," she said, trying to sound authoritative. She knew he liked it when she used his Italian name. "As much as I'm enjoying this line of conversation..."

"You are?" he asked. He sounded half-surprised, half-self-contented.

"I am, but group two just started boarding and I feel you needed to ask me something."

"Many things. You may not want to answer all of them."

"Mare meva! You turn more Italian by the minute. Could you please cut to the chase?"

"Reluctantly," he said, a change in his voice. "Do you remember if there was anyone else in class on February 23? I mean other than you, Josie, Sara, Philippa, Mark, Lashana, and Martha."

"Not really," she said, trying to remember. "Why?"

"There's an eighth person showing for a couple of instants in the recording, but they're in the background, pixelated, and we can't identify them." As much as Sol missed his flirtatious tone, the new twist in the case had caught her attention.

"Could that person be Leonardo Pascual?" he asked, which caught Sol completely off guard.

"The actor?"

"Yes."

"No."

"Are you sure?"

"Believe me when I say I would absolutely remember if Leonardo showed up at my Pilates studio," Sol said. "Sadly, I've never seen him in the flesh. The man is irrefutably sexy."

"That's what everyone keeps saying, yes," conceded Luke, even if he didn't sound confident about it.

"Let me think about it and see if I remember anything about that mysterious person who *wasn't* Leonardo Pascual," she told him. "I have an eleven-hour flight ahead of me, after all."

"That would be fantastic," he said. "Are you about to start boarding?"

"I am." She joined the queue for her group number.

"Any chance you'll want to see me when you're back in London?" he asked.

The last time he'd asked her that, she'd been in Barcelona and much more unsure about the answer.

"I'd like to," she said. "But I really need to go now. Adeu, Luca."

"Ciao, bella, see you in London."

She liked the sound of that promise.

35

"Remember the poster that we thought looked like a Martha Broch design?" Divya asked Luke when he got to T&T's office that afternoon. "It may have been because it was meant to look like a Martha Broch design."

"What do you mean?" he said, absorbed in his phone. He was checking his surveillance schedule for the remainder of the week.

"I was reading the review our Stringer wrote about the first season of the show." The mention of Sol caught Luke's attention. "She liked it, but she mentions *The Privateers* has been mired in controversy and links to an article where it's all explained."

"What controversy? The Twitter hack?"

"No, something about the opening credits and a poster. They were AI-made apparently, and it didn't sit well with the creative community. At the time, Meshflixx said…" Divya checked an article on her phone to read from it. "AI is just one additional tool among the vast array of toolsets used by the artists involved in the making of the show.' But it's almost as if they utilized the tool so that it would resemble Broch's style, eh?"

"Why didn't she tell me anything about this?"

"Who? Martha? Are you also *interviewing* her?" asked Divya, confused.

"What? No," he said, realizing he hadn't sounded very clear. "I meant Sol. We talked about *The Privateers* the other day, and she didn't say anything about this but it's clear she knew about it."

"She could have forgotten about it. I'm sure she doesn't remember all the shite she writes about." That sounded reasonable enough. Or did he just want to believe it made sense? "But I don't care if Martha organizes birthday parties and is still super friendly with her ex, she has a motive," Divya added.

The cab from the airport left Sol at home a bit after nine that evening. She took a long shower, made herself a kale omelet, called her mom, called Laia, texted with Lola to the point of thinking a call would have made more sense, and was deciding whether to keep doing stuff or retire to bed with Sally Rooney's latest emotional nail-biter when she realized Luke had left her a voicemail.

"Welcome to London. I won't tell you that I hope you had a pleasant flight because I know *that's* not possible. I'll be working until late. Text me if you want to catch up," he said.

She was in the mood for a chat with him and texted him right away without thinking much about how late it was.

> Sol Novo: Just heard your message. Are you
> still working?

She sent the message and started unpacking but felt exhausted at the idea of having to do laundry from the trip. She was debating again whether she should try to go to sleep or not—the guidelines around jetlag mitigation had always been fuzzy for her even with decades of supposed experience on the subject—when she got Luke's text.

> Luke (Sexy PI): I'm just done for the night.

> Luke (Sexy PI): Happy you wrote. I've been meaning to ask you something.

She was intrigued.

> Luke (Sexy PI): Is it safe to assume you forgive me?

Sol chuckled. She hadn't actually dwelled too much on his deception since the day of their trip to Harpenden. She'd never been one to hold a grudge.

Had she forgiven him? She had been mad at him in the beginning, especially the night when he finally admitted to everything about his real profession, but her anger hadn't lasted. They were soon embroiled in the mystery he was investigating, and she was simply too intrigued by him.

And even if their latest conversations and text exchanges had been on a friendly and often flirtatious note, Sol appreciated his checking to make sure that she had indeed forgiven him.

> Sol Novo: It may be safe to assume, yes.
> Inexplicable but safe

> Luke (Sexy PI): Mind if I ring you?

Luke (Sexy PI): If it's too late and you prefer
to talk tomorrow, let me know.

She checked the time and realized it was almost midnight. Even if she wasn't the least bit sleepy because she was in California time—and she'd taken a seven-hour nap on the plane—the wise thing to do would be to go to sleep and leave everything for the following day. She didn't appear to play it safe lately though. She called him herself. He answered after one tone.

"Ciao, bella. Happy you're back." His tone was gruff, husky, and accompanied by some background noise that made her deduce he was probably walking on the street.

"Hola," she said. She wasn't sure how to proceed with that conversation even if she'd initiated the call.

It was late, and she was calling a man who had lied to her and had been flirting with her persistently practically from the moment they met. She was also a young Gen Xer trying to communicate with a youngish Millennial, and if years of clickbait-article reading had taught her anything, it was that those two generations didn't get each other.

"Thanks for forgiving me," he said tentatively. He was no longer in his teasing mode. He sounded the most serious he'd behaved since he came clean to her.

"Just don't lie to me again," she said sternly, wanting him to know she meant it.

"I won't," he replied, and she believed him. "I know it's late," he added in a much more playful manner.

"I'm so jet-lagged that I don't really know what time it is." And, in a way, it was true.

"Do you want to go for a drink?" he asked. "We can meet in your neighborhood if that's more convenient. I'm already on the move anyway."

"It's too late. I'm too dehydrated from the plane for alcohol, and I don't really feel like going out," she said. That didn't mean she didn't want to see him. "I know how this could be interpreted, just don't read too much into it: Do you want to come to my place? For tea."

"Just tea?" he said.

"I guess I could also offer you some Hawaiian macadamia nuts."

36

On the phone with Luke, she'd been wearing her *Lilo & Stitch*–themed Primark pajamas. Sol had gotten the tip about their fabulous sleeping sets from *Killing Eve*'s resident fashionista Villanelle. But with Luke on his way to her place, she decided to change into something that still gave the illusion of casualness and homely comfort but was more sophisticated and appropriate for a visitor.

She opted for a pair of high-waisted, wide-legged, cropped faded blue jeans that she'd gotten in Paris recently and a black fitted hoodie that hit at her waist. She was deciding whether to don a pair of Arizona Birkenstock sandals or her furry pale-pink slippers when she heard the doorbell and ended up running barefoot downstairs.

Nina Simone was singing "Nobody Knows You When You're Down and Out" through her home-theater audio system when Sol opened the front door. Her heartbeat picked up speed when she saw Luke standing there. He wore his signature dark jeans with an equally dark T-shirt and a midnight-blue bomber jacket. A loose wave of hair fell over his forehead, and Sol thought he had to have staged such hot tousledness before buzzing the door. It couldn't be fortuity. No one was that casually gorgeous.

"No Greg Knight look tonight?" she asked. She probably sounded relieved by his sexy appearance. Had he changed clothes before heading to her place?

"Two days across the pond, and you forget how to be Mediterranean?" he quipped with his best, most smoldering smirk.

"Perdón." She breathed deeply to compose herself. "Hola."

She kissed him on both cheeks with an ease she'd learned from her upbringing in a very physical country, even if his closeness—and his lavender- and hickory-tinged smell—was melting her insides.

"Ciao, bella," he replied in turn, walking in and making Sol feel even more unsure about the whole thing. What had she been thinking exactly when she'd invited him over? Since when did she get visitors of any kind that late at night?

"Let me take my boots off," he said, sitting on the wooden storage bench that graced the tiny entryway. "Should I also take my socks off and match you?" he added, eyeing her bare feet on the wooden floors.

"Better not," she said, not missing one single detail as he unlaced his rugged classic boots.

"Why?" he asked, lifting his eyes from his shoes and catching Sol's attentive gaze on him.

"I have a thing with naked feet and ankles," she said bluntly, trying not to blush excessively.

"Not into it?" he asked, returning his attention to his shoes.

"Opposite," she whispered more than said.

But he heard her and returned his eyes to hers with a

wicked smile. He took his socks off and rolled up his jeans almost provocatively so that his ankles would be visible.

"Unrelenting flirt," she said, ushering him inside. She would not look around the vicinity of his feet under any circumstance. Unless he was some sort of very tall hobbit with the hairiest of feet and the thickest of ankles, she'd be doomed.

"I liked your Barcelona place, but this is impressive," he said, looking at Sol's minimalist selection of mid-century modern furniture in the professionally interior-designed living room. "I've always liked this street."

"Oh, I fell in love with the street too and then ended up in this cramped old house," she said. She'd tried salvaging some of the furnishings from her California home, but most of the pieces were too big for the London space. Plus, Sol had quit trying to negotiate property rights to a few of her former belongings with her most recent ex-husband.

"Cramped old house?" Luke asked her, sounding perplexed. She recalled he'd talked about renting a tiny, overpriced studio. Sometimes she was totally clueless.

"You should have seen my place in Santa Monica," she said, trying to justify herself. She swallowed, grasping the fact that she appeared to have exactly no wits left about her that night. It wasn't because she was nervous. She was frantic.

"I doubt you had a Georgian cottage from the 1830s in Santa Monica," he said, a tad defensive. And that touchiness, paired with the fact that he'd stopped being a consummate seducer for the first time since he'd arrived, allowed Sol to regain a bit of lucidity.

"I most certainly didn't," she conceded. "Let me show you the skylight above the kitchen/dining room."

They crossed the arched opening that separated the living from the dining area and that had been the closest to an open-space concept Sol had managed to get from the regulation-abiding architect who'd led the renovation of the house.

Next to the almost all-white, modern, and completely remodeled kitchen was a long, six-person wooden table surrounded by four chairs and a bench against the wall. The roof over the table had been replaced by a skylight that provided the room with lots of natural light during the day. It was one of Sol's favorite places in the house.

If one of the upstairs rooms hadn't been devoted to her home office, where she kept all her favorite novels, dictionaries, manuals, and tea-table books, she'd probably work out of her kitchen even more than she already did.

"I'm not in the habit of making tea and having people over at almost 1 a.m.," Sol told Luke, putting the kettle to boil on the stove.

"I'm not in the habit of going to people's places to have tea at almost one at night either." He helped her reach a couple of cups stored on a tall shelf.

"Somehow I don't believe you," she told him, looking him in the eyes and grabbing the cups from his hands carefully so as not to touch him.

"That's only because you weren't actually talking about tea, and you decided to typecast me." His smolder was hard at work.

"As?" she asked.

He thought she looked a bit more at ease than when he'd first arrived, but she was still not her usual confident self.

"Someone who has lots of—I guess let's continue with the tea euphemism..."

"... lots of *tea* with different people, yes." Sol finished his sentence. "I did typecast you. Am I right, though?"

"Not sure if I want to reveal that yet." He smiled, aware of how seductive he could be.

They held each other's gaze for a few seconds—longer, perhaps—daring the other to say something first, to do something first. The kettle whistled then, taking them away from the intense staring competition. Sol went to the stove to pour the hot water from the kettle into a teapot. He followed her movements. He didn't want to ogle at her, at her body, but caught himself already doing it.

She took the teapot to the dining table. Luke helped with a plate of nuts and segments of oranges that she'd prepared before he got there. He was certain there wasn't a single biscuit to be had in that whole house. He'd been misguided when she invited him for tea.

She set the cups on opposite sides of the long, wide table, filled them with tea, and sat in front of one of them, signaling Luke to take the place across from her. But he grabbed his cup and sat at the head of the table, closest to her and at a ninety-degree angle.

"If you don't mind," he told her in a purr, his lips near her ear, their arms practically touching, "I'd rather sit here."

37

"Unrelenting," she said, holding her cup and smelling her Mighty Leaf fragrant African Nectar rooibos tea. She'd been so distracted since he'd gotten there that she'd forgotten to ask if he was okay with that type of caffeine-free brew. That would be a first for her: not asking a guest what their favorite type of tea was, easily reaching into her well-stocked pantry, and providing it.

"I have to live up to the clichéd Italian standards," he said. He was purely Mediterranean charm, and Sol didn't understand how she'd been able to overlook that side of him when they first met. That Greg Knight disguise concealed a lot.

"Oh, you do live up to them," she told him.

"I'm glad you're no longer cross with me."

"Why?" she asked, and she immediately felt like she'd asked the stupidest question.

"Because I've been thinking about the night at your terrace in Barcelona non-stop."

He didn't seem to mind that she wasn't sounding her

sharpest that night. His eyes were fully on her, his gaze starving.

"You liked the views," Sol said almost timidly. If she was going to play that game with him, she needed to find the courage to do it. Now.

"I liked the *view*."

Luke's eyes weren't leaving hers. Not even to blink.

"Are we doing this again?" she asked, suddenly reassured. She closed the minimal distance between the two of them.

"Please." His face was a couple of centimeters from hers, and she could smell the saltiness of the sea on his breath.

She left her cup on the table, reaching with her right hand to his face, wanting to feel that rebellious lock of hair that had been torturing her all night. But she stopped herself. She needed to know something first.

"Are you going to leave like the last time?" she asked, her tone no longer mischievous.

"This time you know who and what I am," he said, looking even deeper into her eyes as if wanting her to know he was being sincere. "So, no."

He drew nearer to her and kissed her, trailing his lips along hers, drawing her mouth apart with his. Even if that was the kind of touch that had been on both their minds when they'd agreed to a midnight meeting, Sol was still surprised by it.

After her latest relationship, she'd almost resigned herself never to relive the thrill of a first kiss surrounded by the night lights of her hometown, a second kiss enveloped in the darkness of her adoptive home city.

London's night flowed in through the skylight of her deliberately dim-lit kitchen as she untangled Luke's unruly curls and surveyed the line of his profile with her hands.

Their kiss was unhurried and tender in a way that almost took her back to the velvety feel of a summer love in her teenage years. How long had it been since she'd caressed—and been caressed—in that unhasty manner?

"Sol," he said. He made her name sound Italian, elongating the final L. She liked the sound of her name in his mouth. It was almost as delicious as that kiss.

"What?" she asked him, dazed.

"Do you want to dance?" Music had been playing in the background all this time, and Otis Redding was currently intoning the notes of "Cigarettes and Coffee."

"Yes," she said, surprised again. She couldn't remember when she'd last danced—alone or with someone else.

He rose, reaching out his hand to take hers. She stood up in front of him, accepting his proposal. She linked her hands around his neck, placing her head at the nook of his neck and shoulder, and inhaled his smokey scent while they circled the kitchen, following the music's sensual rhythm.

She felt so comfortable there, dancing in her London kitchen with Luke, that it took her half the song to finally lift her face from where she'd been resting on his sexy collarbone.She took her hand to his unshaven jaw and kissed him again.

She wasn't prepared for the electricity that hit her when he kissed her back. She felt his tongue in her mouth; his hands on her waist, along her back, under her hoodie; his solid body against hers.

She found herself pinned between the compactness of Luke and the fridge, and that closeness to his whole breadth made her crave him. Impatience had always been one of her least endearing qualities, and she hadn't invited Luke to midnight tea *just* to dance and kiss, after all.

He read her yearning and lifted her with more ease than

she would have anticipated, setting her on the kitchen counter. They were done pretending there was any more dancing going on.

His lips traced the sensitive area behind her earlobe, her neck, the contour of her clavicle.

She moved to the edge of the counter. Her legs were parted, her body claiming his proximity. She took her hand under his T-shirt, pulling him toward her, exploring the contours of his torso.

She felt intoxicated even if she hadn't drunk a drop of alcohol since her stay in Barcelona. He was making her dizzy. The last time she'd been this horny, she was reading a Sarah J. Maas novel and picturing Jessica Chastain and (a perhaps taller) Oscar Isaac in the smut-filled chapters after a swoony joint appearance on the red carpet by the two of them that had her reeling for days.

She suddenly felt overcome and overwhelmed. Stunned, even. *You definitely aren't too old for me,* he'd once texted her. Did she believe him? It wasn't like he hadn't lied to her before. Was she ready to let this thirty-something-year-old get more acquainted with her toned-but-still-not-that-young-anymore forty-two-year-old body?

She needed to collect herself.

"I can't believe I'm saying this, but I think we should call it a night," she managed to mutter under her ragged breath.

He slowly freed himself from her touch. "I'll go," he said. If he was disappointed with the turn the night had taken, his expression didn't show it. "Is it because I lied to you?"

"No," she said. He was still standing in front of her in the kitchen. "Maybe... It's just that I like taking things slowly."

He offered his hand to help her off the counter, but she declined and descended to the kitchen floor by herself. She feared another touch of his skin would cause her to succumb to his allure and make her keep him for the whole night.

But she wanted to maintain her cool. If only for once during her whole history with him, she needed to feel she was making a rational, dispassionate decision.

"Slow is good," he told her with a devastating smile. "Can I kiss you one last time before leaving?"

"Yes," she pleaded more than assented.

So much for keeping your fucking cool, Sol. The moment his lips touched hers, she'd be lost.

But he didn't go for her mouth. His lips chased the line of her cheekbone instead, not kissing her as much as branding her skin with his breath.

"It's going to be five awkward minutes of me putting my socks and boots on before I leave," he told her, fixing his eyes on her one last time then heading to the entryway.

"Awkward is good," she said.

If he was in a hurry to leave her place and get home, he didn't show it. Sol felt a bit like a voyeur following his moves while he dressed his feet in almost deliberately slow movements. When he finished, he stood up, gave her one last lust-filled look, and opened the door to leave.

"We should meet for tea again soon," he said.

38

The following morning, she woke up with the sun and found a new voicemail from Luke the moment she disabled Airplane Mode on her cell phone. She listened to the audio message in bed.

"Ciao, I wanted to call you mid-morning and hear your voice, but I have an awful day at work. Not sure when I'll be done. But text me and we can meet for tea again. There are a couple of things I'd love to whisper into your ear." That last sentence was uttered in Luke's signature gruff tone, and Sol had to fan herself. "Also, please don't take this the wrong way. Traditionally, sex is optional when having tea. But biscuits aren't."

It made her feel giddy and hot all at once, and she wasn't able to listen to it in one go the first—or second—time. But, when she did, she promptly added some McVitie's dark chocolate digestives and Walker's shortbread fingers to her Waitrose online grocery order to be delivered that afternoon.

It was only then that she faced the stark reality of having

to write an article while being very much sleep-deprived and majorly absent-minded.

During the long flight back from Los Angeles, she'd emailed the editors at *Conceit Fair* and explained the Richard Fynn situation. She'd already gotten the okay from Fionna for her proposal of a new angle for the article where Sol would expose a bit of the director's uncooperative attitude during the chat. The editor also replied to Sol's email with a submission date. The piece was due in two days.

Sol had always been a procrastinator who needed the right type of encouragement, and a tight deadline was exactly that, even if that would mean working through the weekend. She soon found herself in a writing groove and making progress.

She cringed in her detailed recollection of the interview with Fynn when she relistened to it, which she only did to verify that the AI system she'd used had transcribed everything accurately.

Every time she felt too dejected about the terrible interview, or when she needed to be persuaded to keep focused, she relistened to Luke's message. It mostly made her horny, but it also had a way of reminding her to stay concentrated.

The sooner she was done with the Richard Fynn story, the sooner she'd be able to direct her attention elsewhere.

Plus, she needed the mental clarity and space to do some thinking because a few questions kept popping into her mind every time she allowed herself to get off track.

What exactly did she want between her and Luke? What did *he* want? Was it just sex? Was there a chance of something else? Did she feel like starting something else though? Hadn't she agreed to be done with committed entanglements? Was he aware that he was too young for her? Plus, wasn't joblessness, financial uncertainty, and the possibility of never finding a staff position again—journalists would start being replaced by AI bots any day now—enough burden already? Did she need more instability in her life?

Those were all questions that Sol needed answers to, but trying to find responses meant she needed to be finished with the Richard Fynn portion of her haphazard career.

...

By mid-afternoon, she was about done with a first draft that needed lots of edits and rereads on her part when her cell phone buzzed and she saw a text from Luke.

> Luke (Ear Whisperer): Sorry to text you for work-related non-tea reasons. But yesterday you distracted me so much that I forgot to ask you something.

She bit her lower lip to prevent herself from bursting into a full smile. Her heart still skipped a beat though. She was delighted with the notion of having distracted him.

> Luke (Ear Whisperer): Did you ever remember if there was anyone else in class on the day of the theft?

> Luke (Ear Whisperer): Still trying to figure out who the mystery person is

Sol hadn't really thought about it, even if she'd promised Luke she'd do it. She returned to her work assignment, deciding to text Luke later and tell him if she recalled anything.

Luke had stopped by the office after an early surveillance shift that had been beastly. His alarm had been set at six in the morning and he wasn't good at functioning with less than six hours of sleep a day, even if he'd gotten accustomed to it since being hired by T&T.

He was aware that he was partially responsible for his lack of sleep. He'd left Sol's place at two the previous night. He'd been so pumped up—and drenched in lust—that he almost involuntarily started walking home.

It had been a gorgeous night, and he never got to enjoy the city so late anymore. London after midnight was a different place, a calmer, dreamier one. He'd started the walk not taking the most direct way home but the route filled with the most beauty through Southwark and the City. He'd taken in the views of the moonlit Tate Modern from the Millennium Bridge and promised himself to never fall out of love with his hometown. It was easier with not a single tourist in sight. He'd stopped at the Christchurch Greyfriars Garden to simply experience the silence and serenity.

The enchantment had lasted past the dormant Smithfield Market, as he walked through some of London's most labyrinthine streets. It was one of Luke's major senses of accomplishment to never get lost in that part of town. Even if he sometimes got distracted, he could always find his way, no devices needed.

But when he'd realized that the whole trip to his studio on foot would still be more than an hour, he'd taken the night bus. Part of his devotion to the city came from its convenient public transportation, after all.

All in all, he'd gotten a bit more than three hours of sleep and was trying to remedy his acute lethargy with a strongly brewed tea he was preparing at Thompson &

Thomson's kitchenette. But P's arrival put an abrupt end to Luke's reminiscing of his nighttime walk and, more explicitly, his flashing back to the heated, kiss-filled session with Sol in her kitchen.

"Did you hear?" the senior partner asked. It was one of Thompson's many aggravating qualities to always assume everyone else was privy to all the gossip he was.

"No," Luke answered. He'd long stopped pretending he was in the loop when he wasn't.

"I just met with Meshflixx," P went on. You didn't even have to prompt Thompson for him to start babbling. "The case is almost done."

"Didn't they say the same last week?" Luke tried not to sound too bored about the news.

"This time it is *almost done*," P said dramatically, as if that made anything clearer.

"Are they going to be upset because we haven't got a suspect?"

"Oh, we'll figure something out, won't we?" As if coming up with something concrete wouldn't require hours of interviews and further investigation when the agency's team devoted to the Meshflixx case had been deployed to the cases of at least three new clients. "One of their top executives shared with me in a confidential manner that they're currently developing a second project with the Daniels sisters. They want the whole mess with *The Privateers* to be behind them."

It baffled Luke that the way of dealing with a script leak would be to ignore who leaked it, but he preferred not to voice his dissent *again*.

"What's the new show about?" he asked, genuinely curious. If he ever found the time to watch it, he'd probably like *The Privateers*, so he was interested in anything else the creators of the series would do. If only because he'd gotten to know them indirectly in those past few weeks.

"A prequel of some sort," said Thompson disdainfully, as if the idea of a new TV show preceding the story of an already released and successful series sounded preposterous. Luke was convinced that his manager's only two acceptable forms of entertainment were reading *The Sunday Times* and counting the days until the start of the horse racing season at Ascot. "Something about the origins of a character who is a quartermaster on a ship or other. But you haven't heard it from me," he added, chuckling.

"The quartermaster is the character played by Leonardo Pascual," said Luke. "Is that why they wanted us to follow him? It's not like we've found any link between him and the case."

"Let's not jump to conclusions." Thompson left the room with the same suddenness and in the same bizarre way in which he'd entered it.

Luke texted Sol the moment P was out of sight.

Luke Contadino: Apparently this is classified information but Meshflixx is planning a prequel of The Privateers starring the quartermaster.

She replied almost immediately.

Sol Novo: Weird

Luke Contadino: Why?

But instead of explaining herself, Sol sent him a link to an interview with Bryana and Sara Daniels from January of that year.

Luke Contadino: Do you want me to read
the whole thing?

Sol Novo: Mare meva Luca! Call me then

He did as he was told, and she picked up after a couple of tones.

"Hola," she answered. "Before you say anything, we're not going to talk about last night. Not because I don't want to but because I'm on deadline and need to go back to writing. But you needed to ask me something work-related, so ask away and we can hopefully plan something for tonight."

"Something like tea?" he asked.

"You really can't help yourself, right?" He could practically hear her eye roll. "Something like tea, yes."

There was silence on the phone for a few seconds while Luke let Sol proceed with the conversation. If he wasn't able to flirt, he preferred her to talk.

"I sent you a link," she finally said.

"I saw."

"You're awfully quiet."

"You basically told me not to seduce you for the duration of this phone call. This is me not seducing you," he said as deadpan as he could.

"Unrelenting." She sounded like she was smiling.

"I don't see how."

"Since you don't seem inclined to read the article I sent you, let me summarize it, I guess."

"I'm ready for the summary," he said impassively.

"Okay, you win." She sighed. "I can't believe I'm saying this, but stop the non-seducer bit. It's driving me crazy."

"Thank you for acknowledging that you prefer me when

I'm being naughty. But I promise to be on my best behavior. I know you need to work, and I don't want to interfere."

"That has to be one of the sexiest things that anyone has ever said to me," Sol said.

"Intriguing. Also, understood. It wasn't necessarily the type of conversation I had in mind for tonight, but I'll make sure to continue supporting you in your career in a very vocal fashion," he told her.

"Going back to the article," she said. "It's an in-depth interview with the Daniels sisters. They talk about their plans for the future of *The Privateers*, rave about the actors and all the usual promotional stuff. They also talk about their process as scriptwriters and TV showrunners and are adamant about the fact that they *cannot* work on two projects at the same time. So I'm not sure how they'd do a second season of *The Privateers*, which still hasn't started filming, *and* a prequel. And I don't know if I mentioned this before, but come May 1, we could be facing a writers' strike. So I don't see much of this happening anytime soon. Who gave you the scoop?"

"The scoop?" He'd only gotten about half of what she'd just told him.

"Who told you about the prequel?" she replied patiently, or as patiently as he'd ever witnessed her.

"My boss. He says a Meshflixx exec told him in confidence."

"Do you believe your boss? Is he the type to be well-connected at Meshflixx and know high-ranking executives privy to that kind of information?"

"I honestly don't know," he admitted. "But can I go back to something you just said? About a strike?"

"You really know nothing about Hollywood," she said, clearly displeased.

"I know I liked the second season of *Bridgerton* more than the first one." Maybe that would make him sound more cultivated.

"Now, *that* is actually the sexiest thing I've heard," she said. "But let's not digress into *Bridgerton* territory."

"We can do that with tea," he said. For the first time in that whole conversation, he was aware of using his husky voice. He caught the timid moaning sound Sol made on the other side of the line.

"Writers' strike, right," she finally said. "All you need to know is that the Writers Guild of America, which represents the screenwriters of pretty much anything with a US-based production company, is renegotiating their contract with the alliance of TV and movie producers. And if they don't come to an agreement, which at this point looks like they won't, they'll call for a strike of all its members, meaning they will stop writing. I won't get into specifics about why it'll happen because frankly, I don't think you care or that it matters for the case. But I'm not sure about the second season of *The Privateers*, let alone this prequel show, happening any time soon."

"Isn't *The Privateers* a British show though?" he asked. Everything she was telling him made sense, but he still needed extra information to comprehend it.

"Yes. But any project in the jurisdiction of the American writers' guild would get impacted by the strike. Both Daniels sisters and half the writing staff of *The Privateers* are from the US and most likely members of that guild. This is not an exclusively British show. I think they shoot and produce here for its locations and for tax purposes."

"I see," Luke said, but he wasn't sure he was getting the whole puzzle yet. That had been the norm with that particular case. He was starting to wonder if it was his total lack of knowledge and plain ignorance when it came to the Hollywood industry—or if there was something else on top of that. Something he was ignorant of.

He hadn't found a way of asking her about the controversy around the show's opening credits yet and wondered if that would be the right time to do it.

"Are you working tonight?" she asked him instead.

"Miraculously not," he said.

"I can offer you biscuits." He decided to drop the controversy subject for another moment. "But I feel I should earn them first. I've been sitting all day. Want to meet for a walk?"

"A walk?" asked Luke, amused. "You're so Californian sometimes!"

"I'll deny having ever said this, but you should be more in touch with your Mediterranean side, Luca." She spoke with the same mirthful tone he'd used. "Californians meet for *hikes*. But a leisurely stroll in the city in the late afternoon or evening is as Mediterranean as you can get. I'm sure you've heard of the *passeggiata*?"

"You know I have. I wasn't aware you *also* spoke Italian though," he teased.

"I don't, even if I'd like to believe I dabble," she admitted. "But we have similar words in Catalan and Spanish—and we certainly share the habit."

"Allora, andiamo a fare una passeggiata," he said.

"Meet me at six at Winchester Palace and we can take The Queen's Walk and do some sightseeing along the river —if you don't mind the tourists."

"Oh, I do mind the tourists." He felt almost obligated to complain. "But I can ignore them. Ci vediamo dopo, Sol."

"Adeu, Luca."

39

Sol got to the remains of the thirteenth-century **palace** that had served as the living quarters of the Bishops of Winchester five minutes before the agreed-upon time and relished in the fact that, for once, she was the first to arrive. Luke got there one minute later. His hair was perfectly disheveled, his clothes ruggedly dark and sexy, and he was smiling. He approached her but stopped himself before touching her as if realizing the etiquette around that greeting hadn't been negotiated.

"Can I kiss you?" she asked him, returning his smile.

"Yes," he pleaded more than assented, as if echoing her feelings from the previous night.

She went for his mouth, trailing his bottom lip and biting it before kissing him. She felt a bit lightheaded when he kissed her back. One of his hands was on her face, the other on her waist, and his smell all around her.

"Ciao," he said when she finally pulled back.

"Hola," she said in turn, realizing they were the object of intense observation from a group of around twenty four-to-six-year-old children on what could only be a school-organized outing. Were she and Luke making so much of a scene? "Since I'm sure you've seen the Winchester Palace many times, let's get moving, yes? Let's passeggiare." She grabbed his right arm and steered him in the direction of the river.

"Are you shy?" he asked as they made their rushed way out of the children's view. "The whole Mediterranean meeting was your idea, and I think we were acting in a completely appropriate fashion."

"For Southern Europe, yes," she agreed. "But let's behave more like proper Londoners if we're in a crowded public space."

"So you're shy." He laughed.

"Before we both forget *again*," she told him to switch subjects and because she knew they truly would forget otherwise, "and then we can go back to all this playful banter you excel at, I don't recall another attendee in class the night of the theft. But I remembered something else."

"I was going to protest your shameless change of subject," he said. "But now I want to know. Also, are you guiding me on this tour of *my* hometown?"

"I'm not guiding, I'm merely following the river!" She signaled the Bankside promenade in front of The Anchor tavern with its brownish brick façade and red-painted wood paneling. "We both know you're a North Londoner, so don't get so possessive about South London, please."

"So what else did you remember?" he asked as they both eased into a more relaxed walking cadence alongside the river.

"Look who's changing subjects now," Sol quipped.

"Sol," he said, once again lengthening the sound of the final letter of her name.

"Okay, I can't torture you when you say my name that

way," she said. She took a deep breath to focus. "So, we established that the class must have ended at 6:40 on the day of the theft. When Josie dismissed us, I went to the locker area to grab my bag but realized that my compartment was unlocked."

"Unlocked?"

"I didn't have to input the four numbers of my combination because the door was already unlocked and ajar. At the time, I thanked the deities of tardiness for such a blessing because I assumed I had forgotten to lock the thing when I came in for class. I was a bit late. And it came in handy on my way out because, again, I was a bit late. And I hate—"

"Being late." He laughed. "Yes, I've noticed."

Sol ignored him and continued.

"But thinking about it, perhaps the same person who opened Sara's locker to get the script also opened mine and maybe a few others on their search for the right compartment. It's not like we have an assigned one. You get to choose your locker for the class on a first-come basis. The first to arrive tend to choose the ones where you don't have to crouch to get your stuff in and out."

"But you're not completely sure that it wasn't you who left the locker open by mistake?"

"Not really. It wouldn't be the first time," she said. "Sometimes I get to class still distracted because I'm rewriting an article on my mind and make some notes on my cell phone and just forget about locking the whole thing. I've never thought much of it because, as I've told you *repeatedly*, I don't think any of Josie's members would steal anything. And you need to get buzzed into the building to get access to the studio. So it's not like someone from the outside could come mid-class and loot the lockers when we're all agonizing through the five series."

"So what else happened that day? You found the locker open, thought nothing of it…"

"Grabbed my bag and left quickly because I was in a rush to get home and from there dinner at this tapas place on Bermondsey."

"Bermondsey?" he said in an almost judgy tone, as if that wasn't one of the boroughs of London but a faraway land in the suburbs.

"Mare meva! You are such a North Bank snob! I go there often with my friend Laia because she lives in the area and for me it's a short taxi ride away. There's life south of the Thames, Luca."

"And you were meeting your friend when?" he said, ignoring her jest.

"Is this still for your case? You need a detailed log of my movements that evening or something?"

"It could come in handy to prove your lack of involvement when we finally draft that wretched report for Meshflixx. But I'm also just being nosey."

"We were having dinner at 7:30, I guess—it's our regular dinner time," Sol said. "When I left the studio, I needed to get home to leave my things and get changed, but since it was late I took the Tube at Charing Cross. I normally just walk home."

"For some reason, I can't picture one of Josie's disciples doing something as mundane—and plebeian—as taking the Tube," he said.

"Please!" she protested. "I do it all the time! I wasn't even the only 'disciple,'" she said, air quoting that last word. "When I got to the platform to wait for my train, I ran into Sara."

"Sara Daniels?"

"Uh-huh."

"Hadn't she left class like ten minutes before you?"

"Don't underestimate my ability to move fast when I'm in a hurry," Sol explained. "Also, apparently there were delays on the Northern line and she'd been at the platform for a while. I think she said she needed to be home to finish something for work."

"Did you ask her what she needed to do?"

"I would never. There's nothing that causes more paranoia than a journalist asking unnecessary questions. She was purposely vague on whatever she needed to do and then she complimented my bag, which is indeed gorgeous. Oh and then Phyllis got there too, actually."

"Phyllis?" Luke asked, confused.

"Philippa! I always mix up her name. You know, the influencer who's at Josie's on a permanent basis?"

"I know who Philippa Majors is," Luke said. "But I can't picture *her* taking the Tube."

"I would have never said you were so prejudiced," she told him, amused. They stopped for a moment to take in the views across the Thames in front of Shakespeare's Globe Theater.

"I'm not prejudiced!" He imitated Sol in her admiration of the city's skyline. "But I assumed she'd have a chauffeured car taking her everywhere."

"She probably does have a driver," Sol conceded. "But she normally walks to Josie's from her place in Grosvenor Street. The woman lives by her daily steps quota as much as I do."

"So what was she doing there then?"

"I don't know! The train arrived then. I said bye to both of them and made my way inside one of the crowded cars. I was in a hurry, remember?"

"Yes, in a hurry to trek to Bermondsey," Luke said, and

Sol laughed. "Don't tell me there are no neighborhoods in Barcelona that you consider far away and where you never set foot?"

"Oh, many of them! Most of them probably," she admitted. "Now that you make me think about it, I tend to limit myself to a walkable and historical part of the city and never venture too far from it. It's funny to meet my London equivalent in a way."

"Why did you move out?" he asked.

"What do you mean?" Sol wasn't prepared for the abruptness of his question.

"You seem so much in love with Barcelona," he replied.

"Oh I am. I guess I needed to leave the place to realize how much I miss it. Don't you ever take London for granted?"

"I try not to," he said, but lately he'd been more aware of how inadvertently that could happen.

"Of course, you don't." He thought he saw not only sympathy in her eyes but also some friendly enviousness.

"But there was also the matter of work," she continued. "Not many prospects for me in Barcelona even with a network of friends and university colleagues working in media. It's such a small market. There are just no jobs."

"California welcomed you with open arms?"

"It's not that." Sometime during the conversation, her manner had changed. She was no longer teasing him. "It was tough. I was homesick. It's so far away. It's so different from Europe and everything I knew. The visa was a nightmare. But there was a sense of things working in a way where I'd be able to find a job based on merits. No need to be personal friends or the sister-in-law of the hiring manager."

"Was it hard moving here after that?" he asked, slightly afraid of her answer.

"Moving is always hard. No matter how many times you do it." She had donned a pair of round wayfarer Ray-Ban glasses at some point during the walk, so he couldn't see her eyes but her voice sounded melancholic. "You have to make new friends, open new bank accounts, get a new cell phone plan, a new internet provider and, what's worse, find a new place to live and a new hairdresser. Plus, I moved here on the eve of fucking Brexit." There it was, the word Luke had been anticipating and dreading since he met her. "I did it on time to be able to sort my immigration status. But, in a way, I felt I was moving to a country that didn't necessarily want me. I'll always feel like an outsider. It's not like I wasn't feeling like an outsider before. I guess it comes with being an immigrant."

"My mom talks about feeling that way as well, and she's been living in London since the nineties. She says the accent doesn't help." He wanted Sol to know that he understood. "I think that's why I don't speak Italian outside of their house and I've always tried to disguise that side of myself." He was surprised by his openness. The only other people he'd ever talked about that with were his sisters.

"You speak Italian with me," she said, smiling again.

"That's only because I noticed how much that side of me attracts you."

40

After the walk, she suggested her place to grab a bite. She was convinced that tossing something together there would be quicker than trying to select a riverside restaurant on the spot and without a reservation, especially since he probably had lots of quandaries when it came to choosing a place in such a touristy area. She knew she did.

He agreed to go to her house even when she told him she could only offer him a lentil and spinach salad, goat cheese, jamón, sourdough bread—and tea, of course.

"Pasta is also my go-to option when I'm pressed for time and want something yummy," she told him, reaching inside the refrigerator in her kitchen to take out some of the ingredients to make the salad. "But I'm not going to make puttanesca with whole-grain wheat fusilli and sautéed cherry tomatoes when the guest is Italian."

"It sounds interesting though," he said, cutting some slices from a dark loaf of bread as she'd requested.

"I would feel judged," she said.

"I *would* probably judge you," he admitted. "But please don't let that stop you from doing anything."

"I won't." She clutched his T-shirt and drew him to her body, kissing him.

"Before we get into this portion of your visit," she said, unfastening from him ever so slightly after a few minutes, "let's eat."

"Can we eat while I ask you some questions?" He had the most devastatingly deep brown eyes.

"I don't think I can say no to you right now." Sol swallowed hard. She hadn't meant to say that out loud.

They sat around Sol's table, reclaiming their spots from the previous night: she by one of the corners on the long side of the table overlooking the kitchen, he at the head of the table by the same corner she occupied, looking at her.

They ate in comfortable silence for a while, their eyes doing all the communicating, not missing a detail about what the other's gaze was implying.

"I thought you wanted to ask me some questions," said Sol, playing with the remains of the salad on her plate. It wasn't often that she found herself feeling this way, but she seemed not to be hungry—for food.

"Are we having tea?" he asked her.

"Yes, in the two connotations we seem to have for the word." She met his gaze unabashedly. "If that's okay with you."

His rakish stare gave her the answer she needed. She scooted over to the edge of the bench to get closer to him and let her mouth find his.

"Before we get too lost," he told her, nibbling at her bottom lip, "remember that I have questions."

"You had all dinner to ask them!" Did he really want to talk about the case right now?

"You're so impatient!" He chuckled. And tried to appease her by caressing her neck with his lips. "I needed to make sure I wasn't presuming anything."

He continued exploring the back of her neck and shoulders unhurriedly until Sol surrendered and started to relax.

"I'm going to need to know what you like." His low, throaty tone made her skin tingle.

"Right, this is the proper way to do it, no?" Sol said. "We talk likes and dislikes, turn-ons and turn-offs, protection."

"You're making it sound transactional," he said, momentarily relinquishing his duties at her nape to look at her. "But it can help us understand each other's wants and needs, and what our boundaries are."

"I'm digging the rationale behind this." She bit her bottom lip and played with her fingers over the edge of the shirt, grazing his neck. "I'll make it brief because I'm impatient. I love foreplay, to a point. *I am impatient.* The top drawer of my nightstand is stocked with toys and condoms. Clitoral stimulation is a must. You can't go wrong with neck play, nipple play—or dirty talk. More details to come. What do I need to know about you?"

"For now, let's say I'm simple." He delicately kissed the most sensible area of her inner right wrist, and Sol moaned at the touch. "I get turned on by my partner's pleasure. And I get better with use."

She swallowed hard.

"I'm going to sound extremely traditional, but is it okay if we go upstairs? I think I need a bed this first time."

"You're in charge," he told her, his eyes fixed on hers.

Sol grabbed his arm and guided him upstairs. When they got to the second floor, they were both panting. She wasn't sure if it was because they'd climbed the stairs so fast —but there weren't that many steps, and they were both supposed to be in relatively good shape—or their frantic anticipation. Still breathless and holding his hand, she showed Luke to her bedroom.

She had fantasized about taking him to her bed for the last few nights—even if during the days she'd pretended she wanted to be just friends and all the other nonsense. She'd imagined how he'd push her against the wall, kiss her neck, take her clothes off.

But when it finally happened—and she was so relieved it was finally happening—*she* pushed *him* against the wall, kissed him hard, helped him out of his T-shirt, and unzipped his pants, all while getting out of her own jeans and top.

She was frenzied by his smell, his touch, his taste.

His lips worked on her earlobe and neck as she pushed against him, corralling him against the wall. He was only wearing boxer briefs by then. She was in her most minimal-istic—and practically sheer—bralette and thong, yet they were both still extremely overdressed.

She allowed herself to contemplate his almost-naked beauty and wasn't the least bit disappointed. He was as sexy and sculpted as all her most recent—and frequent—steamy dreams had anticipated.

She tugged at the waist of his boxer briefs and felt his well-rounded ass underneath it. She lowered the garment, tracing his length with her fingertips, enveloping him and sliding her hand along him slowly. He exhaled in pleasure, and they both smiled. She liked being the one who made him make that noise, feel that sensation.

"Let's get rid of the underwear," she told him.

He promptly replied to her urge with a smug grin on his face as he reached out to slide one of the straps of her bralette over her shoulder, unclasping the garment after that.

"You're the one making the decisions tonight." His voice raspier, coarser than usual. "I'm at your mercy." He smiled wickedly while he helped her finish undressing him and pushed her thong down her legs slowly.

"Are you sure I'm not at your mercy?" she asked, her fears of the previous night suddenly returned now that she was completely naked.

Sol Novo didn't often feel uncomfortable in her own skin. Since turning forty, she'd worked hard to feel that she looked good. She found herself incredibly sexy—something inconceivable in her twenties and thirties. But standing there with no clothes, no armor, in front of such a magnificent man—and his very magnificent erection—she doubted herself and her body.

"You're so fucking beautiful," he told her then, almost as if he'd read her mind, and she *was* fucking beautiful. She didn't need him to remind her, but his admiring gaze delighted her all the same.

He grabbed her in his arms, lifting her from the floor. Her legs automatically wrapped around his waist, and his lips started a slow descent from her neck to one of her breasts and then her nipple. She shuddered in pleasure while he teased, licked, bit. His hands were firmly planted on that ass of hers that he'd brought up in conversation often.

Almost as if remembering she'd told him that she was feeling traditional that night, he deposited her on the bed. Her legs and arms bound by his long, hard body.

"Tell me about your toys," he said, neglecting her breast for the briefest of moments. "Any favorites for a duo setting?"

"The first one you'll reach if you open the top drawer of my nightstand. Hot pink sort of smallish thing," she said breathlessly.

"And you like it?"

"Miracle worker."

"I'm getting jealous," he said, reaching to open the nightstand and easily finding the toy she'd referred to.

"Don't. You really have a lot on it. Like six feet of a well-toned, manly body..." Luke mercilessly bit one of her nipples and one of his hands was now at her clit, teasing it with his fingers. "Plus, that thing doesn't have an ease with words and has never looked at me the way you do," she said, panting.

"How do I look at you?" He lifted his face from her breasts, fixing on Sol's eyes.

"With warm, inquisitive brown eyes."

But Sol couldn't tell him anything else about his beautiful eyes. Her body arched at the sensation of Luke's finger sliding inside her, slowly pulling out and spreading her own wetness over her clit. He turned on her toy then and pressed it against her most sensitive area.

"Still a bit jealous," he told her in between her moans.

"I'm so fucking turned on right now because you're the one using that thing on me. I don't normally relinquish the use of my toys," she said raggedly. She was about to come, but part of her wanted to be in that lulled state for longer.

"Do you want to join in?" she asked on a breathy exhale.

He looked at her with questioning eyes. And she had to admit that he took her consent to a degree that made her even hornier.

"Please," she said. She'd missed sex in the company of another human being—even if none of her toys had *ever* let her down.

She reached for the nightstand, her eyes still fixed on Luke, her body under his. She felt the contents of the drawer with her hand and grabbed a condom. She unfoiled it and wrapped it around his cock slowly, feeling every sensation her hand affected on him.

She moved her legs, lifting them in the air around his body. She caressed his ass with her nails, and at the first sensation of him inside her, she realized she'd been lost since the first time she'd set eyes on him. Even if her mind had not recognized the unavoidable attraction, her body had.

"All good?" he whispered in her ear while pushing inside her.

"You babble too much." She scratched his ass and pressed him deeper.

"Communication is key in this line of work," he murmured while teasing her earlobe. He hadn't let go of the toy, still diligently working at Sol's center and teasing one of her breasts with his pillowy lips.

"Harder," she told him, and the bite made her arch her whole body in pleasure. She was panting, sweating and doused in lust. She could feel the building sensation overcoming her with each new thrust of him inside her, each new nipple bite, each humming stroke between her legs. And to think, she'd read some nonsense article about female blended orgasms being debatable or somewhat controversial or something she couldn't really remember. It had probably been written by an inept dude. And edited by another one.

She lost sense of everything surrounding them, overcome with a spiraling sensation.

"Almost there," she said, and she suddenly realized the whole of Roupell Street was probably aware of her having sex with another human being. She couldn't remember ever being so loud by herself.

"Miracle worker indeed," whispered Luke jaggedly.

"It's having some exceptional help."

He thrust into her again, and the two of them got lost in the bliss.

They laid in silence side by side for a few seconds after.

"You said you get even better with use?" She traced the contour of his clavicle, descending his chest and circling his navel. He shuddered at the touch.

"Should we give it another go and see? I promise some dirty talk this time."

41

She woke up only five minutes before her scheduled 7:10 alarm went off and thought she should try making love to a sexy younger Italian Londoner again as an infallible method to beat jet lag. But even if it was barely day outside, Luke was already gone. She could hazily recall him leaving her place earlier, trying not to wake her up but still kissing her good morning.

There had been no occasion for her to think over some of the big questions that preoccupied her before taking yet another step to further her connection with Luke.

But who had time to reflect on life? Wasn't it better to take things as they came sometimes? The consummate planner in her had always revolted against that idea but wasn't so opposed to it now. Spontaneous sex had a sudden allure.

She wanted to recall every single detail from the previous night, every stare, kiss, and hurried touch. But she'd have to forgo her need to relive all those details since there were more pressing—if undesirable—matters that required her attention.

She needed to finish writing that blasted interview with Richard Fynn.

She went downstairs to put the kettle on and start brewing tea, eating breakfast, and trying to finally rouse herself to a semi-awakened state.

In her kitchen, she found a handwritten note waiting for her on top of the dining room table.

Bella, sorry I left so early. I hope I didn't wake you up. I promise to stay for breakfast next time and get some cornetti. I'll call you at a more appropriate hour later today.

Luca

PS1 Still want to whisper a lot more dirty things into your ear

PS2 Who buys dark instead of milk chocolate digestives?? I hope you don't mind I stole them all though, I was starving!

PS3 I approve of your tea taste. Wordplay intended

Reading it put a smile on Sol's face. She studied the irregularity of his hand. It looked like he'd written the note in a rush and then thought about adding something to warm her that chilly morning with that first postscript. The second, more prosaic one had clearly been added after he rummaged through her kitchen cabinets in search of something sweet. She preferred not to dwell too much on the third one but saw that he'd found her cache of Harney & Sons Royal English Breakfast tea.

Luke had gone home for a quick shower and change of clothes and was now on surveillance mode for the umpteenth time that week. The fact that it was Saturday and he hadn't had a free day in almost two weeks hadn't escaped him.

On this occasion, he was watching the fiancé of a hotel and luxury spa heiress. T&T had been hired by the heiress's parents, who were set on finding some dirt on their daughter's partner. So far, the only dubious behavior Luke had witnessed was his mark's tendency to go to the gym and then get a lemon curd doughnut at Bread Ahead when there were far superior fillings there like velvet chocolate or praline.

Luke was now outside the South Kensington location of the small-chain bakery, still judging Sol for her dark chocolate pick while nibbling on some digestives and waiting for the heiress's fiancé to finish his citrusy breakfast.

Luke made the most of the wait by opening Instagram on his mobile phone and searching for Philippa Majors's account. He checked again the picture Sol had mentioned on a previous occasion taken by the internet entrepreneur before the beginning of the Pilates class on February 23.

Josie wasn't in it but her acolytes for that evening were all there. Sol looked hot—he was partial to her in workout clothes—but she also appeared distracted, as if she didn't want to pose for a picture. Mark Green was in the center, completely at ease surrounded by so many younger and objectively beautiful women. Sara Daniels was on one extreme of the picture, her expression unreadable. Her ex, Martha Broch, was on the other extreme close to her friend and publicist, Lashana Fletcher. And Philippa herself was taking the selfie-type picture, looking as flawless as she always did.

He had hoped the post would yield some more information this second time around, but there was no one else there. There was no mystery person who had appeared on two occasions in the background of the class's video recording and whom Sol didn't remember.

He kept browsing through Philippa's Instagram feed to see if she'd posted anything else that evening and found a short video of the lifestyle influencer on a Tube platform. Her face was closely framed, and she was talking about the benefits of walking over anything else but also taking public transportation when getting somewhere by foot wasn't an option.

The video was bizarrely devoid of substance for Philippa's standards. He'd seen some of her more recent posts, and he liked the content she produced. She was good at giving informed, specific, and easy-to-follow ideas when it came to nutritious meals or strength training activities. Yet that suggestion about taking public transportation was so... obvious.

The Instagram video was time stamped on the night of the theft, and Luke wondered if there had been any additional motivation for its publication. Had Philippa wanted to prove all her movements for that night? The video put her on Charing Cross platform with Sara—and Sol—but by then the script had already been stolen, right?

42

Sol managed to file the damned Richard Fynn interview after a continuous back-and-forth of emails and other forms of communication between her and Fionna's deputy editor at *Conceit Fair*, Christina Jones, who was also in charge of line editing and extreme freelance torturing.

Christina had the not-so-rare quality of reading an article and managing to unnecessarily change every single word for a synonym, in the best of cases, or every single paragraph for something that meant exactly the opposite that had been initially written, in the worst of cases. She was one of those editors who needed to prove how much their input was needed, even when it really wasn't.

Sol fought hard, trying to preserve her voice through the savage onslaught of edits and knowing when to yield—yes, they could use "wrinkled" instead of "rumpled" when referring to Fynn's clothes—and when to withstand—no, using that quote out of context would only damage Fynn's already battered image more, and it would mischaracterize him.

Fortunately, Sol had two decades of editor-negotiating experience and knew how to handle herself with more ease than when she'd first started. It was still not fun.

Christina had also been completely unmoved by Sol's request to add a couple of good quotes from that global press conference the PR team of *Revengers Reunite Redo* had sent Sol after her failed interview with the filmmaker. Richard sounded articulate in the press conference, and even if Sol understood they should disclaim the origin of the quotes in the article, she saw no reason not to use them. They would enrich the piece. Christina didn't agree.

Sol couldn't help but feel there was no Sol Novo left in that article when it was finally done. It read as a generic *Conceit Fair* piece that any other journalist could have written. Her own idiosyncrasies as an interviewer, writer, movie enthusiast, and viewer were nowhere.

She was about to head to Josie's for a much needed Pilates mat class and put everything behind her when she saw Luke's call and answered it.

"Hola. I'm on the move, heading to Josie's."

"Did Sara look nervous?" he asked.

"Sorry, what?"

"The night of the theft, when you ran into her at Charing Cross, was there anything unusual about her?" he explained. "According to the information we have, she should have already realized the script had been stolen by then. That was the whole reason for limiting the investigation to the Pilates studio."

"Perhaps she was a bit on the tense side, but I didn't think much of it," said Sol, grabbing her weekender bag and heading out the door. "She was always like that with me. She knew I was an entertainment journalist, and that can strain relationships sometimes if people think they need to avoid saying or doing anything that could end up being published. I would never do such a thing, but I understand her lack of confidence in the profession."

"So she was tense as usual?"

"Uhhh." She tried recalling that day again but couldn't. "I don't really know. I don't remember much other than what I've already told you. I'd just had a row with my editor about a story I wanted to publish. He didn't want me to pursue it because he was going to go with my idea and write it under his byline. I was furious about that and not paying attention to anything else. I'm sorry to be such an unreliable witness."

"Don't be. I am the one sorry for making you relive the whole thing. It's just, I feel there must be something we're missing. But I have to let you go now. I promise to ring in a bit and be my usual charming self."

"Looking forward to it."

...

"Check that your pelvis isn't puckering forward," commanded Josie as the four-person class was deeply engaged in a side-leg routine. Sol tried following that very specific instruction while pointing her left leg up and flexing her foot on the way down. "Find the feeling of your inner core, engage it as it helps you stabilize. For five, stretch it through. Lift and lower for six, seven, and eight, hold it through. Circles."

Sol's butt was starting to resent her decision to take the Pilates class. The series of little circles made by her elevated left ankle, which was encircled by a two-pound weight, didn't help the building pain subside.

"Sculpt your awareness. Propel your obliques," Josie

went on, and Sol wondered what the hell she meant. "If you feel defined in your elongation, that keeps you from contracting. Sol, check your lines."

Sol double checked the perfect straightness of her back, her abs, her legs, and the balance of her hips. She didn't like being called out for a less-than-perfect form. She tried focusing again, even if sometimes she got lost in Josie's jargon.

"Hover over your bottom leg, make sure your hips are level," continued Josie. "Lengthen through your heels. Find the tone of your hamstring and pulse."

The class was finally over after the same painful choreography was performed with the other leg and they did a few welcome cool-down breathing exercises and stretches.

Sol was ready to get out of there and do nothing for the rest of the day—for the rest of the following two weeks, actually. She grabbed her stuff and was about to head out the door when she overheard Oliver on the phone. The annoying semi-regular had showed up at Josie's that day without his dad. And Mark was the only redeeming quality Oliver Green had.

"I could have written that script better than any of them did," Oliver said. Sol rolled her eyes. He was so full of himself. But her interest was piqued by what she heard next. "*The Privateers* was never a good show. I don't even understand why people liked it. Well, I guess they like all kinds of rubbish."

The dude was utterly oblivious to how obnoxious he sounded. He was disparaging one of the most popular recent shows on streaming and had the audacity to suggest he could have done a better job writing it.

She couldn't understand how someone as sensitive and nice as Mark had fathered such a pretentious troll. But as the proud auteur of a mediocre oeuvre, Richard Fynn, once told Sol: Families could be such a drag sometimes.

It suddenly all made sense. She was already on the street, outside of Josie's and about to head home when she realized what hadn't clicked for Luke in the Meshflixx case. She stopped right there and texted him.

Sol Novo: Does the name Oliver Green ring a bell? Did you check him during the Meshflixx investigation?

Sol Novo: He's Mark Green's son.

Sol Novo: I know this sounds abrupt, but I think he was at Josie's the night of the theft.

Sol Novo: I remember him now

Sol Novo: Vaguely

Sol Novo: Call me when you see this

She finished that last text when she saw Oliver leaving the Georgian building on Henrietta Street that housed Josie's on its second floor.

She happened to be almost perfectly attired for the occasion. She was wearing her trench coat on top of her black leggings and a fuchsia cropped, slim-fit, long-sleeved shirt. She wrapped the coat around her, cinched the belt at her waist, and tied it. She also donned her oversized sunglasses for maximum anonymity and followed Oliver from a distance. He seemed distracted while still talking on the phone so it shouldn't be that hard to trail him and remain unnoticed, right?

It wasn't. Oliver barely managed to drag himself one

block away from Josie's at a painfully slow pace and then sat at one of the outside tables in a nearby coffee shop. Sol lingered in the distance, pretending she was waiting for someone and too absorbed in her cell phone.

She was about to leave, convinced that the whole thing had been a futile errand on her part when someone else arrived, sitting at the same table as Oliver. The person, a forty-something-year-old man with white hair and dressed all in azure, looked familiar to Sol but she couldn't place him. He could be one of her fellow entertainment reporters, a showbiz executive or other, the new stylist at her hair salon, or even a frequent guest actor in one of the dramedy procedurals she loved watching.

She stole a couple of pictures of Oliver and his companion and left, hopeful that at some point she'd be able to remember who the mystery man was. When she was around the corner and out of Oliver's sight, she sent the pictures to Luke with a new message.

> Sol Novo: Followed Oliver to Grind coffee
> shop next to Josie's. He was meeting there
> with someone.
>
> Sol Novo: Seemed familiar but not sure who
> he is. Do you recognize him?

Only after she'd hit send on that last text did she realize that whoever was meeting Oliver for coffee could be completely irrelevant to the case at hand. But playing at being a private investigator had been fun—and she certainly had the wardrobe for it.

...

On her way home, she picked up a call from her finally back-from-vacation accountant. Sol had almost managed to put aside her need for financial information while focusing on the Meshflixx case. Trying to keep her own name clear had seemed the most urgent.

But her money guru didn't have good news.

"Didn't your parents talk to you when you were visiting a few days ago?" the accountant asked, astonishment in her voice.

"Yes," Sol answered hesitantly.

"Well, judging by your expenses, it doesn't really look like it," the accountant said.

"What do you mean?"

"You need to stop spending as if you still have a salary and a generous chunk of money on the side, because you don't."

"I know my salary is gone, but is the rest of the cash all *really* gone? I thought it had just been invested."

"There's no such thing as *just invested*. Do we need to have the conversation about cash flow, short-term investments, and long-term investments *again*?" the money guru said patiently.

"Nope." Sol didn't fully grasp the situation, but she didn't want to hear her economics expert going over tiresome terms.

"Your parents made some long-term investment decisions lately," the guru told her. "And right now the only thing you can do is wait for it to make you some money—and find some other source of income in the meantime because you're what's called *cash-flow poor*."

Finding some other source of income was easier said than done. Also, she thought she had been somewhat thrifty those last few days, but apparently not enough. She didn't voice those concerns though. She instead thanked the accountant for the chat and hung up.

43

Luke knew Sol couldn't see him early that night because she was meeting her friend Laia. So he suggested dropping by her place after that instead. He needed to talk to her about the onslaught of noon text messages.

He buzzed the door at her place and waited for her to open it, only it wasn't her who did. At the door was a woman who looked to be around Sol's age. She was shorter than Sol and sported her chestnut dark locks in a similar cut-above-the-shoulder style. The woman, who Luke knew was Laia even if they had never been officially introduced, carried an adorable little girl in her arms who looked just like her and was probably around three.

"Hola," the woman said, kissing him on both cheeks and letting him inside the small vestibule. "I'm Laia and this is Paula. Sol is upstairs, on the phone with her mom."

"I see," Luke said and then put on his best smile. "I'm Luke, by the way. Nice meeting you and Paula."

Laia and Paula went to the living room area and Luke followed them after taking his shoes off.

"So you're the Italian?" Laia asked. She inspected him from top to bottom with an expression that suggested cautious unfriendliness. She was seated on Sol's boxy anthracite-colored sofa that looked out of a Herman Miller catalog—because it probably was.

"Well, technically I'm British. I'm from London," he mumbled. He was terrible at this kind of casual conversation.

"What, so Sol has lied to me then?" Laia asked, arching her eyebrows. "I thought the one with a lying background here was you."

"It was a misunderstanding. And no, Sol hasn't lied." How did they get there so quickly?

"I thought so." Winning her confidence wouldn't be easy.

"We don't like misunderstandings!" yelled Paula.

Luke managed to laugh, although he wasn't sure how to react to the child. Her mother seemed to be trying to soothe her.

"We don't like you!" added Paula, pointing her chubby finger at him. She didn't seem so cute anymore. Whatever Laia had told her didn't appear to have worked on the girl. Or perhaps Paula was simply voicing Laia's feelings toward him.

"Sorry about that." Sol reentered the room then, descending from the upstairs floor and seemingly unaware of Paula's dislike of him or the strained conversation between him and Laia. "My mom just had an epiphany and wanted to share it with me. We're going to Greece this summer, apparently. Something about consulting the Oracle of Delphi on investments because the market is way too volatile anyway and we could use all the help we can get." She shrugged. "I assume you folks have introduced yourselves?"

"We have," said Laia with a radiant smile. She hadn't directed a smile like that in Luke's direction at any point that evening. Paula shared the same angelical expression.

"Can I offer anything to anyone?" asked Sol.

She was dressed in a pair of impossibly wide-legged black trousers and a cross-back sleeveless silk top that put the accent on her olive-skinned arms and shoulders.

"We should have left ages ago," said Laia, standing from her comfortable position on the sofa.

"No!" protested Paula.

"We can put her to sleep in my bedroom if you want to stay a bit longer," offered Sol.

"No!" Paula repeated.

"I think we are both going to have to go to sleep now," explained Laia, ignoring her daughter. "It's been a long week and I'm tired."

Luke managed to say goodbye to both of them without being yelled at or reprimanded. Sol saw her friends to the door while he made himself comfortable on the now empty sofa.

"Don't think they liked me much," he said when Sol reentered the room. He was afraid they may have mentioned something on their way out.

"What makes you say that?" Sol seemed genuinely unaware of what had happened, and he preferred to leave that question unanswered.

"Right, this may get a little awkward," he said. He realized they hadn't kissed or otherwise properly greeted each other when he arrived. But he needed to get something off his chest first.

"Awkward?" Sol asked, confused. "Please don't tell me

you lied to me *again* and are about to confess something that completely changes my opinion of you."

"I haven't lied," he said. "I won't lie, and please stop because every word you say makes the thing even more awkward."

"Are you ending this?" She pointed to him and then to herself, repeating the movement rapidly several times as if to imply their relationship.

"No, of course I'm not! Why would I? Are you?"

"Am I what?" she asked.

"Ending this?" He imitated her gesture.

"I don't think so," she said. "But you're freaking me out with the whole awkward thing."

"Forget about it. It's silly. I came here ready to scold you," he tried explaining. "But I've already forgotten about it. Can we kiss now?"

"Scold me?" she exclaimed. She clearly wasn't happy— and there would certainly be no kissing.

"Wrong choice of word," he said.

"I would think so," she said, still at yelling-adjacent volume. "I haven't been scolded since I was eight years old and not even then. My parents were into self-directed child-hood education and a lack of intervention."

"Of course, they were." That explained a lot about her fierce independence. "Right, how do I put this?"

"You're on thin ice right now." She crossed her arms in front of her chest, standing very straight in front of him.

"I'm aware. Sorry again for an unfortunate way of phrasing things. But you shouldn't have followed Oliver," he finally told her. "It could have been dangerous. I have no idea who he is or how he's involved in all of this. What if he saw you?"

"I would have pretended I was waiting for someone," she

said. "I have a completely innocent face. People always believe me."

"But you can't go around putting yourself at risk, banking on the fact that nobody would ever mistrust you." He stood up. The whole conversation with him sitting on the low-profile sofa and her towering over him had made him uncomfortable. He was used to being the tall one. "I only gave you so much information about the case because I don't want to hide anything from you anymore and because you've been helping me a lot."

"I was just trying to help you a bit more," she said.

"Yes, but I don't like the idea of you being in a potentially dangerous situation." He was about to touch her arm but stopped himself at the sight of her enraged face.

"As touching as that sounds," she said, "and I'm really not sure if it is touching, who do you think I am? I'm a forty-two-year-old woman. I have *decades* of experience in the art of not putting myself in potentially dangerous situations. Every time I get out of this house, I'm maneuvering how to stay safe! Hell, even being in this house I have to deal with that because I live alone and need to make sure to set the alarm every night before going to bed. I wouldn't follow Oliver in the middle of the night or to a remote place. I know I'm not a trained MI5 agent or anything like that. I just trailed him for two minutes in plain daylight in one of London's busiest areas. I took a picture and then came home." When she put it like that, it all sounded ridiculously innocent.

"Are you seriously getting angry at me because I was worried about you?" he asked.

"I'm seriously telling you there's no reason to be worried," she countered. He was about to admit that he'd been wrong in his reading of the situation. Perhaps he had infantilized her, and he shouldn't have. "And stop acting like a total ass!"

But she wasn't exactly acting like an adult by calling him names.

"Look, I'm tired," she said then in a less belligerent tone. "It's been a long day made even longer by an untalented editor, and I think I need to go to sleep. Jet lag is killing me. Can we talk tomorrow? Hopefully, I'll be less short-tempered."

"Let's talk tomorrow," he agreed.

She followed him to the entryway. He was quick to put his boots on this time. He was about to ask her if he could kiss her—something on her face had changed as if she was no longer mad at him. But then her mobile phone rang upstairs and the moment evaporated.

"It's probably my mom again," Sol said apologetically. "She gets carried away when she's planning a trip."

"Go ahead, I'm leaving," he said. "Let's talk tomorrow?"

She assented one last time before closing the door to her Georgian terraced house. He remained on the street, in front of that door, for a few seconds and realized that she actually owned that house. She had supervised an extensive renovation of it. She was the kind of person who hired an interior decorator and bought a £5,000 sofa, among many other tasteful pieces. There were three types of gourmet salt in her kitchen and quite as many olive oils. She had a mother who was zealously planning a trip to Greece. She had already been on two international trips since he'd known her, and he'd known her for only a handful of weeks.

He was renting a minuscule studio flat where the most luxurious item was the Wayfair Murphy bed generously donated by his older sister Gaia so that there would be some room left in the living/kitchen/dining/sleeping area. The olive oil in his tiny kitchen was whatever had been on sale at his local Tesco. His parents traveled only once every other year and it was always to see their family in Calabria. And, of course, he pretty much had an allergy to going anywhere outside a five-mile radius from Islington.

I don't think so, she'd told him when he'd asked if she wanted to end the relationship. That didn't sound very reassuring.

His phone buzzed and he saw Sol's message.

> Sol Novo: Sorry for being so temperamental (and calling you ass)

> Sol Novo: It's been a bad day

> Sol Novo: I promise never to follow anyone again

> Sol Novo: But don't you get all protective on me!

I won't, he texted her back and continued walking to the Southwark Station. The sooner he got home, the better.

44

After a Sunday in which she'd been purposely unreachable, simply nourishing herself, and thinking about the next steps to take in her career —and seriously considering the option of switching to a different one—Sol woke up that Monday and did exactly what she'd promised herself never to do again. She went online to look for her recently published Richard Fynn story and read it over one last time.

Richard Fynn Is Not Ready for His Close-Up

The eccentric auteur returns to directing with the long-awaited sci-fi title *Revengers Reunite Redo*—but promoting it isn't his forte.

BY SOL NOVO

After a lengthy hiatus spanning over a decade, the veteran filmmaker Richard Fynn is making a comeback with his much-anticipated sci-fi sequel

Revengers Reunite Redo. However, our interview with the mercurial director reveals a man who seems more interested in challenging conventions than publicizing his work, as he refers to the promotional leg of a movie as a "numb, soulless act."

Dressed in a wrinkled green hoodie and equally worn bright yellow shorts, Fynn receives *Conceit Fair* at the famed Four Seasons hotel in Los Angeles focused on the consumption of a salad with fried chicken and not entirely collaborative when asked about his latest film, which he not only directed but also wrote and produced.

This sequel to *The Revengers* (2008) and *Revengers Reunite* (2010) returns to the franchise's post-apocalyptic world ruled by a creed of corrupt demi-droid demi-human law enforcers. But getting Fynn to expand on the inception behind this third film or its plot proved almost unattainable.

"Fuck if I know!" Fynn proclaims, his voice filled with annoyed arrogance when we ask him about the secret behind *Revengers*'s popularity over the years and the desire for the newest installment among the fans.

As the interview progresses, Fynn becomes increasingly evasive, insisting on the idea that the science-fiction franchise hasn't defined him or his filmography but the other way around.

"I was the one who defined the careers of the cast. They were unknowns but I saw their potential," he said, referring to original *Revengers* cast members Lena Moriarty, Jacqueline Jenkins, Monica Holton, and Xavier Dumas. None of them grace this new title though, which instead stars newcomers Thierry Miller and Jason Tartt.

Fynn's evasiveness culminates when he cuts our conversation short and refuses to speak about how technology may have made certain VFX challenges easier in 2023. Rewatching the original *The Revengers* will expose the contemporary viewer to a lot of CGI-overloaded scenes produced almost 15 years ago and during a much less sophisticated moment for computer-generated graphics.

But the visual effects of this movie may prove equally arduous. *Revengers Reunite Redo*'s Public Relations team told us after the troubled interview with Fynn that the director's erratic behavior was due to his low blood sugar level, acknowledging as well that the filmmaker was "nervous" over the fact that his latest movie is technically not finished yet since the team is still working on the visual effects.

In the end, the fate of Fynn's latest film will be decided by the viewers at the box office.

Everything looked good-ish, or as good as it could be, considering the outpour of edits that made her almost not recognize the words in something that was bylined Sol Novo. The piece was also considerably shorter than had been initially intended, but the conditions in which the interview had taken place—and the lack of quotable material from Fynn—had dictated the article's new word count. Sol felt a pang of resentment because of all of it.

She then made a second mistake that morning and opened her email account directly on her phone. It was something she knew well never to do on an empty stomach, yet she did it anyway.

It was barely seven in the morning, and the article had been scheduled to get published two hours before that, at five, but there were already several messages in her inbox about it. Most of them were from Richard Fynn's PR team and the *Revengers Reunite Redo*'s distributing studio. They were extremely unhappy about the article and blamed Sol for mischaracterizing the director. Both Fionna and Christina were copied in all those correspondences.

Fynn's people had especially reproaching objections against the article's title—*Richard Fynn Is Not Ready for His Close-Up*. Most folks only read headlines, after all, they argued. That pointed heading had actually been penned by Christina, despite Sol's many complaints. But the editor had been too happy with the *Sunset Boulevard* reference even if Sol had insisted that *Revengers Reunite Redo* had absolutely *nothing* to do with the 1950 black-and-white classic movie starring Gloria Swanson.

Sol felt an overwhelming weight in the pit of her stomach. Why hadn't she followed the rules she set as a protection against exactly these kinds of situations? Didn't she know from experience that it was better to deal with the shit storm that was headed her way when one had already showered and had her tea?

"Aargh!" she yelled. "Sol Novo, you *know* better!"

Fionna Bennett called her then, and Sol picked up quickly and nervously. She should have at least tried to breathe deeply a couple of times before answering. But she didn't.

"Fionna," she said, trying not to sound too shaky.

"Sol," Fionna said. "Have you seen the emails?"

"I have."

"We're very disappointed," Fionna said, and Sol agreed. These *Revengers Reunite Redo* people didn't seem to realize how the business operated. "We shouldn't have worked with you, considering we didn't have all your references."

"I'm sorry, what?" Surely, Sol had misheard or misunderstood.

"You've misrepresented Richard Fynn," Fionna said.

"No, I haven't," Sol stated. "I've been very clear from the beginning about the issues during the interview. Your team got a transcript of said interview. I've worked with Christina closely. She analyzed and went over every single comma. I had to be careful because *she* wanted to add some stuff that would have been a misrepresentation. But in the end, we found a text that met the standards both for me and your many editors and copyeditors and was approved by them."

"It's still your byline," Fionna said.

"I'm aware." Sol was completely awake now even if no caffeine had entered her system yet.

"We'll talk, but I don't like this."

"I don't like it either," said Sol and they hung up.

She went straight to the shower. She'd need to have her full armor on, and she couldn't pull on her empowered persona if she was still wearing her Grumpy-from-Snow-White pajamas. Even if she felt exceedingly grumpy.

"Meshflixx is shelving the stolen script investigation," Thompson told the team during their weekly debriefing meeting. "This time for good," he added. There had been warnings about the termination of the case for weeks now.

"So they're good not knowing who stole their copyrighted property, then?" asked Luke.

"Of course they aren't," said P. "We're meeting them tomorrow and letting them know their thief is most probably, with a 90 or even 92 percent probability, Sol Novo."

"What?" Luke couldn't mask his alarm. "She didn't do anything!" Also, those numbers were pulled out of thin air.

"Now, we haven't really established that, have we?" Thompson reasoned. "She has the most motive and looks the guiltiest from those who had the opportunity to take the script."

"I'm telling you, she didn't do it," Luke repeated.

"That's for Meshflixx to decide, isn't it?"

Luke couldn't keep disputing the most insane statement coming from his managers to date.

"The meeting is over," Sweatshirt intervened with his usual hostile manner, cutting Luke's protest short. Sol's career wasn't the only one at stake in this affair. "You all have things to do. Don't you? Or should I be checking if we need to restructure the team once more?"

Luke exited the meeting room seething—and worried. He hadn't had a chance to look into Oliver Green since Sol had sent him his name. What was worse, their chat two nights before had been so fraught that Luke hadn't asked her how she'd remembered Oliver and why she thought he was the other attendee at Josie's on February 23. He needed to ask her about it, but he felt they needed to talk about themselves first, about what had happened on Saturday night. Even when they both had been appearing to avoid the other on Sunday.

Everything was getting enmeshed in a way he didn't like, which was why he should have waited until the Meshflixx case was finished before pursuing something with Sol.

And after what had just happened during the meeting, Luke didn't think there would be time for much personal talk between them. He called her number and hoped she'd pick up when she saw his name on the screen.

"Hola," she replied after a few tones. There wasn't the slightest hint of anger in her voice. "I'm glad you called."

"Me too, but I need to tell you something," he said.

"Please don't tell me it's going to be awkward."

"I won't, but you won't like it. It's about the Meshflixx case," Luke went on. "My managers are going to suggest your name to Meshflixx."

"What do you mean?"

"They'll suggest your name as the most likely to have stolen the script."

"But I didn't!"

"I know." He kept his tone soothing.

"Then why haven't you told them so?"

"I have, but they're idiots," he said. "Look, I called to let you know because I promised there would be no more lies. I'll do everything I can to keep you out of this, but it'll be hard. So be prepared."

"Luke, if Meshflixx believes I'm the one who took and leaked the script, they'll block my access to all of their content and talent. And they'll make sure every other movie studio, TV channel, and streaming service does it as well. I won't be just an out-of-job journalist who has to hustle and freelance, but one who's never going to be hired to write anything else."

"I know," he said. "That's why I'm calling you. I need to get to the bottom of this. You texted me something on Saturday, and I still haven't had the chance to ask you about it. You said that you remembered Oliver Green at Josie's on the afternoon of the theft."

"Vaguely," said Sol.

"What exactly do you remember?"

"I think I saw him. When Philippa was organizing us to take a picture of the class for Instagram, he was walking in the background, on the other side of Philippa's phone, which was pointing at us. I remember thinking, *Oh no, he came too*, because I've never liked him. But he never showed up for the picture or in class, and I didn't think about it again until the other day when I overheard him trashing *The Privateers*."

"How long did the whole picture-taking thing take?"

"A good five minutes. Philippa took her time to make sure everything and everyone looked perfectly lit and photogenic," said Sol. "She's very considerate about those things."

"So he could have had time to go through the lockers when you were all making sure to look your best for Philippa's snapshots?"

"I guess so," said Sol.

"Could he perhaps be working with his father?"

"What do you mean?"

"We've overheard Mark Green having a go at Meshflixx a couple of times. The second time, he may have been talking to a journalist."

"Mark has been extremely vocal over the years about his dislike of how the industry is evolving. It's no secret that he's not a fan of not just Meshflixx but pretty much any streaming service. You could probably find clips of him online having a go at Supreme Video and all the others. He's complained about the lack of transparency, lack of residual payment, inadequate display format... you name it," she told him. "It's weird though..."

"What's weird?"

"I think a couple of days ago I read about him possibly unretiring and making his streaming debut." Her words were slower as she tried to remember the details of whatever article she'd read. "He never said anything to me, and the piece was all unconfirmed reporting, but he's been rumored to direct a couple of episodes for Meshflixx. But I swear I saw him in Los Angeles about to take a meeting in Supreme Video, which is Meshflixx's main competitor. It could all just be rumors or a coincidence or nothing at all…"

"It could," he said. "I'll check into all of it."

"Luke, I know I keep saying this about almost everyone," she added. "But I don't think I can stress how much of a good guy Mark is."

He acknowledged her comment, wished his pride hadn't prevented him from calling her the previous day, and decided to share something that had been bothering him during that whole conversation.

"Listen, we still need to talk—about us—but I feel I should try and clear your name first."

"Not being involved in a case of theft that could ruin my career would be great, yes. And we can figure *us* out in a couple of hours or a couple of days," she said. She sounded unhappy and tired.

They hung up shortly after that because she needed to answer another phone call, but he couldn't help feeling she was distancing herself from him.

We can figure us out in a couple of hours or a couple of days. She could have easily added *or a couple of weeks or months* as well.

Since they'd spent the night together, they seemed to be further away from each other with every conversation they had. And the urgency to crack the case didn't help.

45

After a conversation on the phone with Luke that left her seriously worried about her future as a journalist—ruined reputations didn't do well in her line of work—she'd had to field yet another call with Fionna Bennett.

Fionna informed her that after a lengthy chat with Fynn's people, in which Sol hadn't been included and that she wasn't even aware had been taking place, *Conceit Fair* had decided to unpublish her story from the website and cancel the plans for it to run in their print magazine.

Not only was her article going to be taken down, but since *Conceit Fair* would need to hire an additional freelance writer to take care of the now empty space in the upcoming issue of their magazine, Sol would not be compensated for her work. Fionna had even floated the idea of not reimbursing Sol for the expenses of the trip to Los Angeles.

Sol was fuming, among feeling many other sentiments. Had she known that she'd end up paying for the trip to LA herself, she'd have booked a first-class flight! She had instead bought a ticket that complied with the magazine's travel guidelines, and for what? Pure discomfort.

Then she remembered that she was *broke* and panicked. She had forgotten what it was like to constantly worry about money, and now her only source of income had vanished.

If all that wasn't bad enough, she was receiving hate messages and all kinds of colorful emails and direct comments on her personal mail and her social media accounts from some Fynn and *Revengers* fans. Her favorite so far was a dude under the account name @DroidCop99 who called her an "ignorant feminazi" and argued women shouldn't be allowed to write about action flicks because they didn't get them.

She knew she needed to switch her phone and computers off and go out of the house, but she was feeling so exposed and vulnerable that even the idea of going for a walk seemed too daunting. She was debating whether to call her mom, Laia, Lola, Laura, Lali, Lurdes, or some other L-friend but definitely not Luke, when she heard her doorbell.

She checked the camera on her phone, convinced it would be Fionna Bennett, Christina Jones, or some *Revengers Reunite* executive producer coming to berate her in person, but it was Luke. She went to let him in.

"Hey," he said when she opened the door. No *ciao* and certainly no *bella* for Sol on that miserable day. "Can I come in?"

"Sure," she said, a bit surprised by his abruptness. "Is everything okay?"

"Not really." He followed Sol to her kitchen.

"If it wasn't because I've already had the worst day ever and nothing else could go wrong, I'd be a bit worried," Sol told Luke as they both sat around Sol's table.

Luke avoided his semi-usual spot tucked into the corner with her, instead sitting across the table.

"Since I don't really know how to put this, the best will be for you to see it." He unlocked his phone and handed it to her over the table. "Play the video."

She saw a CCTV video of her leaving what looked to be Josie's building. The video used the feed from several security cameras and followed Sol until she stopped at a traffic light. The recording zoomed into the big weekender bag hanging from her shoulder. The bag, which she always brought to her Pilates excursions, was half open and there seemed to be a stack of papers inside. The video zoomed further into the papers, but it wasn't clear what they were.

"This was published to *Voyeur* an hour ago," Luke said. "I came here the moment I saw it. The *Voyeur* article that embedded this video is implying that the papers inside your bag are the stolen script. The CCTV appears to be from February 23."

"What?" Sol's heart fell. Could her day get any worse?

"Do you know what the papers may have really been?" asked Luke.

"No! I carry all sorts of things everywhere, that's why I always buy giant bags and purses. I'm old-school and analogic for some things. I print everything: articles I'm working on, recipes of things I want to cook, lists of questions for my next interview subject—or for my doctor. Those papers could be anything: bank statements, some writing notes, a letter from the V&A museum asking for a donation..."

"There's something else," Luke said.

"Nope!" Sol refused to acknowledge it.

"I shouldn't be the one telling you this, but you need to

know," Luke continued. "There's a quote in the article from your ex-husband."

"What?!" she yelled. She thought she knew who the quote was from, but she needed to make sure. "Which one?"

"Your ex-husband?" said Luke, his brows furrowed.

"There are two of them, remember?"

"Right." Luke took his phone from Sol's hands and went through something on it. "Here, David Sparrow."

"The fucking bastard!"

"Yes, that he is," Luke agreed. "He says something about you being oblivious to the idea of earning a living and having probably grabbed the script by mistake but then perhaps turned it into a way of making some quick money—"

"The scum! I'm gonna kill him!"

"I won't tell you how to deal with your ex-husband—either of them," Luke said cautiously. "But perhaps talk to a friend about this, talk to your family, talk to me if you want, but don't call David. I don't think he deserves the attention."

She was sort of sedated by the severity of the situation, but perhaps Luke was right. Even if she did want to kill David fucking Sparrow and call him all sorts of profane, terrible things, she didn't feel like having a conversation with him, not even then.

"I know this is a mess right now," Luke told her while she was still toying with the many options to get revenge on David.

"You don't even know the full extent of it," Sol said.

"Did something happen?" he asked. "Something else, I mean?"

"Let's say I had a very bad day at work."

"Worse than Saturday?"

"Worse than most. Maybe not worse than the first time I

got laid off—*and* the second time I got laid off. But ranking pretty up there."

"I'm sorry about that, mate."

Mate? Had he really called her *mate?* Was that what they were now? No longer sort of together, not even friends, just *mates?*

"I was saying I know this is a mess right now," Luke continued, apparently unaware of having downgraded her from occasional lover to *mate.* "But I want you to know that I'm still trying to figure this out."

"Yes, sure. Thank you." She was exhausted, and being in his presence didn't help.

"I think I should probably leave now," he said as if reading her thoughts. Or perhaps he didn't want to be there. She wasn't the best company at the moment. "But ring me if you need anything and I'll come. And I'll keep you posted about the case. I'm not forgetting about clearing your name."

"Sure," she said and she accompanied him to the door.

She wasn't sure what pleasantries they exchanged before he left. She was in shock and only half-listening, and she hadn't been able to look him in the eye for the whole visit.

...

Laia called her half an hour after Luke had left her place and as soon as she'd seen the *Voyeur* article. Sol was reminded of a libel case her friend had been involved in a couple of years before and asked Laia for the contact of the lawyer who'd helped her with that.

"She's used to dealing with these types of situations," Laia assured her. "Those *Voyeur* people don't know what's coming for them!"

She also told Sol that she would personally handle the David issue in a painful way and Sol thanked her for it, even if she wasn't sure what Laia was planning. She just hoped it would be nothing illegal. Trusting her friends and letting them help her in difficult moments had been one of her recent learnings.

Sol explained what had happened with the Richard Fynn interview, and after twenty more minutes of chatting, they hung up. There had been something that Sol decided to conceal from Laia though—how she was convinced that whatever had been between her and Luke was now irredeemably over.

...

She was trying to take care of herself with a bit of pampering by rewatching an episode of the feel-good romantic procedural *The Mallorca Files* and eating a warmed Franco Manca vegetarian pizza. She thanked her organized self for always keeping frozen pizza and Amorino yogurt gelato at home for emergency cases such as this, and she was beginning to evolve from miserably destroyed to profoundly glum.

Then she got Miquel's text message. He'd seen what *Conceit Fair* had done, taking Sol's article down, and he wanted her to know that he'd removed Fionna from his good-wishes list. *Conceit Fair*'s editor would no longer be getting happy-birthday and merry-Christmas messages from Miquel. And forget about getting the scoop on any other secret sales from Catalan natural-leather purse designers or artisanal shoemakers.

Sol couldn't help but laugh out loud. She didn't know anymore what she could or couldn't afford. She'd been belittled online and offline, her name had been dragged through the mud, and perhaps the police would come knocking and ask about a stolen script. She wasn't sure if she'd be able to work as a journalist again. But she still knew who her friends were.

46

Personal assistant, editor of AI-generated content, PR and media relations specialist, ghostwriter for corporate materials and—Sol's favorite—AI trainer to help robots become better writers. All those professions were now a wide-open opportunity for her. There was really no reason why she shouldn't consider one of them as the next step in her professional life. One thing was clear: all signs pointed to the fact that she needed to pivot.

In the past, there had always been the unattractive option of following her family members and opting for wealth management and administration of family assets. As unfascinating as that sounded, she had to admit that strategic investment had tended to be lucrative for her relatives—until her parents had proved that it was also a risky endeavor.

Besides reconsidering her taste for expensive travel, she needed to figure out what to do when it came to applying a more judicious model to her spending. Should she move to a cheaper place? Was she going to be forced to sell one of her two places?

She was still lost in her thoughts—and horrified at the prospect of having to pack a house—when her telephone rang, and Sol saw Luke's name on the screen. She'd edited his contact information *again* on her cell phone. He'd been demoted from *Luke (Ear Whisperer)* to a very boring, very basic—and almost lacking any sexual connotation—*Luke*.

"Hey," she answered, imitating him in his latest impersonal greeting. Cold and unemotional.

"Hey," he quipped. Whatever had been between the two of them had been completely—and officially—annihilated with that way of saluting one another. "So, I asked my mate Sanjay at T&T to take a look at the CCTV video, and it looks legitimate."

"Meaning?" Was it bad that she really didn't care about the damn video? It had to be.

"Meaning it's not some deep fake or anything. It's actually you on the street, leaving Josie's with a stack of papers in your bag."

"Unless you're some sort of zealous ecological activist, carrying paper around is *not* a crime, correct?" The whole situation was almost too surreal to bother taking it seriously.

"I'm glad you still conserve your sense of humor," he said, not a drop of irony in his voice.

"Are you actually mad at me right now?"

"I forgot you're the only one who's able to react in a dramatic way."

"Are you serious?" She was about to lose it. "In the last twenty-four hours, I've been accused of stealing, of mischaracterizing an asshole, and—what's worse—of not knowing how to write a five-hundred-word profile-ish puff piece. The last thing I need is you calling me, greeting me with a fucking *hey*, and telling me I'm a drama queen."

"How should I have greeted you?" he asked, and the warmth in his voice softened her slightly.

"You used to talk to me in Italian." Her voice was on the brink of breaking. "But I don't think you're interested in me in that way anymore."

"Would you believe me if I told you that up until two seconds ago, I thought it was you who wasn't interested in me anymore?" His voice was honeyed and caring once more. "I was trying to give you space while still being on top of this mess. Allora, bella. Come posso aiutarti?"

"You can start by promising never to call me *mate* again."

"Done. I never thought it suited you. You're more of a cara or a regina," he said huskily.

"Okay, let's focus. Why have you called me, Luca?" She took her use of his Italian name as an indication that her subconscious had forgiven him for any word misuse directed her way in the past.

"My colleague Sanjay did some image processing with the CCTV video *Voyeur* published," he said. "Those papers in your bag do look like *The Privateers* script. A portion of the title is partially visible and so is Sara Daniels's name watermarked on the page."

Sol was so angry, she could no longer hide it. "First your agency gets me in trouble—I've reread *Voyeur*'s so-called article this morning. There's a quote from one of your managers saying their investigation led them to think I was the culprit!" She realized how much she was yelling only once she started doing it. "I'm sure it was your agency who gave them the *scoop* about this supposed story in the first place! And now you tell me this!"

"If you had let me finish," Luke managed to interrupt her. "I would have told you that someone could have planted the script in your bag and then made sure you were caught on video with it. But you're such a cliché of the passionate Mediterranean sometimes, it's impossible to reason with you."

"I'm not sure if you're insulting me."

"I'm not!" Luke told her almost defeatedly.

He'd been uneasy since he'd seen the CCTV video again that morning. He'd genuinely contemplated the idea of Sol as the script thief for the first time then, despite the fact that he should have done it weeks earlier. When it came to her, he couldn't be objective. He'd made many assumptions about the case based on Sol's account of what went on. But what if she'd lied? Could his supposed good nose have been misled all these weeks by the attraction he felt for her?

"Why didn't you tell me about the AI controversy surrounding *The Privateers*?" he finally asked her. He was trying to figure out one of the things that had been bothering him in order to eliminate her as a suspect once and for all.

There was silence after his question. Was she thinking? Was she coming up with a plausible explanation?

"The fact that the credits weren't designed by Martha Broch but an AI imitator, you mean?" She sounded surprised.

"Yes, you never told me about it."

"Because I didn't remember it! Do you have any idea how many scandals and controversies Hollywood has in a single week?"

"You mentioned this particular one in your review of the show."

"Do you know how many of those I write in a year?" she

yelled. "Do you really think I remember everything I've written? Sadly, I don't."

"So you weren't concealing information on purpose?"

"Why would I do that?" He could hear the frustration in her tone. He also couldn't help it—he believed her even if he wasn't sure he could totally trust himself when it came to her.

But it made no sense that she would hide something like that when it gave Martha Broch a motive—unless they were working together.

There was something else he needed to ask her.

"And you're sure you've never met Leonardo Pascual?"

It still bothered him that he'd run into Sol at Fortnum & Mason while he'd been following *The Privateers* actor. It could be a coincidence, but did that really happen in a city the size of London? What if Sol and Leonardo were meeting there for some reason?

"To be honest, I've interviewed so many actors over the years that I've forgotten most of them at this point," she said. "But believe me when I say I would *not* forget him."

"Oh yes, irrefutably sexy," Luke said. A pang of jealousy immediately made him forget anything else he wanted to ask her.

"Basically that, yes," she said. "Are we done yelling and throwing allegations?"

"Please." Once again, when it came to her, he preferred to stop digging whenever he felt he was getting too close to unearthing something potentially unpleasant.

"Okay, whatever happens today—and, if yesterday is an indication of anything, I could either be accused of not knowing how to properly conjugate a verb in the subjunctive mood in Spanish or of murder—would you come to my place tonight and we can talk?"

"Red or white?"

"What?"

"The wine I'll be bringing because we need it. I'm not sure tea will be enough—double meaning intended. So red or white?"

"We're talking about wine, all answers are right. You know that." The wine allusion took them back to the first time they had dinner together in Barcelona, changing the mood.

There was a long silence on the phone after that, and he wasn't sure how to proceed. Was the conversation over? Were they saying goodbye? And, if so, what was the proper way of doing it so that no one called each other *mate* or simply said *bye*? Sol would probably view that as the goodbye equivalent of *hey*, which was unacceptable in their once-again-tending-toward-scorching relationship. He opted for candidness.

"Sadly, I need to go and keep following a bloke with questionable taste in doughnuts," he told her.

"Are you investigating him because of *that*?"

"Basically. But all the bloody time I can steal, I'm devoting it to your case. And I'll see you tonight." He paused. "Let me rephrase that: Ci vediamo stasera, cara."

"Adeu, Luca."

47

Sol was taking a long and supposed-to-be-soothing bath with the intention of forgetting about everything going on in her life. The whole endeavor was feeling like a waste of water when it suddenly hit her.

She'd never found any mystery script inside her purse that day when she came home. But Sara had been admiring of her weekender bag at the Tube platform. Perhaps too much, considering it was just a gray gigantic canvas tote.

She grabbed her phone to message Luke from the tub, which felt sexy and comfortably warm all of a sudden.

> Sol Novo: I think Sara must have grabbed the script from my bag when we "ran into each other" on the Tube. I also don't think the encounter was casual

She edited Luke's contact on her phone once more, had a sip of her still lukewarm cup of tea, and thought she should do the whole long, potentially calming bath thing more often. If only she'd remembered to bring her book to the bathroom. She saw Luke's message then.

> Luke (Tea Connoisseur): On doughnut duty but my colleague Divya Bakshi will call you right now

> Luke (Tea Connoisseur): You can trust her

She had barely a couple of seconds to read Luke's messages when she got a call from an unknown number and picked it up.

"Hello?" she said hesitantly. What if it was another obnoxious *Voyeur* staffer trying to get a quote? She'd been screening all her incoming calls even more zealously than normal since the previous day, letting all unknown numbers go straight to voicemail.

"Is this Sol Novo?" a woman with a strong Mancunian accent said. "This is Divya, Divya Bakshi. Luke Contadino told you I'd be calling, right?"

"Yes," Sol answered, still unsure about the whole situation.

"He's, unfortunately, taking care of some useless surveillance so that our bosses can charge a lot of money to some rich clients." That fit what Luke had previously told her about his agency. "But he asked me to ring you and ask you a couple of questions."

"I see."

"Is this a good time to talk?" Divya asked. Sol had to admit this detective seemed to have a nose.

"As a matter of fact, can I mute you for a few seconds while I take care of something?"

"Go ahead."

Sol muted her cell phone, got out of the tub, and wrapped herself in a gigantic plush organic-cotton bathrobe while drying her wet hair with a towel.

"Okay, what do you need to ask me?" she finally told Divya from her office, still enveloped by towels.

"Let's see if I have all the details straight. On the day of the theft, you went to grab your bag but your locker was open. Since it was late, you took a different route than usual and walked to the Tube station. Did you at some point notice something weird inside your bag?"

"Like a TV script?" Sol said. "Nope. But, as I've told Luke, I carry papers around all the time because I'm—"

"Old-school and analogic, yes, he mentioned."

"He's described me as old-school and analogic?" Perhaps Luke had realized how old she was.

"No, he said *you* had described yourself that way. Do you want me to tell you how he describes you?"

This detective could *really* read her mind—through the phone! She seemed to know what she was doing.

"No. I'll let him do that," Sol told Divya, trying but not quite accomplishing a nonchalant tone.

"I see." Sol could almost hear the smirk in her voice. "What happened when you got to Charing Cross station?"

"I was waiting for the train, and I saw Sara standing next to me on the platform. I said hi because I'm polite that way."

"So you first approached her?"

"I did. It would have been rude otherwise. Has Luke talked about my Mediterraneanism?"

"He has," said Divya almost too formally. Sol wanted to ask about the specifics but didn't. "What happened then?"

"We had some small talk until Sara commented on the gorgeousness of my bag and asked to try it on."

"She asked to try on your bag?"

"She was looking for something big enough to carry all her work stuff and workout stuff, but she's kind of, like, not the biggest—shorter and definitely skinnier than me—and she wanted to make sure she wouldn't look ridiculous with a bag the size of mine."

"I see. So did you let her?"

"Of course."

"And you didn't think anything of it then?"

"I mean, the bag is fabulous. It's from this boutique design studio in Florida, of all places. All their products are made with high-quality standards and they're all manufactured in the US. The thing is even machine washable and water resistant. I can send you a link to their website if you want."

"You needn't do that," Divya said. Sol couldn't help but feel the detective was all professional and not much of a fashionista. "So could Sara have grabbed something from your bag when she was checking it out?"

"I suppose so. It's not like I was intently looking at her to make sure she wouldn't steal something from me. I was probably more focused on seeing if the train was any closer."

Divya made a humming noise. "I have slightly bad news. Please don't get upset as I'm sure there's a perfectly reasonable explanation for it. Even if we haven't found it yet."

"What do you need a perfectly reasonable explanation for?" Sol was aware that her tone was a bit elevated.

"Your encounter at Charing Cross," said Divya, still perfectly calm. "Sara Daniels called Luke and me earlier today. We've been trying to talk to her for days. She says she never took the Tube on February 23 and, as a result of that, she didn't run into you on the train platform. According to her, she left Josie's at half past six, couldn't find the script inside her bag then but didn't think much of it at the time, hailed an Uber, and went directly home to finish some work. Of course, she could be lying."

"She has to be!" Sol wrung her hands.

"She's offered to send us the receipt for her Uber ride. Hasn't done it yet though."

"Are you still there?" Divya asked Sol after a few seconds of silence.

"I'm speechless," Sol admitted. Never in a million years had she pictured herself saying that.

"It happens." Divya's composure was comforting. In a way, it was easier talking to her because Divya had kept her cool the whole time, unlike Luke—who was Mediterranean to the core, even if he didn't always admit it. "Listen, we're trying to figure this out. Don't worry, and let us professionals handle it."

"When did she realize the script had been stolen?" Sol asked. She was going to let the professionals do their thing, but she needed to understand what had happened. "You said she realized the script was missing at the studio but still went home."

"I guess she was hoping to find it at home and, once there, she called her office at Meshflixx. Her creative liaison told her the script wasn't there either, and then she started thinking she could have misplaced it and worried," Divya explained. "But Sara says she didn't realize what had happened until the script appeared online hours later. Know what I mean?"

"I see."

"There's something else. Luke told me you may get cross if I brought it up though..."

"Sounds promising." Sol couldn't imagine what the subject could be.

"He says you told him Josie could not be involved in this in any way because it would put the studio at risk," Divya said.

"Uh-huh. That, and Josie is not the kind of person to steal."

"We did some digging. She was ready to sell the business a couple of months ago."

"What?!" The last thing Sol needed in her life right then was for Josie's to close or change in any way.

"In the end, she didn't, but we're wondering if she needed money and found another way of getting it. Did she ever suggest that she was thinking about selling, or that business was tight?"

"Never. She's a very private person though. She never talks about her personal life with her clients. She's sort of a mystery to all of us, which I think contributes to her aura," Sol said. "And you're sure she's not selling now?"

"We think she isn't," said Divya. "But there's also the fact that it was her who caused the class to run long that day. Even if you've told us she's normally extra punctual."

"I still think Josie as the thief doesn't make sense." Literally, the last thing she needed then was for her perfectly crafted exercise regimen to be altered in any way. Then she realized she had *bigger* problems at present and ordered herself to stop panicking about what could be construed as nonsense.

"Listen, you have my number now," Divya told Sol. "If you remember anything else or if you need an update or even if you just want to talk, you can call me. Of course, you can ring Luke as well, but we both know he can be a bit overdramatic sometimes. So you can call me for the fuss-free experience."

"Thank you. You and Luke are devoting way too much time to this." Sol was genuinely moved.

"We feel bad that you're in this position due to our agency's incompetence. We're better detectives than this."

...

She decided to listen to Divya and leave the investigative part of the mess she was in to the actual private sleuths. But that didn't mean she couldn't do anything about her situation. She was going to do everything she could to restore her ill-damaged reputation. She had to be in control of at least that aspect of her life.

She was still wearing a bathrobe and she hadn't even bothered drying her hair—a beauty inattention she only allowed herself if she was vacationing at the beach—but she was happy with the writing she'd done since hanging up the phone.

She read the draft once again, this time for possible typos, and clicked the *publish* button. When the post was live on the online publishing platform she used, Sol copied the post's link and pasted it into a message on her Twitter account that read: "In case you want to know what actually went on in that Richard Fynn interview. TL;DR: He didn't want to talk about Revengers. Also, I didn't steal no script!"

What Really Happened in My Interview With Richard Fynn

You'll never read about these behind-the-scenes Hollywood details in traditional media. Plus, I didn't steal that damned script!

BY SOL NOVO

What do you do when a director tells you "It's not like I had too much of an option" when—at the very beginning of a one-on-one interview—you thank him for taking the time and talking to you? You shrug it off and move to the next question.

What do you do when that same director follows that up by telling you that the promotional portion of making a movie is "the numb, soulless act of trying to charm the likes of *you*"? Also, did I mention he was eating when I got to the Four Seasons suite where the chat was taking place and never bothered closing—or wiping—his mouth while doing it?

I don't know why filmmaker Richard Fynn didn't want to be there during the press day for his upcoming sequel *Revengers Reunite Redo*, which opens on May 5, but he didn't. "Why do the fans care about my return?" he told me when I asked him what made him decide to return to the iconic franchise. He seemed oblivious to the reasons why *Revengers* has been so popular over the years. "Fuck if I know!" were his actual words when prompted about it.

He also kept manifesting his dislike not personally for me but for journalists in general, referring to us as "you people" and our need to "over-analyze every single frame" of his filmography. He refused to talk about his longtime collaboration with director Mark Green—together they made over 20 action-adventure movies during the 1980s and 1990s in a time when Fynn was still only producing and Green was directing.

And he also didn't want to talk about how the changes in technology over the last fifteen years—the first *Revengers* was released in 2008 and *Revengers Reunite* opened in 2010—may have been a game-changer in the production of this third installment. If you watch the original films now, you'll see that the special effects on those movies don't look exactly current.

In a chat with a publicist for the studio releasing the movie that took place after the peculiar Fynn interview, I was told that the filmmaker was "nervous" because the film was technically not completely done. So whatever VFX or other post-production work is taking place, it's making Fynn uncomfortable.

"I've been babbling about the damn movie all morning already!" were the words Fynn used when he decided he was cutting our initially agreed upon 20-minute chat short. He left the room, fried chicken thigh in hand, never to return.

And that's basically what went on, to the best of my recollection—plus the relistening of the recording of the actual interview and reading of my detailed note-taking—during my recent chat with Fynn, which was initially published on *Conceit Fair* but was later taken down because I was accused of "mischaracterization."

I didn't have to fight twenty editors to get this story approved, edited, copy edited and published. What's best, I could even write my own headline.

Also, and this has nothing to do with *Revengers* or Fynn, but don't believe everything you read on the internet, especially if you saw it on *Voyeur*. No, I didn't steal a script for the second season of *The Privateers* that made its way online.

She closed her laptop and promised herself not to look at it for the rest of the day. She even went as far as deleting the Twitter and Mail apps from her cell phone.

48

Luke was at her door two hours later, wearing Greg Knight's most unstylish attire to date and a mischievous smile that absolutely compensated for the lack of wardrobe smartness.

"I'm sorry I look like this," he told her, acknowledging his ill-fitting white polo shirt tucked into maroon-colored chino pants. "But I come bearing gifts." He handed her a bottle of Aglianico del Vulture.

"I don't care about the clothes." She urged him to come inside and got rid of the bottle, putting it on the storage bench in her home's narrow entrance hall.

"I don't believe you," he said almost defiantly while Sol rushed to close the door.

"Could you please just shut up?" She balanced on her tiptoes, bringing her hand to his mercifully bearded jaw, and chasing his lips with hers.

"Better?" he asked after a few minutes of urgent reacquaintance.

"Better," she admitted, scarcely annoyed. The words had

been spare, but they were interfering with the making out. "But still not great."

She grabbed his unfortunate shirt, untucking it while pulling him toward her, letting her lips find the last place they'd been feeling on Luke's mouth and then making her way through the contour of his neck and collarbone.

"Are you super hungry?" she asked, managing to sever her mouth from his body—briefly.

"For food?" he asked with a smile that could only be described as roguish.

"Mare meva! You and the wordplay!"

"You *know* I do love a bit of wordplay, yes." Right then, he was all magnetic sex appeal and beauty. "*If* you were talking about food, I can wait."

"Good."

Eventually, they made their way upstairs. Sol had always abhorred the steep narrowness of those stairs, but they apparently hid so many nooks conducive to letting him toy with the sensitive skin behind her earlobes. They also appeared almost designed for her to meticulously remove every single odious garment he'd been wearing.

Their bodies had recognized one another when Sol first kissed him downstairs, but once undressed, they found each other in a different, more profound way.

Sol was more relaxed this time, more confident—not only in herself but also in him. She knew she could trust him. Completely.

She shut all the voices inside her head that told her she should be worrying about her career, her public image, her future, and even her heart, and that this wasn't a good moment for a relationship, for flirtation, for commitment, or even for just sex. She was present, her only aim to take and give pleasure.

...

They sat in Sol's kitchen. The red Aglianico del Vulture bottle was open and generously poured into two wine glasses, the leftovers of the Ottolenghi take-home selection of salads and char-grilled salmon still on the table.

"Divya discovered the identity of the mystery man," Luke told her. He was devouring the stash of double chocolate cookies she'd gotten that afternoon at the Spitalfields location of the same popular restaurant and deli where she'd bought dinner. "She's been in touch with Sara Daniels's creative liaison, and they recognize the person who had coffee with Oliver Green the day you followed him."

"Who is it?" Sol nibbled on a cookie herself, even if she had a strict no-baked-goods-or-other-sugary-foods-on-weekdays policy.

"Some senior vice president of scripted TV content at Meshflixx called... Let me check my notes." He got up to leave the room, tracing the naked outline of Sol's shoulders with his fingers on his way. An electric charge shook her whole body.

"Eduardo Callaghan," Luke yelled not a minute later from what sounded like the entryway. "Eduardo Callaghan," he repeated at a more measured volume while making his way back into the kitchen. He sat at his now officially usual spot at one of the ends of the table. A spot she was sure he'd chosen because it gave him direct access to her ear, in case something needed to be murmured.

"Why would Oliver meet with a higher-up at Meshflixx? Especially from the scripted TV division? He's always been happy to proclaim he only works in long feature documentaries." Luke's semi-disrobed state made it almost impossible for her to think clearly. He was wearing boxer briefs and a long silk robe of hers that looked kind of small on him.

"Maybe his father made the introduction?" Luke asked.

"You're right." Luke was wearing the black-and-pale-pink robe completely open. No wonder Sol had missed something so obvious.

To make things worse, he wasn't only showing chest, abs, and muscled legs, he was also showing shoulder as the robe slipped from his left arm. And since he'd stolen her favorite getting-out-of-bed-and-feeling-sexy garment, she'd been forced to don a suggestive vintage sleep gown herself.

"Mark is great and all, but that doesn't mean he wouldn't arrange a meeting for his son, even if he probably knows better than I do that Oliver lacks any kind of talent," she said. "Could this have anything to do with the article I saw about Mark possibly working on Meshflixx's projects? Maybe the reporter got the facts wrong, and it's going to be Oliver and not Mark doing work for the streamer."

"Divya is checking into the reasons for the meeting. Oliver's undisclosed presence at Josie's the night of the theft is kind of suspicious," Luke said. "Then again, it could also be that he didn't feel like having his arse kicked that day."

"It could, I guess. Would you thank Divya for me for everything she's doing? It was reassuring, talking to her today."

"More reassuring than talking to me?" He raised his eyebrows.

"Only because she wasn't flirting with me the whole time. And I didn't feel like I needed to measure every single word coming out of my mouth," Sol said. "You have to admit that this investigation has interfered with our relationship from the beginning, and the other way around. We don't seem able to do either one right."

"I think we're really applying ourselves on both fronts," he said, an insinuating smirk on his face. "And we're making some palpable progress when it comes to..." He pointed to her and then to himself, repeating the movement in a rapid gesture that imitated the one she'd used two days before.

"This wine is delicious, but I'm drunk," she said then. "Should we move to tea?"

"If you were trying to brush off my comment on sex and relationship progress, I think you made a mistake in your choice of a subject change." He looked intently at her while savoring some more wine. "Tea is a charged word for us, remember, cara?"

"Oh, I do. Who said I was trying to brush off your comment?" She straddled his bare thighs, shifting the placement of the robe on his body so that suggestive shoulder would be completely naked.

49

He woke up early knowing there was probably no surveillance job to go to that day once everything had been released.

He was checking the maps app on his phone to see where he'd have to go on that side of the Thames to get some cornetti that would end up being some British reinterpretation of croissants. He was partial to GAIL's—it was the closest, and he was a semi-regular at the Islington branch. But a text message from Sanjay about his mate at the Metropolitan Police broke Luke's train of thought.

"Fuck!" he growled, not even trying to keep quiet. "Sol, you need to wake up."

She groaned, turning over so that her back was to him, ignoring Luke and covering her head with a pillow.

"Sol, you need to wake up," he insisted.

"¿Por qué?" she managed to utter. She sounded half unconscious, with notes of early morning grumpiness. Under normal circumstances, he'd never force her awake, or he'd proceed with extreme care and coax her in some pleasurable way. But there was no time.

"The police are on their way," he told her as commandingly as he could, considering he was a bit afraid for his life. Sol didn't look like someone who woke up with a smile.

"What?" She sat up on the bed, trying to open her eyes and not being completely successful.

"The police are on their way. They want to talk to you about your possible involvement in the Meshflixx case."

"Let me call my lawyer," she said.

Of course, Sol already had a solicitor on call. The woman never ceased to amaze him with her deliberate preparedness for every single situation.

...

Twenty-five minutes later, Sol and Luke were fully dressed and sitting around Sol's kitchen table. Two detective sergeants from the Met were also there, and Sol had even offered them tea and leftover cookies from the previous night. Sol's solicitor, Victoria Sifuentes, was on speakerphone and currently talking through Sol's mobile phone.

"I'm sorry I can't be there in person, but it was impossible to get to the South Bank on such short notice. I live in Mayfair," Victoria said, and Luke almost chuckled. He could see Sol rolling her eyes at the lawyer's words. Mayfair wasn't even that far from there, but it was across the river. "But tell me, to what do we owe the pleasure of a visit from the Met?"

"We just want to chat with Ms. Novo about her involvement in the Meshflixx case," DS Steve Fleming said—pronouncing Sol's last name with long vowels and a fricative "v" sound that Luke knew she didn't use.

Detective Sergeant Fleming was in his fifties and wore an ill-fitting suit that made Greg Knight's attire look almost fashionably acceptable in comparison. Luke immediately took a liking to him.

"Can you be more specific when you refer to the Mesh-flixx case?" Victoria went on while Sol sipped her tea. The lawyer had told the stringer to let her do the talking, and Sol seemed to follow the directions with perfect self-control.

"I'm sure you've heard about the theft of the script from the pirate show at Meshflixx," the detective continued.

"My client has read about it in the press. And that's the extent of her involvement," Victoria said.

"I'm sure you've read the *Voyeur* article that maintains it was her who took the script?" Fleming continued.

"Is the Metropolitan Police basing their investigations on non-researched online posts that get published regardless of their factual content? We're suing *Voyeur* for defamation."

There was a brief, almost unnoticeable glance between the two police detectives when they heard Victoria say they were going to sue *Voyeur*. Luke wasn't sure if Sol had perceived the gesture, but he sure had.

"There's also the private detectives' agency saying she's the culprit," Fleming added. That was Luke's cue.

"As a junior detective at Thompson & Thomson, I can tell you that Ms. Novo"—he made sure to pronounce Sol's last name properly—"has been cleared of all involvement in the theft and leak of *The Privateers* script."

"That's not what your boss says," the other detective, a woman in her early thirties who had introduced herself as DS Kate Arnott, intervened then.

"Have you actually talked to Archibald Thompson or Alistair Thomson?" asked Luke.

"No, but there's a quote from one of them here in the article," the sweaty detective said, signaling to his mobile device.

"If you check the news, you'll see *that* quote no longer stands." Luke couldn't avoid smirking.

The two detectives focused on their phones while Sol raised an eyebrow at Luke. He hadn't had time to tell her about that particular topic before the police got there.

"Is there anything else we can do for you detectives?" Victoria asked after a few minutes during which, Luke was sure, she also had been browsing and probably found an article corroborating what he'd just said.

"This is going to be all for now," DS Arnott said.

"Excellent. Please remember to address any further requests directly to me as my client has been instructed to not talk to you unless I'm present," Victoria said. She added the only thing Sol had asked her to inquire if the occasion permitted it. "May we ask what prompted this questioning?"

"There's been so much noise and coverage about this case, we thought we should look into it," Fleming said.

"The script was stolen weeks ago," Victoria protested.

"No one cared weeks ago," the chatty detective continued.

"Do you mean Meshflixx didn't care when their script was leaked online?" Luke stepped in again. He knew Sol wanted to ask exactly that, but he preferred she remain silent while the police were present.

"Meshflixx never reported the theft," said Fleming.

"What about Sara Daniels?" asked Luke.

"I think we've talked enough," DS Arnott interrupted her colleague before he could say anything else. "We'll let you get back to your lives."

Sol and Luke accompanied the detectives to the door in silence.

"How convenient for you to already be in the neighborhood before we got here," DS Arnott told Luke as they were leaving. And even though he knew how it could look for him to be at Sol's place so early in the morning, he'd decided to stay and offer his support. Victoria had agreed that it was a good strategy, especially since she couldn't be there herself.

"What can I say, detective? The South Bank has many charms," he said, his best smile shining.

And with that, the officers left. Sol thanked Victoria—she was still on speakerphone even for that; Sol took professional counsel that diligently—one last time and hung up. Once Sol and Luke were alone again, the stringer was finally able to speak freely.

"Please tell me what just happened."

"I guess you're feeling as clueless as I normally do when dealing with matters pertaining to your profession," he said.

"I'm sorry if this is how you normally feel, because I'm totally lost. Why are they talking to me now? I mean, I understand the whole *Voyeur* thing, but Meshflixx never reported the case?"

"It never hurts to get involved in a popular case. If you can't solve it, no one will care, but if you do..."

"Fame and glory." He smiled at her. "Now tell me, what is this thing you referred to about T&T's quote no longer standing?"

"I may have sent a press release using T&T's PR agency to state that you're not, after all, the script thief and that our investigation has cleared you of any wrongdoing."

"Why would you do such a thing?"

Her reaction wasn't exactly what he'd envisioned. Especially considering that up until the previous day and only after Divya had talked to Sol and came to the same conclusions he had, Luke hadn't been confident enough in his belief in Sol's innocence.

"I wanted to clear your name," he said, a bit uneasy.

"But you're already doing that by investigating who actually did it. Once that gets out, my name will be clean. There's no fucking need for you to put your job on the line!"

"I have to say, this is not the reaction I was expecting from you," he told her with a tone a tad harder than he'd anticipated.

"No, eh? What did I tell you a few nights ago? Don't you get all protective on me! And you went and did it again."

"I'm sorry, I forgot you didn't need any help!"

"Oh, there you're wrong!" she said, and by then they were both yelling at each other. "I do need help. I need you and Divya to crack this case. What I don't need is you going behind your managers' backs to send a press release and losing your job because of me."

They remained perfectly still at Sol's entryway for a few more seconds, looking at each other cautiously, her last words reverberating in the air.

"I think I get it," he told her then, his voice suddenly serene, and he did. He'd just figured out the bizarre logic behind her words and feelings. "You're going through a tough moment because you lost your job, and you don't want me to go through the same."

She stared at him in silence, as if trying to figure out the next words to yell at him but not managing to find them.

"Sol, I wasn't trying to be protective. I was trying to right a wrong." For once, he was happy that she was speechless because he wasn't quite sure that he'd made his argument with her yet. "I've been unhappy at my job for months now. I was troubled about the agency's methods long before I met you or I realized that I was, quite simply, mad about you. And then all of this happened, and you were in the middle of it... So forgive me for reacting the way I did."

"You're mad about me?"

"I think it's pretty obvious."

She was silent again, her eyes focused on him, her expression stunned. She looked as if she was going to say something a couple of times, only to remain quiet yet again.

"Sol, you're freaking me out. You're never this quiet." He feared the whole thing had been too much, too soon. "Please yell at me or something."

"The part of me that's been through two divorces and a lot of disappointments and rejection in life wants to pretend like you didn't say anything, tell you to go home, ask you to put the brakes on whatever this is, and take a break," she said. Luke could feel his heart as if it was going to beat out of his chest. "But you've managed to remind me of another Sol these past few days. Someone I like a lot but who I had neglected for a long time. And you've done it even if this bloody case keeps getting in the way."

"It does get in the way," he said, drawing nearer to her, not touching her but close enough that he could feel her warmth.

"Do solve it soon because, as hot as it is sometimes, I'm getting tired of fighting with you over nonsense."

"Can I kiss you now?"

"Please."

50

She was still ambivalent, but she'd decided one thing: to give that burgeoning *romance* between Luke and her a chance. Her dispassionate side resisted the temptation to use that very specific, charged word, but the writer in Sol who always tried choosing the more appropriate word knew better.

Even if the circumstances in which they'd met and where they still pretty much found themselves made the whole thing much more tumultuous than what she would have preferred, given the choice, she was willing to stay in that situation and explore whatever this thing with Luke was.

When it came to relationships, she had tried twice in all seriousness in the past. And it wasn't that she'd failed—she'd never seen divorce as such—but she'd also not succeeded at it. She loved excelling, but perhaps she'd have to learn to simply try.

Luke had left not long after the police—after they'd fought and reconciled once again.

Considering the abrupt circumstances in which she'd woken up that day, given everything else going on in her life, and taking into account the fact that she hadn't had all her beauty sleep—even if she'd traded some sleep hours for an equally soothing activity—Sol decided to take the rest of the day easy.

She had breakfast and a second long and strongly brewed tea. She took the longest of showers and carefully chose what to wear for the challenges coming up. Only after her hair and skin looked flawless, and she felt comfortable but sexy wearing her favorite cropped sweatshirt and leggings, did she go to her office and open her laptop.

She wasn't prepared for what was waiting for her. She almost felt as if she needed to hire a publicist to filter through all the noise directed her way.

The self-published article she'd written the day before was trending online after a few industry blogs had picked it up.

The story had also been tied to T&T's press release about Sol's innocence. There were a couple of quotes in it from Luke that she hoped didn't sound as evident to strangers as they did to her; he appeared to really be mad about her. She'd become an overnight sensation and the epitome of what journalists faced daily.

One of the first people to link to the story and contribute to its virality had been Fynn himself. It looked like the director had decided to go rogue once again and use his official Twitter account to share Sol's article. He'd added, "Had an awful time with interviewer @SolNovo. She would only ask the blandest of questions. But I was not an easy subject. She tells it exactly how it went here." She felt tempted to like the message but didn't.

More than two hundred emails had flooded her inbox, as well as a significant amount of mentions and direct messages on her Twitter account. She was still happy to have taken the initiative of telling her own story but decided to close her laptop. She felt better just by doing that.

She signed up for Josie's mid-morning Pilates reformer class on her phone—she'd finally done some of the mandatory math, and giving up Josie's exorbitantly expensive classes wasn't an option. She would go as far as renting her place in Barcelona or selling her car before leaving Josie— and got out of her house, ready to be sore.

...

She was leaving Josie's studio filled with endorphins from the workout and some lingering dopamine and oxytocin from the night before when she felt her cell phone vibrate.

"Hello, Divya," she answered, a note of cheerfulness in her voice.

"Someone sounds happy," the detective said.

"I guess I am," Sol realized. "I've just exercised. And Josie just announced the new schedule for the remainder of spring and summer, so it doesn't look like she's going to be abandoning me any time soon."

"So your cheeriness has nothing to do with Luke being out of reach all night?"

Sol blushed. "Talking to you is bizarre. I feel like I'm having a conversation with a very sagacious therapist who is also a clairvoyant."

"I think it'll be better if I don't read too much into it," said Divya matter-of-factly.

"As usual, you're perfectly spot-on."

"I called to tell you we figured out what happened at the Tube the night of the theft."

"You found a perfectly reasonable explanation?" said Sol, her mood rising even more.

"We did," replied Divya. "We've had a chat with Philippa Majors. She corroborated your story about Sara Daniels being at Charing Cross the night of the theft."

"So Sara lied to you."

"Not really. Philippa didn't think it was *really* Sara at the Tube. It only appeared to be her."

"What do you mean?"

"Philippa said she's always admired Sara's perfect posture, but the person at the Tube, even if she looked like Sara, didn't carry herself with a completely straight back."

"Such a Philippa observation. Now I want to ask if she mentioned anything about my posture," said Sol, straightening her back. She struggled to take the case seriously sometimes. "Could it have been Bryana pretending to be her sister? The whole twin swap is such an easy plot twist though..."

"Luke is talking with Bryana right now," said Divya.

"He is?" Sol realized she hadn't heard from him since he'd left her place that morning. It had only been a few hours, but still. He'd said he was mad about her, after all.

"He's hopeful that Bryana, at least, won't lecture him about his Pilates practice and counsel him on how to improve it. Both Sara and Philippa have done it so far." Divya chuckled.

"Did he seem to care about the advice?"

"Not really," admitted Divya.

"I thought so."

"He gave me a message for you though. His mobile died because he didn't remember to charge it last night. He says he'll meet you for a passeggiata—I really don't know if I'm bodging the pronunciation of that word. Be at your usual spot at six. Does that work? I'm seeing him in ten minutes and can relay any messages."

"It works," said Sol. "Thanks again for everything."

"Don't mention it."

51

Luke had gone straight to Meshflixx after the chat with Philippa and a visit to *Voyeur*'s office that had confirmed *The Privateers* script had been sent to them anonymously.

Divya was dealing with some of the fallout at T&T after he'd coordinated the release of the statement disassociating Sol from the Meshflixx mess. Luke had also asked his colleague to ring Moon for him and get the creative liaison to arrange a chat with Bryana Daniels.

When he got to Meshflixx, he checked in at the reception and was told Bryana was expecting him. He found her waiting by the lift's doors on the building's top floor. She indicated he follow her and guided him to one of the company's diaphanous meeting rooms. They sat across from each other at a clear round table before Bryana uttered a single word.

"So you *think* you figured out who stole the script," she said.

"Yes," Luke admitted.

There was a silence then, but Luke hoped getting Bryana

to talk wouldn't be hard. She'd agreed to see him already. She'd brought up the subject of the stolen script herself. And he could almost see her willingness to explain how it all had happened. She just needed a little more encouragement.

"You temporarily disabled the wi-fi on February 23 here, forcing your sister to take a physical copy of the script with her. Oliver Green took the script from your sister's locker and put it inside Sol Novo's bag. Later on, you pretended to be Sara and bumped into Sol at the Tube, where you took the script from her bag." He tried to be as straightforward as possible.

"And exactly why would I do such a thing, detective? Especially when I had access to the script the whole time and no need to enact a ruse like the one you're describing."

"I was hoping you'd actually tell me why," he answered with his best, most professional smile.

...

Luke saw Sol standing with perfect poise by one of the brick arches of their meeting point. She wore one of her mostly dark, elegant dresses and the same pair of espadrilles he'd seen her don in Barcelona. Her bob was tussled, her oversized sunglasses were on, and she looked regal. Best of all, there were no school children anywhere in sight.

"Hola." She smiled at him when Luke got closer.

"Ciao, bella," he said before they kissed, and, for several minutes, they were quite unaware of their surroundings. "Should I guide this time?" he finally asked.

She acceded even though he knew she liked leading. He

grabbed her hand and steered in the direction opposite from the river, making his way to the Borough Market.

"Are you going to tell me what happened with Bryana? Did she take the script?"

"Yes," he said. "Care to know how Divya and I figured it out?"

"Other than the fact that Sara Daniels seemed to be in two places at the same time the day of the theft and she happens to have an identical twin?"

"Other than that, yes," he said.

"I'm getting impatient," she warned him.

"I have been so off with this investigation because you've distracted me so much," he started, stopping underneath the train tracks on Stoney Street by one of the market's entrances.

"I'm distracting you?"

"Deeply." He gazed at her, and she seemed to struggle with a response. It was oddly entertaining to watch her fighting to find the words, especially after praise had been directed her way. She almost didn't know how to take it.

"Let's go back to the case, and we can deal with the distraction issue in a less crowded place," she said, lowering her sunglasses momentarily and looking him directly in the eyes.

"Sure." He smiled, resuming the walk. "I dropped by *Voyeur*'s offices this morning after I left your place and talked to a couple of people there. They were quick to tell me that they hadn't paid for *The Privateers* script—even if it brought them lots of traffic. Whoever stole the script wasn't looking to make money with it."

"And that's peculiar?"

"That paired with your encounter at Charing Cross

pointed toward Bryana. But it wasn't until we spoke to Philippa and she corroborated your story—"

"Still don't know why my story needed to be corroborated."

"I never doubted you," he told her with his best smile.

He hoped she wouldn't make a big deal out of it, but he was also getting weirdly hooked to their frequent yelling contests. And the truth was that he *had* doubted her—briefly and against all his instincts.

"The day of the theft, Bryana called Josie, pretending to be Sara, and asked her for some specific workout routine that would be added to what Josie had already prepared for the day. It was what made the class run long and forced you to take the Tube. Sara went to class prompted by her sister, unaware of Bryana's petition to Josie. Oliver took the script from Sara's bag and put it in yours. And Bryana retrieved it at the Tube."

"Why?"

"Bryana wasn't happy with the notes from Meshflixx," Luke explained. "They wanted them to kill off the quarter-master to develop a second show with him, the prequel my boss told me about."

"Wasn't it simpler to talk to Meshflixx? She arranged this thing with the hopes of what?"

"With hopes of the fans getting ahold of the script resulting from Meshflixx's notes and demanding a change, voicing their disappointment because the character was killed off and making Meshflixx doubt the decision."

"Did Sara know anything about this?"

"No, the sisters had quarreled. Bryana was unhappy because she sees her sister as too soft, conceding to all the studio's demands. Bryana didn't want to kill off the quartermaster, and she didn't want to make a second show. It was *her* who said she couldn't work in two overlapping series in the article you sent me a few days ago. But Sara didn't mind working on several projects at the same time, apparently."

"And Bryana told you all this today?"

Luke shrugged. "She was eager to finally come clean since no one seemed to care about it. Meshflixx didn't report the theft to the police. They were rushing the private investigation, and she feared the writers' strike would force some of the changes she wanted not to happen. She thinks they'll be stuck with the actual leaked script, even if the fans have raged against it. That's why she decided to surface the CCTV video now, to try and get people angered about the script again."

Sol frowned. "So how did Bryana manage to pull this elaborate thing off? Was I always collateral damage?"

"Yes. Bryana and Oliver knew you'd be at Josie's that Thursday because you're always there on Thursdays. She knew you'd have to take the Tube because she made sure the class ran late, and she knew you always have dinner at half past seven and hate being late."

"Mare meva, am I this predictable?"

"You're reliable," he tried soothing her.

"Why the Tube though?"

"CCTV coverage is better on the streets leading from Josie's to Charing Cross than the usual route you take when you walk home."

"And I always take the same damn route home," she said. "But why me, other than my unwillingness to be late and how boring I am?"

"Perfect scapegoat, everyone automatically suspected the journalist. Plus, she didn't like the review you wrote of their first show."

"What? I loved that show!" she protested.

"Bryana said something about an untasteful headline," Luke explained.

"My editor wrote that fucking headline! I've been in purgatory all week and it's all been due to my poor taste in editors."

"Fortunately, you have excellent taste in private detectives."

"That I do." She turned to him. It seemed they were due for some Mediterranean public display of desire, after all. But, before she acted on it, something hit her. "I just realized that Josie's best, most challenging class to date was also the result of a nefarious request from Bryana Daniels."

"The fascination you and the rest of Josie's people have with the whole practice still baffles me," he said, laughing. "Philippa tried turning me toward the Pilates way this morning."

"I've heard. I was also told she had no luck."

"Let's say that now that I've finally figured out my way to seducing the sexiest Pilates practitioner I've met, there's no need for me to continue pretending I care for it." He was happy to see her blushing. "Now, will you yell at me if I tell you I'm sorry about the damage my former agency has done to your name?"

"Why would I be mad at you for apologizing?" she said, then her expression shifted. "*Former* agency?"

"I resigned this morning," he said. "I mean, they would have probably sacked me anyway..."

Sol's gaze softened. "I'm not going to yell at you for being jobless," she said.

"Sol, it has been a long time coming. I wasn't happy, and I was seriously questioning some if not most of the methods employed by the agency."

"You're trying to make me believe this wasn't because of me," she said.

"It wasn't because of you." Her answering stare was severe. "Okay, it wasn't *only* because of you. But do you seriously think I could stay at the place that tried to ruin your reputation?"

"At least tell me you have some savings or some plan B or something, and you won't be on the streets because of me." She sounded genuinely worried.

"Fortunately, I'll still be able to afford the rent," he said. As of that afternoon, he had an inkling of what the future would entail, and the prospects looked mildly optimistic. "So you're not angry with me?"

"Of course I'm not angry. I'll even buy you a drink, if you're up for it..."

"Why not. I've heard there's a good tapas bar not that far from here anyway." He directed them to Bermondsey Street.

52

Sol had asked to meet Mark at the Café at Foyles on Charing Cross Road for a cup of tea and some mandatory explanation while Divya and Luke met with Meshflixx.

When she got to the store, she breathed in the smell of books and felt the comfort of being surrounded by so many bound pages. Mark was already waiting at a table on the fifth floor. He was pouring some green fragrant brew into a cup. Sol sat across from him and thanked him for meeting with her on such short notice—she'd texted him the day before after the walk with Luke.

"Other than some reading, rose pruning, and maybe dropping by Josie's later on, it's not like I had that much to do," Mark replied.

"What I wanted to talk about is a bit delicate," said Sol, which was why she'd preferred to meet him there instead of trying to tell him about Oliver at Josie's. Too many prying ears at the studio, even if everyone tended to mind their own business.

"You have something embarrassing to tell me about Oliver." Mark gave a pained expression. "Please don't tell me he tried pursuing you romantically. He's been expressly warned not to harass any of my Pilates classmates—or Josie!"

"It's not that," said Sol, hoping to be as reassuring as possible and immensely glad that it wasn't *that*. "But he was involved in the theft of *The Privateers* script. Did you read about it?"

"I did, only because the rumors said the script had been stolen at the studio. I never believed it..."

"It was, actually, stolen there. Oliver took the script from Sara's bag and put it in mine. He was working with Bryana Daniels. But Bryana, who has confessed to everything, hasn't offered any explanation behind Oliver's involvement. And it doesn't make much sense really."

"The little dickhead!" Sol was sure it was the first time she'd heard Mark cursing. "Even if I no longer read the trades, I saw that your name was mentioned for a couple of days in connection to this. I'm sorry it was due to the shortcomings of that son of mine."

"Not your fault," Sol said, and she really believed it. Oliver was a grown-up even if he didn't act like one. "I saw Oliver chatting with a Meshflixx executive a few days ago, some senior vice president of scripted TV—"

"Eduardo Callaghan?"

"Yes."

"We're tennis mates," explained Mark. "I complement my Pilates workouts with some tennis so that I balance strength training and cardio."

"Tennis, huh?" said Sol. "I've been doing lots of brisk walking and that 12-3-30 cardio thing that went viral a few months ago, where you walk fast on a treadmill with a steep incline. But I'm wondering if I should switch to swimming, honestly."

"Oh, it has the lowest impact," Mark conceded.

"And it's a full-body workout for sure," Sol added.

It was great to talk with a like-minded person who was equally, if not more, worried about his health and overall fitness. But the chat needed to get back to Oliver.

"Oliver has been pestering me to make an introduction with Eduardo for months. Said he had a pitch that was perfect for him," offered Mark.

"Wasn't Oliver adamant about only developing documentary-long feature content?"

"And Eduardo is a scripted TV person, yes. I asked Oliver the same, and I didn't get any sort of satisfactory answer, so I decided not to make the introduction. Please don't think I'm a terrible father."

"Oh, I'm not judgy in that way, don't worry." And she wasn't.

Mark continued, "I've introduced him to so many people over the years. He's had so many opportunities and basically done nothing. He's the ultimate nepo baby. I thought it would teach him a lesson to find his way toward a pitch meeting at Meshflixx the regular way. Then a few weeks ago he started gloating that he'd finally figured out how to get introduced to Eduardo without my help."

"Do you think Bryana put them in touch in exchange for Oliver's help getting the script from Sara?"

"I would bet my beach house in Truro on it. Bryana and Oliver have been somewhat simpatico for years. I introduced them when the sisters did their first TV show."

"Right, you almost went back to directing with the pilot of that one!" Sol had to admit, even for showbiz standards, Josie's disciples seemed to be extra connected with one another. "Are the rumors true though, are you going to be directing again soon?"

"I toyed with the idea. I've actually had meetings at both Meshflixx and Supreme Video—two of my most hated streaming services—if you can believe it." Sol did believe him among other things because she'd seen him get to one of those meetings. "And then I realized that being back in the director's chair would leave me little to no time to maintain my physical regimen and keep up with my social life. Plus, my wife wants us to travel more."

Mark told Sol, strictly off the record, that he'd called Meshflixx and Supreme Video that morning to politely decline their offers.

Family, friends, and health had taken precedence even for someone with such a successful filmography as Mark.

...

She met Luke for a drink after that but told him that she really couldn't keep up with that much alcohol intake. Between her recent trip to Barcelona and her many encounters with him, she was consuming quite above average for a worried-well like her who regularly never drank more than one or two glasses a month. Alcohol had high sugar content and inflammatory qualities.

"How did it go with Meshflixx?" she asked him after they'd adequately greeted each other.

"We told them everything. Sara had no opposition to us telling the streamer about her sister."

"Were they surprised?"

"Not really," Luke said. "They suspected it could be someone on the inside who wasn't happy because with the leak of the script—and the Twitter hack you told me about

—the aim was always to reverse one of Meshflixx's decisions. That's why they didn't go to the police. They just didn't know who it was but hoped T&T's investigation would clear it out. They didn't appreciate the agency's style and decided to cut the investigation short before being charged way too much money."

"So the hack was also Bryana?"

"They think so. They may have indicated that they weren't going to hire Leonardo Pascual for *The Privateers* role. He was Sara and Bryana's first choice, but he wasn't very well known outside of theater at the time. The whole hack indicated there was a lot of interest and fandom around him. It's funny though."

"What?"

"They didn't want to hire him two years ago, and now they would work with him in anything he'd wanted to do. That's why they wanted us to follow him for a while, to check if he was meeting with any other studios."

"Is he leaving Meshflixx?"

"Not sure, but Divya has followed him several times to a West End theater."

"Is he going to be back on the stage?" asked Sol enthusiastically. "I need to get tickets for that!"

"You don't even know what play he'll be in!" protested Luke. "But now that I know for a fact that, even if you find him *irrefutably sexy*, you didn't conspire with him to steal the script, I'm not jealous."

"Good because I don't do jealousy." She really didn't. "So is Meshflixx happy with the investigation after all?"

"They're happy that we cleared Sara from all this mess. At least now they can continue working with one of the Daniels sisters."

"I'm glad that's worked out," Sol said. "What will happen to Bryana—and Oliver?"

"Professional purgatory," said Luke. "Meshflixx has banned them and will be sharing their dubious practices with the other networks, streamers, and studios so that they do the same. I'm told their showbiz careers are over."

"So fitting," she said. "Especially after they tried getting *me* in professional purgatory!"

"But I have bad news. It looks like *The Privateers* will have to be canceled after this mess because Sara can't see herself working on it without her sister." Luke frowned. "She'll be developing something new for Meshflixx, and Martha Broch is already attached as title designer. But I think Sara is going to wait until that strike you told me about gets sorted out."

"I'm a bit sad there'll be no new adventures of the captain and the quartermaster on *The Privateers*," said Sol. "But I'm happy they had their happy ending together, even if it looks like they were one more victim of the *Moonlighting* curse."

"Look at you, Sol Novo," Luke said. "I didn't have you pinned for a romantic. Are you sure you're feeling all right?"

Sol was about to tell Luke to go to hell when she got a text message from Laia.

"Laia's new-ish babysitter just quit," she told Luke while reading her friend's message. "She's canceling our dinner plans for tonight."

"I may regret this, but why don't you tell her I can take care of demonic Paula while you two have dinner together?"

"Are you crazy? That kid is all cuteness and I love her to pieces, but she *is* a little demon. I've never babysat her, and I'm her mom's best friend in London!"

"Oh, I know I'll regret this," Luke said. "Deeply. But let's say I feel I need to pay my dues with Laia, or I'll never be on her good side."

"I see." Sol thought about how Laia could be. "She's been giving you the rude treatment because you lied to me."

"She has. I feel that, unless there's some kind of grand gesture coming from me, she'll stare at me with a judgmental, impassive gaze forever. And I don't like not being liked. Also, since she's your friend and all, I should find a way to make her at least tolerate me."

"Probably," Sol admitted. "I have extremely good taste in friends."

"They take care of you," Luke agreed.

"And I take care of them, lending them sexy private investigators who can pretend they know how to babysit," joked Sol.

"Minding Paula for a couple of hours shouldn't be that hard, right?"

"You wish!" Sol laughed and texted Laia with Luke's proposal.

Laia's answer came immediately.

"She says okay, be at her place promptly at 7:15. She says she doesn't like tardiness, but I can tell you *that* is not true." For the first time in days, Sol wasn't worried about anything. "Also, she says she won't pay you because liars don't get any money from her."

53

When she finally remembered to disable Airplane Mode on her cell phone the following morning, she found a couple of voicemails from Luke highlighting his signature gruffness and inviting her to a party at his place that evening.

She also got a text message from someone she had managed to put out of her mind for days.

> The Boring One: I was woken up this morning at 5 a.m. by your moving company! They took all your stuff but made me pay for the service myself!

Sol smiled. She was sure it had been Laia's doing. Her friend knew Sol still had some things that she hadn't been able to retrieve after the divorce from David—mainly books but also some decorating objects and furniture.

> The Boring One: They took stuff that's mine!

Sol doubted it. She was sure Laia had given them precise

information about what to take and what to leave, the same precise information Sol had compiled three years earlier while trying to get some of that stuff back. Even if taking revenge on David herself directly could have been more satisfactory, Sol was perfectly happy. If there was something she'd learned how to do well as she aged, it was embracing her friends' constant offers of support.

> The Boring One: I demand an explanation and compensation! Call me urgently

She texted him one bit of information: the telephone number of Victoria Sifuentes. She hadn't liked her divorce lawyer, but she loved how Victoria was dealing with the whole *Voyeur* situation. The story about Sol's involvement in the Meshflixx case would be removed from their website after they publicly admitted to it being unfounded, and they were negotiating an agreement where Sol would get financial compensation. Victoria was ironing the deal, but it looked like it would be enough for Sol not to worry about flying economy anytime soon. And even if Victoria wasn't a divorce lawyer, Sol was sure she wouldn't mind dealing with David at her usual hourly rate.

After that, Sol blocked David's number from her phone once and for all.

The only remaining thing now would be to properly thank Laia for taking revenge on David for her and doing it in a fitting way. She'd get her an expensive Catalan wine or olive oil—or both—and Sol could let her borrow Luke for babysitting duties again if she wanted. She'd heard he'd done a semi-decent job the night before by reading *Ada Twist, Scientist* a record of twenty times and managing to make different voices almost every time.

...

Luke hadn't given her much information about the party other than it started at seven. If there was one occasion for which Sol never showed up on time it was parties, where she preferred to be a good twenty minutes late. She was trying to follow her usual guidelines that evening and yet she had the feeling she'd be the first to arrive—people in their thirties had better things to do than get anywhere early or even fashionably late. And for some reason, that knowledge made her oddly uncomfortable. She'd never been to Luke's place, and she'd get to meet a few of his friends that evening.

She was afraid she'd be the oldest—and uncoolest—person at the party, which was why she'd forgone one of her customary going-out little black dresses and was instead wearing her favorite pair of baggy, cropped trousers from Lurdes Bergada and an asymmetrical top that put half her midriff on display for what—she hoped—was a punk-rock look.

She brought a couple of bottles of wine from Montsant and hoped that this alone would help make people like her.

She made sure she was at the right address one last time and checked the time on the steps tracker at her wrist, which read 7:07. She cursed her inability to ever be late anywhere even if she tried, and knocked on Luke's door.

He opened almost immediately, a smile already on his lips, his waves in perfectly composed disorder, a lightweight sleeveless tank clinging to his chest, and plenty of sweaty skin on display.

"Are you just back from running?" she asked in disbelief.

"Afraid yes, but come on in," he said, showing her inside

the tiny studio. "I assumed everyone would be here late, but I was counting on you being early."

"Were you?" She eyed his workout clothes and sweat one more time.

"Maybe not this early," he conceded, grinning. "I'm going to have a quick shower, but feel free to show yourself around. Although this is basically it. The moment you set foot in, you see it all. There's not much else I can show you other than the shower room and the Murphy bed."

"Right." She examined every single detail in Luke's small but sunlit place, from the gray IKEA KLIPPAN sofa she recognized, because she'd had the same minimalist model in her late twenties, to the framed poster of *Moonlighting* featuring Cybill Shepherd and Bruce Willis clad in a white T-shirt that read "Medicate Me."

"Heading to the shower," Luke said as if he wanted to make sure she agreed to be left there alone.

She eyed his bare arms and shoulders. "I'm actually joining. If you don't mind the company."

"I was hoping you'd want to join," he said with a smug grin. "I may have told everyone else the party started after eight..."

Sol closed the distance between them and kissed him. She didn't mind that he was sticky and wet or that his usual notes of hickory overpowered the lavender with some muskier scents.

"But you have no idea how small that shower room is," he warned.

She took his tank off while still urgently kissing him, first his lips, then his neck, collarbone, chest, nipples. He was saltier than she'd ever tasted him.

They tumbled into the shower room. She tried getting rid of his brief-lined running shorts, but they clung to Luke's sweaty skin and she demanded he do it for her with a frustrated grunt. She took off her own tank top and pants, leaving them on the floor to wrinkle. She almost couldn't recognize herself. She was needy.

She liked this new Sol, and Luke seemed to like her even more. He was looking at her flushed face, at her disheveled hair, at her body with the most ravenous eyes. He drew nearer, biting her earlobe.

"You look so hot right now," he told her in a growl that she felt between her legs.

She did feel hot wearing nothing but a black bralette and cheeky high-waisted panties. But even that seemed like too many clothes when she could touch Luke's erection hard against her hip. He trailed down her collarbone and neckline with his mouth. She helped him unclasp the bra, and he bit one of her nipples greedily.

She didn't know where all this urgency was coming from. Five minutes before, she was just a girl—no, not a girl —a woman arriving early to a party. Now she needed this bathroom sex to be quick and extremely pleasurable.

"Did you bring one of your toys?" he asked, as if he'd heard her thoughts. She was always so damned impatient.

He was still mercilessly playing with her earlobe and nipple when he'd asked her that, and Sol almost couldn't reply. She uttered a primal noise that meant she hadn't brought anything.

"We'll have to take it easier then," he murmured again in her ear, and she could hear the delight in his voice. "And rely on the smutty talk."

His lips descended on her body while he lifted her in the air and seated her over the edge of the small sink at the shower room.

"This may get a bit uncomfortable," he told her, trailing

her stomach with his lips and kissing her bony hip. "Cramped." He took her panties off, parted her legs further. "And hot," he said, then brushed her clit with his tongue. "But tasty."

She arched her back instinctively, breathing heavily. He licked, kissed, drank her. If she'd been able to articulate any complete thought, Sol would have admitted that he was proceeding with the same level of proficiency as her suction vibrator. And she'd done lots of research before buying what she *knew* was the best in the market. That thing had caused a frenzy among people with clitoris—or was it clitorises?

Luke added two of his fingers then, diligently sliding them inside her, and she knew she wouldn't be able to take it much longer.

"Luc—" She wanted more of him but couldn't say anything else.

He unrelentingly used his mouth on her, his fingers inside her, until she spasmed in unwavering, severe, exquisite pleasure. One thing her favorite sex toy didn't have: the ability to surprise her.

He went back to facing her only once her ragged breath had steadied a bit. He touched his lips with hers once again and she tasted herself on his sea-flavored breath. She wanted to say something, to urge him to have mercy on her. She wanted him. No, she *needed* him, all of him. Ya.

"Inside," she demanded.

"I like it when you're bossy," he told her, the same smug grin on his lips that he'd had since she'd told him she'd join him in the shower.

"Now."

Acquiescing, he reached behind Sol and grabbed a few

condoms from the armoire above the sink. She took them from his hand.

"Deixa'm," she ordered and unfoiled one of them. She was still dizzy from the orgasm.

She wrapped the condom around his cock, feeling him on her hand.

He lifted her again, her legs wrapped around his waist, and lowered both of them to the closed-lid toilet. He sat there with her straddled on top of him. She didn't even think and simply took him all in.

Their movements got rougher and more urgent then.

"You're getting me hooked," she confessed.

"To?"

"Fucking you," she told him, in pure sensuous agony.

"I'm addictive," he said, sounding as breathless as she was. Another nipple bite had her panting.

She felt the release starting to build again and chased it, pushing against Luke's body. She heard herself moaning, screaming with the notes of release, not a care clouding her pleasure.

"Fuck," she said, feeling his orgasm inside her. Her heart rate was almost uncontrollable.

"Fuck," he agreed, reaching to her face and pulling a lock of her hair behind her left ear. "And we haven't even made it to the shower yet."

54

By 9 p.m., Sol was munching on some funghi pizza, comfortably seated on the IKEA sofa and wondering why she ever got rid of hers. Oh right, she'd moved to California and couldn't fit it inside the suitcase with so many other things she'd left behind over the years.

"You look lost in your own thoughts," Divya said, sitting next to her and giving her the glass of water she'd just brought from the kitchenette area. She had a beer for herself.

"I would tell you I wasn't," Sol said, "but I think you'd see the lie."

"So you *were* lost in your thoughts but don't want to talk about it."

"I guess, as usual, you're spot-on," said Sol. "Any chance I could hire you as a therapist?"

"I'd love to have an excuse to ask you all sorts of intrusive personal questions, but I'm afraid I won't have much time for extra gigs now with the new agency and all."

Sol tilted her head. She didn't know anything about a new agency.

Divya clearly noticed her confusion. "Luke has told you, right?"

"No..."

She was one hundred percent sure that none of the things Luke had whispered to her in the shower before the guests started arriving were about a new agency.

"Luke!" Divya yelled. He promptly made his way from the kitchenette, where he'd been talking to Sanjay and another T&T colleague. "Why does your woman not know about us?"

Sol almost choked on her water. There was so much to unpack in one short sentence that, for a moment, she wished she hadn't switched to water and still had some wine left. She was going to ignore the whole "your woman" thing, which would have offended her as sexist coming from anyone else, but it sounded somehow endearing coming from Divya. Only because Sol had labeled her as a feminist. So she'd let go of the comment, even if Sol didn't know exactly what she was to Luke, and she would *never* define herself that way.

And she absolutely had no clue what the thing between Divya and Luke could be.

"Right. I haven't had the chance yet," said Luke, sitting between the two women on the two-seat sofa, not seeming to care about the ample space he was taking. He turned to Sol. "Divya and I are going into business together."

Luke and Divya looked at Sol expectantly, as if waiting for her cheerful reaction.

"I'm sorry I'm not sounding more enthusiastic," she finally told them. "The read I'm getting from this—based on your smiles and general demeanor—is that I should congratulate you. And I am happy. But I'm going to need more info, Luca."

"Luke, mate, you really don't know how to sell it properly," Divya admonished him. Now she turned to Sol. "I left T&T and we're opening our own detective agency. Meshflixx is our first client."

Sol gasped. "You are? And they are?"

"They liked our work with *The Privateers* and want us to look into something else," explained Divya. "They don't trust T&T after that last case."

"What's the new case?" Sol asked eagerly.

"Oh, some boring showbiz nonsense. One of their showrunners is being sued because there's a bloke who says the showrunner stole the idea for his hit show from him," Divya answered before Luke could say anything. "But we're not going to tell you *anything else* about it this time, because that's how it should be."

"Congratulations! I'm so happy for you both." Sol scooched over to hug Divya over Luke's legs.

"Don't I get a hug too?" asked Luke as Sol was returning to her place on the sofa, and she did hug him. She didn't linger too much between his arms though, because even if the two of them were far from strangers, the gesture felt odd. They'd never shared an almost innocent and simply friendly gesture like that before.

Luke returned to socializing with the rest of the guests after that, and Sol got better acquainted with Divya and then Sanjay, but that was about it. She didn't do well with big or even medium-sized gatherings. Luke's place wasn't even that big, and there couldn't have been more than ten people there, but it still felt like a crowd to Sol.

People started leaving after eleven, some of them headed to a nearby pub. Divya and Sanjay helped Luke tidy up the place, and Sol felt almost obliged to do the same but managed to only pretend like she was doing it. She was aware that she was the worst, but one of the reasons she'd stopped throwing get-togethers at her place with her book-club group was precisely that she hated cleaning after.

Luke's party had been quite different from what she'd anticipated or imagined. There had been no smoking—Luke absolutely forbid it at his place; no drugs—not even the marijuana-laced edibles that had become so popular during her last few years in California but were illegal in the UK; no overly drunk people throwing up—Divya had had perhaps a beer too many, but Sanjay was seeing that she got home safely; no dancing—although a nice selection of jazzy indie pop music was playing in the background all evening; and no people fucking in the bathroom—not *during* the party, at least.

Everything had been so grown-up after all, and she suddenly became aware that Luke and his colleagues were in their early-to-mid-thirties, not their early twenties. Sol could be such a provincial, prejudiced snob sometimes. Perhaps there wasn't such a humongous age gap between her and Luke after all.

When Divya and Sanjay left and she was alone with Luke again, she asked what had been plaguing her for the previous half an hour.

"Should I also get going?"

"Only if you want to," he said, looking genuinely surprised. "Do you need to leave?"

"Not really." She wasn't sure if she was making the right decision. What if Luke wanted to be alone but was too polite to say otherwise? On the other hand, she had brought a medium-sized purse, and the many cosmetic products necessary for her nightly skin routine didn't all fit in there. "Are you only telling me to stay to be nice?"

"I'm not telling you to stay," he said, smiling. "I'm saying there's no need for you to leave if you don't want to. I distinctly remember the terms around me staying at your place not being so thoroughly discussed and analyzed."

"I'm just trying not to overstay my welcome." It was that and also making sure that her mature skin got all the extra moisturizing it needed.

"I don't think you overstaying your welcome is possible," he said. "Not here. But I understand if you'll be more comfortable at your home. This place is not much."

"What? I love your place!" She really did. It was notably small, but he'd managed to make a tasteful home imbued with his personality, and she liked that the most.

"Sol, you said your place was cramped. Look at this," he told her, gesturing to the studio.

"This is the same size as the first apartment I rented in Barcelona. Only there, the shower pressure was nonexistent. The first apartment I rented in Los Angeles wasn't much bigger either, and I had to cohabit with a nesting family of spiders," Sol said. "Please don't forget I've also been young and poor. Not that I'm implying you're poor or anything." Why couldn't she stop blundering?

But he seemed not to fixate on that last part.

"You're still young," he protested, and his earnestness warmed Sol's heart.

"You know what I mean," she said. "Forgive me if I've been a bit stiff tonight around you."

"I don't remember any stiffness," he said, getting closer to her.

"It's just that I'm coming to terms with the fact that I am... perhaps... how did you put it? Mad about you," she said, relieved that she'd been able to find the words but also a bit scared of having uttered them out loud.

"You are?" he asked, almost hesitantly, but then he smiled. "I warned you I was addictive."

"To be honest, I decided to let myself be mad about you once I saw the good taste with which you've decorated the place and the cleanliness of your kitchen and bathroom. I would have talked myself out of it if this place looked even mildly unkempt."

"What if I told you I cleaned because I knew you'd be coming?" he asked playfully, pulling her closer to him and kissing the back of her neck.

"I'll have to live with the possibility of you not being as archetypically ideal as I initially thought, I guess."

She was hooked.

55

July 2023

The man who'd been standing on a quiet corner of Fitzroy Road was starting to wonder what was taking so long. It wasn't like her to be late, yet she should have been there ten minutes before.

He returned to his perusal of real estate porn on Rightmove where he verified, once again, his almost nonexistent chances of ever affording a bigger place on his current pay. He switched to the Kindle app and kept reading Manuel Vázquez Montalbán's *Southern Seas*—the misadventures of a Barcelona-native and private investigator that had been recommended to him by a certain Barcelonian—while he waited for his partner to finally get there.

"Dreading the gig already?" Divya's voice interrupted Luke's reading as she approached from behind, ready to fill in for him for surveillance duty.

After the second Meshflixx case had been solved, they had returned to a stable procession of divorce cases, child custody disputes, background checks, and work-harassment inquiries. With them came the necessary surveillance hours. But Divya and Luke were trying to stay away from some of the less ethical practices that took place at their former agency.

"Not dreading this one," Luke said, smiling at his partner. "And not dreading much lately."

"I see," Divya said, a knowing smile on her face. "Please say hi to Sol for me. And tell her I'll be there tomorrow at ten sharp to answer all her pressing questions about the job. Are you still fine with me doing this instead of you?"

"You know I don't get jealous," Luke said.

"Yeah, right!" Divya teased him.

Sol was typing all of it before it escaped her mind when she heard her front door buzz. She checked the time and realized that was probably Luke already. And it looked like he hadn't yet installed the smart lock app on his phone to be able to let himself in!

"Ai!" she protested, running downstairs.

She opened the door, pulled him inside by clutching his T-shirt, kissed him hurriedly, and left him standing at the entryway.

"Ara torno!" she told him, already climbing the stairs. "I need to finish writing just the one sentence."

Ever since she'd decided to take the plunge—inspired by Divya and Luke's entrepreneurial endeavors—and write a mystery novel set in London—inspired by Divya and Luke's work—she had been in an almost frantic writing spell. She had pivoted but, in the end, she hadn't turned to a boring profession.

"Okay, done!" she yelled from the upstairs office a couple of minutes later.

She went downstairs and found Luke making himself a cup of tea in the kitchen.

"Did I kiss you?" she asked. She'd been so absent-minded while opening the door that she wasn't really sure.

"You did," he said, his smile the same seducing one he'd directed her way from the first day they met. "But there's really no reason you shouldn't do it again."

"Right?" She embraced him and realized something. "Are you going like this?"

Luke checked his work attire, which was directly out of Sol's worst nightmares involving Greg Knight.

"I brought clothes and will change after tea," he explained.

"After tea tea, or you mean there's time for *tea*?" she asked, suddenly thirsty.

"As much as I'd love to have both kinds," he said, checking the time on his cell phone, "the thing starts in thirty minutes and we'll barely make it as it is."

"And you're sure I'll like this place?" she asked, not even trying to conceal her disappointment.

...

A change of clothes, a Tube ride, and a rushed on-the-go cup of TWG's 1837 Black Tea later, they were both taking their shoes off.

"Will I have to chant *om*?" she asked, horrified. Why had she agreed to join him? Right, he'd used all his magnetism to charm her.

"You won't if you don't want to," he answered, amused.

Even if yoga was the sort of low-impact but full-body workout that seemed to fit perfectly with Sol's lifestyle and checked all her favorite fitness boxes, she'd never gotten into it. She was spooked by its whole spiritual side, and she'd fallen soundly asleep during Shavasana when she was first getting acquainted with it. She'd never bothered trying it again.

Yet Luke had managed to drag her all the way up to Kilburn, which wasn't even close to his place, to try a yoga class he'd swear she'd love. Sol had no idea what he'd based that statement on until they got inside the studio, yoga mats in hand, and she saw her.

She had already placed her mat in the middle of the wooden-floored room and was doing some stretches over it. She saw Sol and Luke as they arrived.

"Oh, hi Luke," she said. "I see you brought company."

"Hi Emma," Luke said, placing his yoga mat not far away from the stretching actress. "This is my partner, Sol. Romantic partner," he added, using the term he and Sol had agreed on. Luke loved differentiating between his professional partner and his romantic one.

"Nice meeting you, Sol," Emma said, and she returned to her stretching.

Sol remained immobile in the middle of the studio for a few more seconds until she sat next to Luke, still not sure of what was going on.

"Why didn't you tell me fucking Emma Thompson was your yoga buddy?" she hissed.

"I wanted to see your face when you realized," he said, and she wasn't able to even qualify his ridiculously teasing smile. "It was worth it."

Sol's eyes sparkled. "I just want you to know that I totally forgive you for making us skip *tea* for this."

~

Thank you for reading *Cluelessly Unscripted*. For a bonus scene featuring Sol and Luke vacationing by the Mediterranean, visit this link: https://BookHip.com/PGPFWHT

And please leave a review of the book on Amazon, Goodreads or your favorite platform. Gràcies :)

ACKNOWLEDGMENTS

What do you do when you find yourself recovering from breast cancer surgery and being laid off from your journalist job in the same week? You write a feel-good book where everyone looks fabulous because that's the best kind of therapy you can think of.

Thanks, Xavi, for realizing before me that this was exactly what I needed.

Martín Piñol, thanks for all the books, endless advice, and long-lasting friendship. I hope we never learn how to have a short conversation.

Marta Gené Camps, I know having a Hollywood screenwriter and producer read a first draft of this book and give me notes is a luxury.

Thanks, Marta Franco, for being such a supportive reader and friend. Not only were you super happy when I asked you to read the first version of this book, but you also told me you got hooked!

If Sol Novo has a remarkable affinity for people whose names start with L, mine is for people whose names start with M. Mireia Giró Costa, Maura Vallverdú, Mar González Martí, and Margarida Garcia Ruiz—I thought of you while writing this book. But thanks as well to my non-M friends. You've all been quite a supportive bunch these last couple of years.

Sonia Fabre, thank you for introducing me to Singaporean tea and for realizing that I needed an author persona. I seriously wouldn't have figured it out.

Diana Biller, thanks for your books and your generosity. In the end, I didn't find an agent, but chatting with you was inspiring.

Joan M. Griffin, talking with fellow authors has become one of my favorite activities. Thanks for your words.

Brenna Bailey-Davies, working with you has been an absolute delight. Thank you for making my writing better and for being such a refreshing contrast to Christina Jones.

All the Pilates, yoga, running, and fitness instructors who've inspired me throughout the years and made sure to keep me strong.

I really need to thank my younger sister Marta for being a pest when we were little and forcing me to make up stories for her. Thanks, mama y papa, for all the unsupervised reading I was allowed growing up. And thanks to my tieta for sharing all her literary knowledge—and her books—with me.

ABOUT THE AUTHOR

Patricia Puentes is a Barcelona native, expat, and recovering entertainment journalist. She has a soft spot for romance mysteries where the leads actually hook up early. She's been a Pilates devotee since 2018 but has no qualms with yoga. She lives in Oakland, California, with her romantic partner and their rambunctious Border Collie, Boira (aka Peluchín diabólico).

Find her online at www.patriciapuentes.com/clueless. To subscribe to Patricia's newsletter, visit this link: www.patriciapuentes.com/newsletter.

TikTok: @patriciapuentesbooks

Goodreads: www.goodreads.com/patriciapuentes